L[illegible]

Humanity Inmortal

Anatiposi

Laurens P. Hickok

Humanity Inmortal

Reprint of the original, first published in 1872.

1st Edition 2023 | ISBN: 978-3-38213-000-8

Anatiposi Verlag is an imprint of Outlook Verlagsgesellschaft mbH.

Verlag (Publisher): Outlook Verlag GmbH, Zeilweg 44, 60439 Frankfurt, Deutschland
Vertretungsberechtigt (Authorized to represent): E. Roepke, Zeilweg 44, 60439 Frankfurt, Deutschland
Druck (Print): Books on Demand GmbH, In de Tarpen 42, 22848 Norderstedt, Deutschland

HUMANITY IMMORTAL;

OR,

MAN TRIED, FALLEN, AND REDEEMED.

BY

LAURENS P. HICKOK, D.D., LL.D.

BOSTON:
LEE AND SHEPARD, PUBLISHERS.
NEW YORK:
LEE, SHEPARD AND DILLINGHAM.
1872.

Stereotyped at the Boston Stereotype Foundry,
19 Spring Lane.

PREFACE.

In closing the work of "Creator and Creation," it was noted that the full Idea of Humanity could be comprehended only in a history of man through his trial, fall, redemption, and resurrection to eternal Life; and the design to give, in an anticipated opportunity, such a history was intimated. That history, as then contemplated, is here accomplished. In that speculative work we found the Universe constituted a Cosmos of order and beauty from essential Forces, both material and ethereal; and such essential Forces, put in motion round their creative source, worked themselves into separate spheres, and distributed the spheres into revolving suns and planetary Systems. However other worlds may have their dead matter quickened into life, on our earth an Organizing Instinct was, by the Creator, superinduced upon a portion of the ethereal Atoms as an assimilative life-power, communicating itself to and working in other mechanical forces to build them up in living bodies, and so from the Mineral kingdom were formed the plants and trees of the Vegetable kingdom; and out of and above this were wrought the nervous organisms for sentient life in the Animal kingdom; and in the union of sense with reason in Humanity, the whole creative work was crowned by installing over all the sovereign prerogatives of a Spiritual kingdom. All the former find their end in entire subserviency to the imperative claims of the last.

The life-instinct in the vegetable kingdom never rises into consciousness; the animal kingdom has sentient life in persistent consciousness only so long as it may hold the nervous organism in combination, and the dissolution of the nervous system is the destruction of all sensibility; but the spiritual kingdom has immortal life and intelligence. Absolute Reason neither begins nor ends, and the inspiration of finite reason in the human individual secures for him perpetual personality. Vegetable and animal organisms fall asunder and perish, for the life-power which builds and holds them in individuality is the causal efficiency of nature only; but reason is supernatural, and wherever it comes it carries with it eternal rights and claims, and no power less than the creative, which first breathed rational spirit into man, can take back his immortal prerogatives from man. The primal forces, in which the individual human life begins, must be perpetuated through life to preserve its identity; and the bond which holds the identical forces in human individuality is rational Spirit, which cannot work in the sentient life it is set to control without awaking claims that forever attach sentient soul and rational spirit together; and hence every human individual must have also its immortal sentient identity. No matter how many, nor how often, adventitious elements may assimilate with, and dissolve from, these primal essential forces which perpetuate the man's identity; his spiritual individuality will hold those essential forces to be his, unless God withdraw his own in-breathing, and so himself undo his own original creating.

Every human life has thus a perpetual ongoing experience, and as each is a propagation from an original stock by natural generation, so the primitive life sends down its connections through all, and makes for humanity a universal history. In that which is peculiar to man must human experience and history differ from other spiritual communities in other spheres; but since the one Father of spirits is Creator and Lord of all spirits, so in this one source of all authority and responsibility must all rational beings, in all worlds, be necessarily implicated in common interests, and stand each to each in reciprocity of rights and obligations. The work now before us is to trace, in general outline, the specific History of Humanity from its beginning to its consummation in the eternal state, with the communings and collisions that may occur with other orders of spiritual intelligences; taking as our guide the offered light from speculative reason, and from divine revelation, and, so far as the facts of experience may be gathered, from the records of past ages. The light shining from all these sources must give in all readings the same one meaning, since all are reflections from the one pure source of Absolute Truth and Wisdom.

In the same foregoing work referred to, it was noted

that the creating Absolute Spirit cannot be an object of knowledge except as contemplated in three distinct agencies, each as Will working in consciousness through its peculiar appropriation for itself of the one Absolute Reason-consciousness. As originator of the pure ideal universe, the first is the Father; as expressing this in overt manifestation, the second is the Word; and as holding all comprehensively in one, the third is the Holy Ghost. But not only in Creation; in governmental administration and frequent communication, the same threefold agency in the one Absolute Being must also necessarily be recognized. The second reveals the secret purpose of the first in such communications, and the third secures the execution, in human heart and will, of that counsel which the first has and the second publishes. The Holy Ghost has its more special dispensation in the later experiences of the race, but the expressing Logos is from the start the appropriate Mediator between God and Man, openly exhibiting the inner heart of Deity, and intimately commingling his agency with the experiences of the human family. An exclusive Mediatorial kingdom is by him established among men, which in legislation and administration has nowhere else its parallel. Both the Word and Spirit make here their disclosures of the Mystery of Godliness in ways altogether else unprecedented, and greatly adding interest and importance to the spiritual history of Humanity. We proceed to relate it as we shall carefully find it.

AMHERST, MASS., 1872.

CONTENTS.

CHAPTER I.

SECTION I.

SECTION II.

SECTION III.

CHAPTER II.

SECTION I.

SECTION II.

SECTION III.

SECTION IV.

SECTION V.

SECTION VI.

SECTION VII.

CHAPTER III.

SECTION I.

SECTION II.

SECTION III.

CHAPTER IV.

SECTION I.

SECTION II.

SECTION III.

CHAPTER V.

SECTION I.

SECTION II.

SECTION III.

SECTION IV.

SECTION V.

SECTION VI.

HUMANITY IMMORTAL.

THE highest elevation attained in nature is the gratification of sentient life in the animal kingdom. But in man sense has been crowned with reason, and as supernatural, man has dominion over nature, and an end of life far exalted above all animal happiness. His highest prerogatives stand in his endowment of reason, which renders him competent to attain moral character, and in his spiritual integrity to possess that true dignity which secures the respect and approbation of all rational intelligences. The manly valor which holds all sense-appetite in subordination to spiritual integrity is true virtue, and this must be attained and persistently kept, or self-reproach and public condemnation must follow.

Confirmed and stable character in virtue can be attained only through full trial and discipline. From the very constitution of humanity, "the flesh lusteth against the spirit, and the spirit against the flesh, and these are contrary the one to the other," and from self-conflict alone can there be found self-conquest; and without the trial which opens a way for defeat and shame there cannot be victory and honor. It is no matter of choice, but necessity in the case itself, that humanity must be fully tested, since veteran courage and inflexible integrity can be gained and established only through the discipline of sore temptation and intense opposition. It is not paternal faithfulness, but parental weakness, which will withdraw the child from rigorous tests to his fidelity and allegiance. The virtue which has endured the severest conflicts is the most precious, and the love to truth and duty, which has in its way made the most sacrifices for truth and duty, is the most strong and reliable; while no seeming fidelity, which stands only amid favoring interests and congenial inclinations, can be trusted in the day of adversity and persecution. The sterling character is matured in the process of struggle and conflict, and the "patience, experience, and hope that maketh not ashamed," are only attained by having passed through "divers temptations." The first necessity for the newly created humanity is a fairly arranged discipline for the trial in virtue.

CHAPTER I.

THE PRIMITIVE TRIAL OF HUMANITY.

THE nature of the case determines the necessity for human discipline; and if there be other orders of rational beings, the only way in which they also can be established in virtue, and maintain the integrity of moral character, is by an applied trial appropriate to their constitution and condition. Many things, both from speculation and the facts connected with the Divine Revelation of the trial of man, indicate that his trial was at the same time an occasion for the discipline and trial of other and higher grades of intelligent beings; and that while some sustained the trial and gained confirmation in loyalty, others wilfully revolted from their allegiance, and in their fall became also direct sources of temptation and corruption to the human family. Nothing in reason or revelation contradicts, while much in both indicates, that all sin which has come into the universe found its first entrance in connection with man's trial and primitive disobedience.

Repeated irruptions of sin and rebellion in separate

orders or worlds of the divine government, making necessary varied methods of vindicating God's authority by retribution or redemption, can hardly be reconciled, by any rational speculation, with the majesty and integrity of the sovereignty; while ready relief in reconciling the admission of sin with the divine attributes is attained, by supposing all ranks of moral beings to have stood firm in allegiance through previous discipline, till, in the new circumstances occasioned by man's creation and trial, they came to a sharper test of fidelity, which many improved for firmer confirmation in loyalty, and some perverted the occasion and fell off in rebellion. If but slight hints that this was so, be found in revelation, their plain conformity with the reason of the case would make slight intimations grounds of safe conclusion. One occasion for sin, and one interposition for divine vindication in permitting it, will, then, be sufficient for all worlds through eternity. With such supposition, man is at once made the central point of moral interest for the universe, according with Scripture representation, that angels intently watch God's dealings with our small world. He is revealing himself here as he does on no other theatre, and all orders of spirits look on and wonder.

SECTION I.

PRINCIPLES NECESSARILY DIRECTING IN THE TRIAL.

Humanity, from its constitution and relation to its Creator, presents many points from which the reason sees determining principles, relatively to the discipline which must be applied, and the trial it should receive at the hand of the Father and Sovereign of the human family. It does not lie open to arbitrary arrangements on the part of the sovereign, nor admit that there be any claim to consent on the part of man to arrangements divinely made. It cannot be viewed in the light of covenant-making, binding by mutual contract; but from the state of the parties, the fact and the manner of trial must be settled by the Creator himself, on considerations which he shall see to be equitable and reasonable, in view of his own honor, and what also shall be seen to be the most favorable to a happy issue on the part of man. The paternal heart of the sovereign is more deeply interested in securing confirmed loyalty and perpetual safety to the human race, than any other being; and just as the divine perfections make God sovereign, so they also determine that he is to appoint the mode of discipline and direct in all the trial. Absolute Reason must control and guide himself in all his arrangements by eternal principles of rectitude and benevolence.

1. The Integrity of Human Character is in the Control of Sense by the Spirit. — Humanity is constituted of sense and spirit, and to one or the other must the supreme control be given. There can be no neutral position between the ends of gratifying sense and honoring the spirit; and the point of danger is the disposing of the spiritual activity to the end of sense-gratification, and therein incurring spiritual degradation. The alternatives presented are not at all of degrees in the same thing, but of utterly distinct kinds. Gratification of sense and approbation of spirit cannot be included under any one term, as happiness, or blessedness, so that it may become a question of policy or expediency in taking that which shall on the whole give the most; the question of virtue, or integrity of character, is only in taking the spiritual end, and this is wholly lost in taking the end of sense. An animal may be guided by prudential considerations in attaining highest happiness on the whole, since sentient gratification is the end of animal life, and by no way can the animal attain integrity of character in virtue. But for man to attain the highest gratification possible, as end of his life, would be not only the missing of all virtue, as in the case of the brute, but the incurring unmitigated sin and guilt. The highest possible happiness sought and

attained against the end the spirit claims, subjects the spirit to perpetual debasement and shame. And with the spirit so subjected to sense, and self-disposed to carnal indulgence, it is also ready for all spiritual wickedness in its own high sphere of mere spiritual agency. The spirit itself has in this become alienated from the ends of all other spirits, and in its selfishness it will manifest its pride, and scorn, and hate, and envy, and jealousy, and revenge, as the devils do, who can have no carnal lusting. The birthright of humanity is perpetual self-approbation, securing eternally God's approbation; but in fixing on sense-gratification and self-ascendency, there is inevitable self-degradation and divine abhorrence.

Any one appetite allowed to control the spirit will keep the door open for every appetite when its occasion comes; and only by putting and keeping "the body under" can the man be safe, or his conscience peaceful. The fruit of the fleshy disposition is in all forms of iniquity, and the fruit of a spiritual disposing is every virtue.[1] The entire moral man is in his disposition, and out of it, as carnal or spiritual, come all the vices or virtues of his life. To be complete, then, the trial need not be made in reference to every sensuous appetite, nor any more in regard to every spiritual claim; when fairly made in reference to some one opening for sensual indulgence, it will be conclusive for all, and the test will need neither repeating nor varying. The trial must be, or the virtue cannot be

[1] Gal. v. 19-23.

confirmed and established, but fairly and fully to put the man between the ends of the flesh and the ends of the rational spirit, for the issue of his sense-disposing or his spirit-disposing, is all that is needful; and as the disposition which he shall there give to himself may be, such will be his radical character on his own responsibility. In some way the trial and the issue must come, and the only question is, whether the trial shall be left to a fortuitous occurrence, or whether it shall be divinely and thus paternally ordered. The first must be unreasonable, the latter must every way be desirable.

2. THE TRIAL MUST BE IMPOSED AT THE VERY OUTSET. — Were humanity left to its own way, and the first man started upon his practical course under the light and influence which daily experience alone might give, the issue between sense and spirit in his constitution would be soon joined and the disposition taken. Appetite would immediately prompt to gratification, and reason must soon assert its claims, and the occasion come for a conflict between passionate impulse and conscious obligation; and the disposing of the spirit in servile compliance with the appetitive impulse, or the imperative behest, would form and fix the radical character accordingly. But for the sake of God and man, such fortuitous trial should be prevented. God's love to righteousness, and his kind care for his intelligent creatures, will certainly secure that the most favoring conditions and influ-

ences for the integrity of the spirit, consistent with the completeness of the trial, shall be interposed.

And such divine arrangement and interposition must be at the start, for the discipline immediately commences with the opening experience, and any delay will endanger the issue in a fixed disposition before the paternal arrangements are made. If, in such delay, an issue should be disastrous, although man would have fixed his character by his own act, and on his responsibility, yet must there ever be the unhappy reflection that the prompt benevolence of the Creator had failed in doing for human holiness all that full equity and justice would have allowed. To satisfy his own fatherly heart, and show to mankind forever his earliest love and regard for human welfare, God will infallibly begin his dealings with humanity by putting man amid arrangements for discipline and trial as salutary and kindly influential as possible, consistent with its necessary strictness. The very first point in human history must, therefore, be the account of God's arrangements, under which he wisely determines that the character of the first human pair shall be formed. This, and the general facts of the process and result, will stand upon the very first page, and all subsequent pages of human history must transmit the hue which colors the transactions of this earliest record.

3. The Test must put the Sense and Spirit squarely in Conflict. — In many cases appetite will

stand in accordance with obligation; or if at variance at all, it may be remotely and obscurely, and sometimes the motives may present themselves in a blended form, as partly sensual only, and which may plausibly be taken as wholly spiritual; and while in any position the man would be bound to carefully discriminate, and act upon his full responsibility to the honor and dignity of his spirit, and could acquire no virtue except as he was spiritually disposed, yet would not any mixed and confused appeal appear reasonable, as an appointed and formal method of trial. If God should interpose and put his own arrangements in order for human discipline, and test the human spirit the most fairly and decisively, it is manifestly reasonable that the issue be directly joined, and the sense and the spirit be set clearly and squarely one against the other.

Any constitutional appetite may be taken, and the desire of gratification strongly excited, and in fact but one act of tried gratification can occur at one time; and over against this there may be put, and strongly pressed, any claim purely spiritual, and between such conflicting appeals the issue will be fairly joined, and the strength and integrity of the spirit directly put upon trial. The claim of reason, in the end and honor of the finite spirit only, might lack both in clearness and strength for a fair and favorable issue; but if the finite spirit be thrown directly upon its allegiance to the Absolute Spirit, and made to stand under the pressure of positive divine authority, the utmost clearness and strength of spiritual claim may thus be applied. When a positive command, a known "thus saith the Lord," stands over against an excited sensual impulse, and is put at the time as a known occasion for testing the fidelity and strengthening the virtue of the finite spirit, there then comes out an unmistakable spiritual behest against a sensuous appetite, and the trial is plainly and unavoidably secured. If appetite prevail, and the spirit consent to serve the sense in such a test, there can be no apology made, that the highest possible spiritual obligations were not pressed upon the conscience for the preservation of its purity and integrity.

4. The Destruction in subjecting the Spirit to the Flesh should be strongly announced. — The good gained in holding the sense subject to the spirit did not need to be formally announced. The intimate immediate communion with God and his fostering presence with the first pair on their opening consciousness at creation, secured the first exercises to be spiritual confidence in and obedience to their Creator. The daily life had the consequent peace and conscious self-approbation, inseparable from this original trust and love. This was their opening experience, all tending towards perseverance and confirmation in virtue. But the strong guard needed as a warning was, the disclosure of the evil necessary upon spiritual subjection to sense. The terrible consequences of yielding

to excited appetite, and taking on a carnal disposition, should be most emphatically announced in connection with the statements appointing the trial. Man's debasement and defilement in the indulgence of sense and dethronement of reason, and God's deep abhorrence of such moral pollution, are required vividly to be set before him.

All this was intended and effected in the primeval threatening to man, "In the day thou eatest thereof thou shalt surely die." The act of self-indulgence would carry in it the spirit's consent, and fix a radical sensual disposition. Self-gratification would henceforth be dominant, and the debasing of the spirit and depraving of the character become entire and lasting. The spirit would henceforth be in bondage, and though still the alternative to persistence in sensuality, in a return to spiritual recovery and supremacy, would be open, yet would not the defiled spirit choose it, but would basely cleave to its shameful servitude. In sinning, it goes down assenting, and then has nothing in it which dissents; and so, in its own choice, its bondage, because free, is final, and hopeless of all self-emancipation. Such was the helpless and dreadful condition disclosed in the warning against transgression, and was all involved in the death so peremptorily threatened. The bare dissolution of the body was not the evil primitively intended; that may be a sentence subsequently pronounced in mitigation of the first threatening; the warning designed in it was that of endless shame in the spirit itself, and eternal abhorrence in the sight of God. Nothing was arbitrary in the trial or the penalty, but all ordered and announced in kind fidelity to human interest, and necessarily putting the issue upon human responsibility.

5. The Capabilities for an Eternal State of Blessedness can be attained only in passing the Hazard of such Trial. — While virtue can be acquired and confirmed only amid conflicts and trials, so, moreover, the very use of the immortal faculties, freely and completely, can be attained only in the exercises of the spiritual life, which find their source directly in the spiritual disposition. In the speculations followed out in the work of "Creator and Creation," we found life to be an instinctive want superinduced upon ethereal forces, and thus the life literally uses the light. In this use the material forces are also assimilated and organized into living bodies. The instinctive life-want builds up the organisms of the Vegetable kingdom, and in further completeness of sentient life the organisms also of the Animal kingdom; and only by the control of the rational spirit can the "fleshly mind" be disciplined and governed. The human spirit controls the human appetites, and thereby constitutional inclinations are held in moral restraint. And as this subjects the mortal body to the free determinations of the spirit, so, when "the mortal shall have put on immortality," the "spiritual body" shall much more be subject to the directions

of the reason; and only as the spirit has reigned in time can the resurrection-body be made the ready instrument for spiritual employment in eternity.

There is a perpetual balance of combined forces, which perpetuates the identity of the individual body amid all its changes of elements in the present probationary state, and this will be still held in balanced unity by the comprehending spirit in the experiences of eternity; and so the same body in perduring essence, which was ruled by the spirit here, will much more be the spirit's flexible and facile instrument, in the world of triumphant glory. But only as the spirit has ruled the flesh on earth, can it control the essential organism which accompanies it in eternity. Its fleshly sympathies and propensities remain when its dissolved and cast-off elements are left behind; and these will go earthward, and not heavenward, if not guided and used by spiritual affections. The spirit which has bowed in bondage to the flesh here, can never carry the resurrection-body to the central source of light and glory there. The employments can only be as the character and disposition of the spirit permits. In the distinctions of sensual and spiritual disposition the great separating gulf is "fixed."

SECTION II.

THE TEMPTATION AND FALL OF MAN.

Humanity, in the persons of the first man and woman, continued for a time in allegiance to the Creator, and the sense in subjection to the spirit. On the part of God were paternal care and nurture, and on the part of man were confiding docility and reverence. The communion between them was as Father and children; and as the parent helps the child in opening speech and knowledge, so the Lord God brought beast and fowl to Adam "to see what he would call them, and whatsoever Adam called every living creature, that was its name." The abode of man was prepared by God as a Garden in a warm climate; and dominion was given to him over all animals; and the herbs, and plants, and fruits of Paradise were his food. The occupation of the first pair was the dressing and keeping the garden in which they dwelt.

As above noticed, it is most reasonable to assume, that during the period of human innocence, and from before till the temptation of Eve, there was sin in no part of the universe. All moral beings may best be considered by us as having hitherto stood in unbroken loyalty and blessedness. The sacred history gives fair intimation, as we may soon note, that sin began in connection with the trial and fall of humanity. An older and higher spirit than man found his first inducement to sin, in connection with man's creation and God's primeval dealings with him. Other exalted spirits were induced to join in his rebellion, and he also was the direct tempter to the first human transgression. Ever before an angel of light, and prominent among the heavenly host as the morning star; the new experience opening before him in witnessing the creation in flesh and blood of human beings, and of a grade below his own, and they yet receiving the special intimacy and fostering patronage of the creating Logos; and especially, if we suppose him to have been commissioned by the Logos to watch and serve the best interests of these first parents of an inferior race, we may readily see, might become the provocative to feelings of envy, and jealousy, and growing hate unknown before in his bosom; and which at length induced that arrogant ambition and lifting up of pride, which the apostle has affirmed was "the condemnation of the devil." The malignity towards man, and the quenchless spite and enmity towards man's Mediator, everywhere exhibited subsequently by fallen angels in all the revelation made concerning them, is best interpreted through such intimations, as that their depravity originated in their new acquaintance with this lower order of moral beings, and witnessing their Creator's special interest in them, and perhaps their own required ministry to them But we follow the intimations of the introduction of sin in the universe, and in humanity, through the Mosaic account of the trial, temptation, and disastrous fall of man.

1. THE MANNER IN WHICH ADAM AND EVE WERE TEMPTED. — The trial of man, eventuating in his first transgression, had all its particular steps, and successive events, as actual occurrences; but the minute record of the facts have not been given. The inspired account by Moses is general and summary, particularizing only in the items important for the instruction of future generations. This account in Genesis is not to be interpreted as myth or fable; nor yet as truth in poetic figure; but as veritable fact, and occurrence according to sense-appearance and apprehension. Nothing is recorded which was not phenomenally observed; yet many of the appearances have a deeper truth and meaning than was recognized by the human agents at the time, and which became fully disclosed only in later periods. The serpent was the tempting agent immediately appearing, and yet the prime agency of Satan as the responsible tempter, invisibly present, is repeatedly afterwards noted. As up to this period in holy allegiance, the devil here became an apostate and rebel, and began his sinning in the deception and destructive temptation of the new-made human pair. It is to these specific transactions that the Saviour

refers when he calls the devil "a liar and the father of it," and "a murderer from the beginning."[1] And from the issue of this successful temptation he is said to have "the power of death."[2] And from his crafty use of the serpent's subtle instrumentality in this deadly work, he gets the emphatic name of "the Dragon," and the "Old Serpent."[3] All these are personal, permanent characteristics of the devil, as if meant to indicate that he began to be a devil and satan, a deceiver and an adversary, in these very tempting transactions; and that "the beginning" from which he was a liar, and a murderer, was in the deceptive and destructive work of the temptation and fall at man's beginning. The perpetuated malice of fallen spirits towards man, and the malignant enmity towards the Saviour of men, which the devil so bitterly exhibited in the days of his flesh, and the complete destruction of the works of the devil by the Saviour in his incarnation, evince a one great conflict, commencing on occasion of man's creation, and forever settled in the triumphant issues of man's redemption.

And so the principle in the parable of "the lost sheep" has here its broadest application, that all heaven rejoices more for the recovery of one lost world, than for all others that have needed no repentance. And still further, the one short but explicit declaration is given by the apostle, that our

[1] John viii. 44. [2] Heb. ii. 14. [3] Rev. xii. 9 and xx. 2.

redeemed race is enough to vindicate God in the integrity of his wisdom before the Universe, and that the mystery of Christ was "to the intent that now unto principalities and powers in heavenly places, might be known, by the church, the manifold wisdom of God."[1] The sin of devils and of men stands in one view to the moral universe; and the redeemed church of human believers, through Christ, God meant should settle his truth and authority in dealing with all sinners.

The subtlety of the serpent in its power of fascination seems designed to represent the devil's crafty insinuation to Eve, and here with Eve was the devil's first use of the serpent's instrumentality. The human victim did not know that there was an assault from any spiritual adversary. Later revelations determine that the responsible agent was the devil, and this serpent-like power of fascination had here its earliest satanic exhibition.

It is remarkable that not until so late as the time of Job, and then successively in the times of David, Ahab, and Jehoshaphat,[2] do we have any recognition of demoniac interference with mankind. The ministry of good angels was abundant in the age of the Hebrew Patriarchs; and prohibitions of necromancy and witchcraft in the Mosaic law refer to the spirits of dead human beings; but not till beyond the writings of the Pentateuch do we hear of fallen angels. This is quite

[1] Eph. iii. 10. [2] 1 Chron. xxi. 1; 2 Chron. xviii. 21, 22.

conclusive for the antiquity of these books, for any writers of a later age would have recognized a devil.

2. THE PROCESS AND SUCCESS OF THE DEVIL'S TEMPTATION. — The primitive permission and prohibition to man was, "Of every tree of the garden thou mayest freely eat, but of the tree of the knowledge of good and evil, thou shalt not eat of it; for in the day that thou eatest thereof thou shalt surely die."[1] The direct and kind intent of God, here, was to set the man and woman directly between an impulse of sense and a dictate of conscience, giving the necessary alternative to either a sensual or a spiritual disposing, in which permanent character would rest. So plain a test, and the act so deliberately taken, would inevitably carry along the spirit in it, and become a disposition of the proper selfhood of the person in a governing state of will, henceforth controlling the subordinate executive volitions. We have noted reasons sufficient for believing that the sin of the devil originated in connection with the trial of man, and shall further on find still more conclusive proof for it; and we need here only see the fitting occasion for trying with man the loyalty of other than human spirits. Angels are not, as human beings, creatures of sense, and could not be tested by any appeals to sensual appetite. Their selfhood stood directly over against other personalities, whether of fellow-creatures or of God, and their trial must be in the alterna-

[1] Gen. ii. 16, 17.

tive of subjecting the selfhood to the clear claims of others, or arrogating to self against another's right. Up to this point, we may believe, all had subordinated self to others' rights, and remained holy; but here in man's lower state, and God's requisition in behalf of man, opened the occasion for scorn, and jealousy, and envy, and hate, towards man, and impatience, and haughty resistance, and even arrogant defiance, towards God; and so angels stood here upon their personal responsibility, as well as men. But our attention is specially to man's trial and its reasonableness, leaving the devil's tempting interference to his own responsibility.

It was not sinful in man to see the forbidden fruit to be good for food, nor to apprehend it as desirable to make one wise, nor yet to have the appetite stimulated by it; nor any more was it yet holiness to have the conscience excited to the obligation of persistent integrity. Such awakened impulse of sense and claim of the spirit were alike necessary in the case, that there might be probation or discipline. This quickening of appetite and of conscience in conflict was conditional for any trial, and wholly constitutional on the part of man. But at just this point opened the occasion for temptation. An influence from a malign source might here be intentionally exerted upon the complex agency of sense and spirit, stimulating the former and stupefying the latter, and thereby intensifying the discipline and augmenting the efficacy of the trial. It can be at once seen, that the tempting influence must be at the responsibility of the tempter; the tempted is no further responsible than for the act of resisting or yielding. The pressure of the tempting solicitation upon the sensibility brings no guilt to the tempted till the spirit yields its own consent. It only becomes an occasion for more firm endurance in "letting patience have its perfect work."

The devil had already learned human nature sufficiently to calculate the hopeful result to him, in inflaming appetite and stifling conscience; and this process he most cunningly pursued, that thereby he might induce a perverse disposition, and fix the race in a fallen state at the opening experience of the first progenitors. The woman was the more susceptible and the less suspicious, and he carefully directed his approach to her when alone; and although now his spirit had disposed itself in malicious enmity to God and man, and was secretly and artfully plotting the ruin of the new race, yet from what has been before seen it is safe to assume, that here was his first overt act of rebellion against God, and determined injury to man. The first angelic sin was the devil's tempting, and the first human sin was the woman's listening and consenting. On the devil's approach, he had already a rebellious and malicious purpose, but she was loyal and innocent. The tempter's first aim was to remove the pressure of obligation and acquiescence to authority, by suggesting some severity and overstrictness in the just announced prohibition of the fruit of a particular tree. This was skilfully done with the least possible alarm to an innocent mind, awaking no suspicious apprehensions, yet effectually lodging the insinuation there of a somewhat rigorous exaction on the part of God. As if in surprise and doubt whether such a prohibition could have been made, he asks, "Yea, hath God said, Ye shall not eat of every tree of the garden"? The answer of the woman clearly evinces that the poisonous insinuation had at once taken, and the designed course of thought and feeling had been already started, Yes, we may eat of the fruit of the trees of the garden, but the one conspicuous tree "in the midst of the garden" is forbidden; "ye shall not eat of it, neither shall ye touch it, lest ye die." We can hardly help connecting with these words an impatient look and querulous tone, which abundantly evinced a discontented spirit. The tempter could have had little hesitation in following up his purpose, by saying to such a ready temper, "Ye shall not surely die." The direct contradiction to God's declaration neither shocked the woman's sensitiveness, nor dispelled her easy delusion, but rather emboldened her rising presumption.

How fully prepared had Eve now become for the devil's next suggestion! There has been a selfishness on the part of God, that has made him unwilling you should attain the elevation and wisdom you might, lest you approach his position too nearly. "God doth know that in the day ye eat of it, then your eyes shall be opened, and ye shall be as gods, knowing good and evil." In all this the devil attained what he wanted in stifling conscience and blinding reason to authority, by awaking hard thoughts of God, a vain curiosity, and selfish ambition; and then the fair fruit presented to her passionate desire, unchecked by spiritual control, prompted at once to sensual gratifications. "When the woman saw that the tree was good for food, and that it was pleasant to the eyes, and a tree to be desired to make one wise, she took of the fruit and did eat."

The woman's sin made her at once the tempter of the man. Satan, through the serpent, had finished his temptation; he retires, and the woman takes up his deceptive work. She so persuaded Adam that he also yielded. "She gave also to her husband with her, and he did eat." As in every sinful gratification since, so here in the first transgression, "Lust, or sensual appetite, when it hath conceived, bringeth forth sin, and sin, when it is finished, bringeth forth death."[1]

3. The Sin of Man was wholly of his own Origination. — The devil was the first sinner, and his sin, in connection with the opening history of humanity, was at his sole responsibility. His defiance of God and malice towards man make his tempting act altogether another and darker sin than the forbidden gratification of sense by his victim. The curse upon the serpent race is to be taken as the index of God's

[1] James i. 15.

direct retribution upon the devil as the responsible agent. His first sin was not man's sin, though in close connection with it. The malicious temptation was demoniac; the yielding to sense-gratification was human; and sin entered humanity in the latter only, not at all in the former. Other spirits with the devil, and through his instigation, followed in rebellion against God and malignity towards man; and the terrible conflict here began between man's tempter and man's Deliverer that is finally to issue in the destruction of the devil and his designs; but the fall of humanity was sense-gratification against conscious obligation.

The first human sin was woman's, incipiently in her listening and leaning to temptation, and fully consummated in the outer act of eating the fruit which God and conscience prohibited. The sin of inducing Adam was Eve's, but that of assenting and eating was his, and in the deliberate transgressions of both the entire humanity was ruined. Conjunct humanity, created male and female, conjointly sinned and debased itself in its primitive stock. The spirit subjected itself to the sense by its own act. Its trial was a necessity in the case itself, and required as a special formal arrangement by the best interest of man and the benevolence of God; paternally supervised and ordered by Jehovah, in a way that opened the best and freest occasion conceivable for confirmation in virtue, and yet eventuating in a sensual instead of a spiritual disposition. The essence of the sin and fall of humanity was in this primitive disposing of itself upon the end of sense-gratification; and this could not be from any other agency than the human itself. The devil did not, and could not do it, for humanity; God did not originate it; man only did or could make himself a sinner. The mystery of original sin does not lie in the subject who committed it, but in the Creator who made the being capable of originating it. And this can find its solution only in the consideration that, to have beings capable of virtue, involves also capability of sinning; and, as reason demands the former, it must, even in sadness for the issue, leave the door open to the latter.

SECTION III.

THE CHANGES INDUCED BY THE SIN OF MAN.

Sin has entered humanity and debased it, and in connection with man sin has also first reached the world of higher spirits, and the ruin is both widespread and dreadful. How God deals with lost angels we do not here inquire, although as their sin was in connection with his, so there is full evidence that God's dealings with man were designed to throw their influence upon other worlds. God's moral universe is one as truly as the material, and what occurs in one part is to have its bearing on others; and to angelic spirits, confirmed in virtue or fallen, the field of humanity is doubtless more fully in their view, than the spheres in which they move are to us mortals. We therefore cannot learn from them, as they learn from God's way with us; but to us, gleams of revealed light disclose that good angels rejoice in man's recovery, and sinful angels are confounded at his redemption. Principalities and powers in heavenly places read the manifold wisdom of God in what through long ages he is doing for his Church, and for the lost world in the extension of his mediatorial kingdom. The single world of human inhabitants is a spectacle for all intelligences.

But while we leave other worlds to learn, as they may and do, from God's interpositions towards us, we turn with strong and saddened interest to contemplate the changes which the introduction of man's sin has induced. The very knowledge of the fact carries wide changes with it. The conscious sinner is debased and ashamed in his own conviction; and a disturbing blast spreads through the ranks of those yet steadfast. No moral personality stands as he before did. That has come in which all know ought not to have been; and conscious feelings and solicitudes arise which were never stirred before. A loathing and abhorring of the intruding abomination seizes upon all the good, who would fain repel the moral pollution from all approach to them. Anxiety arises as to what is to come of it, and how God will deal with it; while the remorse and forebodings of the guilty are still more direful. God himself is so affected by it that he cannot stand towards his creation as when no sin was in it. The change is universal and deplorable, and no good being can contemplate the sin and its consequences without rebuke and displeasure. We shall note these changes more in detail, having reference to the parties affected.

1. Changes on the Part of the Fallen Man and Woman.

1. *The radical change is the domination of sense over spirit.* — The gratification of the forbidden appetite was not a passionate impulse, suddenly breaking out in vehement intensity, and surprising to a desultory assent while the radical disposition was itself unchanged, but it carried the assent of the spirit, and so the perversion of the disposition, along with it. It had been a deliberate rejection of a conscious spiritual claim and a purposed acceptance of sensual indulgence as the chosen good, and such a disposing of the spirit fixed its voluntary state and settled into permanent personal character. This is the comprehensive change in Adam and Eve; they have become carnally-minded; persistently inclined towards sense-indulgence, and a renunciation of the self-respect and conscious peace which spiritual ascendency perpetuates. The animal part of humanity tyrannizes over the rational, and the spirit consents to the servitude, while every fresh indulgence leaves the spirit poor and

empty, and so fleeing from one gratification to another in constant unrest, continually deluded, and necessarily never satisfied. And such a soul has already in it the baseness, malignity, and desperate hate and enmity infused by the depraved spirit. There needs only the check and stern rebuke of righteous authority, and the "earthly and sensual" soul will manifest in the fiendishness of its spirit that it is also "devilish." The entire selfhood is alien from God, and determined solely to self-serving and indulging.

2. *Self-respect and divine trust has changed to shame and fear.* — The spirit knows its own baseness in consenting to serve the flesh, and in this is essentially the blended shame and remorse of a guilty conscience. The spirit infuses its own bitterness into the sentient soul, and bites back in self-torment with every repeated indulgence. The new gratification stings with a new conviction of vileness, and awakens also the foreboding fears of deserved retributions about to come. The intrinsic excellency and dignity of the spirit, standing in personal responsibility and integrity, Adam and Eve have both manifestly lost. They consent to give up personal prerogative and free self-possession and full responsibility for what they know to have been respectively their own acts, and which personal prerogative is above all price, and both admit that they have let another control them. "The woman whom thou gavest to be with me, she gave me of the tree, and I did eat," says Adam; and "the serpent beguiled me, and I did eat," says Eve; and so

both plead the baseness of renouncing their own selfhood as an excuse for their sinful sensuality. In all that ennobles personal action and character they have confessedly changed, and they manifestly carry with them the consciousness of their degradation, and are their own witnesses to the world of their folly, guilt, and madness. For self-approbation and universal respect they have taken self-reproach, divine displeasure, and the contempt even of the devil, their deceiver, and they still anticipate worse yet to come.

3. *They have fallen to a state of impotence and hopelessness.* — The free perversion of their disposition determines this. The spiritual is supernatural, and should control the sense, which is nature. Where there is only sense, from the necessary connections of cause and effect, the strongest impulses to gratification must prevail; but the endowment of man with the rational, which is spiritual, takes his agency out of the necessities of cause-and-effect connections, and capacitates to resist the impulses of appetite, and yield to the imperatives of reason and integrity of spirit. Brute-will has no freedom, and must follow the stronger appetite; but human will is in liberty, and should, as it can, comply with the claim to self-respect and moral worthiness. In the case of our first parents, the will has already yielded, and the personal spirit has taken self-gratification as the end of life, and so has basely bowed to the flesh and become carnal; and the carnal mind, restrained and rebuked, becomes malignant, implacable, and incorrigible. The

perverse inclination or bent of the soul becomes set and steadfastly fixed by the disposition the spirit has given to it, and in its own way persists in the accomplishment of its own purpose. The whole energy is intent in this one direction, and it has made itself impatient to action in another direction, and therein it has become hopeless to any self-recovery. It chooses madness and folly, and will not seek, and so cannot find, the paths of wisdom. The man has enslaved himself in his self-determined degradation to sense, and his self-restoration to his abdicated dominion over the flesh is most hopeless. His very liberty lapses in chosen impotence.

2. There were Changes towards Man on the Part of God.

1. *There was manifested deep disapprobation.* — Till now there had been nothing to move divine displeasure; but immediately upon the fall came God's arraignment and conviction of the guilty. Their own consciousness of the shameful change made them attempt to hide from his authoritative arrest, and forced to the acknowledgment of fear and nakedness, which was itself a clear disclosure and confession of sin, and was followed at once by stern, vindictive retribution. God is Absolute Reason, and his treatment of a sinner must be reasonable exactly. No passionate anger may be on one side, nor fond indulgence on the other. The exposed shameful guilt of man was regarded by God with precisely deserved

abhorrence. There was admitted nothing of palliation in the apologies presented. The disobedience had been wholly inexcusable, and the sensuality was strictly condemned just in accordance with its exact demerit. The man and the woman had each the same disposition which would gratify appetite at the expense of conscious disapprobation, and God revealed his equitable hatred of it.

2. *There was paternal compassion.* — The change just noticed, from precedent approbation to subsequent disapprobation, had also this important modification, that it was the disapprobation of a friend exclusive of all enmity. God was still their Father, though they had lost the disposition of children; hence the deep disapprobation was mingled with deep paternal pity. They were the creatures of his power, and their being had its source in his creative will, and there was more and other than sovereignty offended; there was fatherly goodness grieved; and this last could only find an expression in ways of compassionate regard. The strict condemnation for violated authority had with it also the yearning of fatherly tenderness. There was no extenuation of man's guilt in the acquired carnal disposition, nor any allowance for it, as if it had been an unfortunate calamity merely, and not determined apostasy; but with all the known guilt and debasement, there was the pity which prompted to the interposition of all that might help the case, or open any measures of relief and deliverance. The very Reason, which in

its own end had made and tried humanity precisely as it behooved reason to do, and which was saddened by man's delinquency and apostasy, moved to commiseration in even its intense disapprobation.

3. *From this displeasure and compassion came the purpose of redemption.* — God was both offended Sovereign and compassionate Father, and the sin of man put this double relation of God to him in such conflict that both could not peacefully stand together. The former demanded justice, the latter asked mercy. Absolute Reason alone saw in its profoundest depths the one way to put them both in harmony. As Sovereign he abhors and condemns, as Father he pities and would spare; and he can stand to man in no position which can abolish this double relation. What Absolute Reason must find, for his own tranquillity in view of man's apostasy, is some expedient to mark his sovereign abhorrence of sin, together with the full flow of fatherly compassion for the sinner; and in the disturbance which sin everywhere introduces, even within the bosom of Absolute Reason himself, we may well expect the plan of human Redemption to be a mystery too deep for the race to receive, until many of its generations pass through special processes of divine instruction.

The indications in inspired Scripture are clear, that antecedently to man's creation, in the eternal ages, a peculiar relationship was purposed between the Logos, as Son of God, and the humanity yet to be constituted; and that an unprecedented covenant transaction, on the part of the Father and the Son, sealed to the Son complete satisfaction for a coming travail of spirit he was to undergo, in the possession of a seed that should arise, and in whose prosperity the pleasure of the Lord should be consummated.[1] But if our first parents could not yet apprehend the presence of a spiritual tempter, much less must it be possible for them to comprehend the coming and work of a Divine Redeemer. A promise was given them involving the certainty of some coming deliverer, and that he should be found in some future "seed of the woman;" but all further peculiarities of character and work were left to the progressive unfolding of prophecy and ritual foreshadowing, till the actual advent and work of the Redeemer should plainly disclose God's method of "peace on earth and good will towards men." It was intimated that continual enmity would exist between man's descendants and the serpent race, hereafter to be interpreted as meaning the devil's hostility to man and man's Redeemer, and that the injury on one side would be severe, and on the other side fatal. "I will put enmity between thee and the woman, and between thy seed and her seed; it shall bruise thy head, and thou shalt bruise his heel."[2] It discloses God's attitude to man to be such as relieved from despair and opened future hope; yet the promised redemption left abundant tokens of divine displeasure at man's sin, while faint-

[1] Isa. liii. [2] Gen. iii. 15.

ly opening the light of God's gracious coming interpositions.

4. *God's open communion with man changed, to be only through mediation.*—The opening a way of redemption opened an occasion for a new probation. The first trial necessarily stood upon equity, giving an even-handed discipline in the cultivation of spiritual integrity and the control of sensual appetite. As this failed, eventuating in sensuality, and followed by a dispensation of grace resting upon a divine interposition, so it behooved to open a further trial for humanity on this new and more favored footing. But here God may no longer permit man to approach him in open communion, and he stand to his fallen and sensuous creatures with unchanged tokens of his former satisfaction. As a sinner, God, with all his compassion, must disapprove and rebuke man for the carnal disposition he cherishes, and refuse an immediate communion face to face in the light of his approving smile. This was signified by his exclusion from the "tree of life," and the guard of flaming cherubim which barred all future approach to its fruit from every quarter. God's favor is life, and man, spiritually dead in his carnal disposing, cannot appropriate that favor, nor taste its living peace and joy. He can come to it again only through the medium of the new dispensation of Grace, and standing before God in another's name, and not his own. His prayer and his thanksgiving, his whole worship of God and communion with him, must now be only through faith in

the promised mode of pardon and reconciliation. Hence so soon began offerings and sacrifices; and hence the clear interpretation of God's respect to Abel's sacrifice, and his rejection of Cain's. The former looked to God through a Mediator, the latter presumed upon the direct offering of his own gift.

5. *God's dealings with man changed to blended severity and kindness.* — A determined and promised plan of redemption afforded an adequate ground for God to mitigate the original threatening, and confer much positive kindness, while putting man upon a new probation. There must be manifest severity in his dealings, to enforce the conviction of his displeasure against their depravity; and this immediately began, by driving the first pair from the prepared Paradise which had been theirs in their innocence. The open world, in its uncultivated ruggedness, received them, and its thorns and thistles blasted and choked the vegetation they cultivated, and forced them with toil and sweat to eat their bread. The mind was to be burdened with care, and the body worn with labor; weariness, pain, and sickness must supervene to their exposures and privations till at length their fleshly tabernacle should fall again to the dust from whence it had been taken. In all this severity there is not the retribution in strict justice of the original threatening of eternal death, and yet it is a curse which even in a gracious administration makes "the creation groan and travail together in pain until now."

But though God thus manifested his abhorence of their sin, there were many ways in which he proved himself placable and graciously inclined to help their wretchedness and restore them from their ruin. Their deepest suffering was yet so far a mitigation of their just penalty as to teach them clearly that by so much "mercy had already rejoiced against judgment," and that in their very misery God was gracious still. Many good things were left for their enjoyment. Shut out of Paradise, but yet living in a world of many offered benefits; the earth yielded its harvests, though only through toil, and the brute bowed his neck in service, though more stubbornly and impatiently than before the fall. The sun shone and the seasons cheered, and social life offered its gladness, and communion with God was permitted through a Mediator, though no longer face to face. Earth was a wilderness compared with Eden, yet such as man might make to "bud and blossom as the rose." All good was forfeited, and unmingled evil deserved, and yet direct acts of kind care and help from God awakened hope and joy. The one recorded interposition where "the Lord God made coats of skin and clothed them,"[1] had much more in it than the conferring of present relief and comfort. It told them plainly of God's regard for their welfare, and spoke strongly in present consolation, and for future expectation of further bounty. And this was doubtless but one of many instances of paternal minis-

[1] Gen. iii. 21.

tration to the need of his fallen children. He was in it dealing with them in kindness and pity, not in anger; his own hand was helping them, and revealing him to be their benefactor, and not an inexorable avenger.

3. Changes in Regard to Humanity in General.

1. *After his fall Adam ceased to act as public head of his race.* — Had the first parents continued spiritually disposed, their descendants would have formed their disposition and fixed their character under the conditions which the parents of the race must have induced for them, and which could then have been more advantageous for holding sense subservient to the spirit than was even the arrangement made for Adam. The body would have been "put under and brought into subjection" by both man and woman; God would have communed with them face to face; all would have been tranquil and serene within and without; and in such inner and outer conditions, it might strongly be expected that the successive generations of the race would open their moral agency in spiritual integrity, and grow more confirmed in virtue. But Adam's sin closed irrevocably all such opportune conditions. The ascendency of sense has put his spirit in bondage, and all such favorable prospective propagation of the race from him is blasted. The first parents now stand condemned and excuseless; self-convicted of guilt, and subject to the penalty; and if justice be allowed its course, final condemnation must

immediately ensue; and thus at once would come the exclusion of any posterity by the infliction of eternal death upon the first sinners. All this is settled for Adam in Adam's first transgression. If God now, as he does, provide a way of redemption, and by this open the occasion for delay of punishment, and put Adam upon a new form of probation, and admit the incoming of a rising race of descendants, this cannot reinstate Adam in his former public headship, that he may act again for them as he necessarily must have done in his first trial. His fall has already shut up the bowers of Paradise, and precluded open communion with heaven, and the harmony of fleshly appetite with spiritual rule; and no subsequent act of his, under any form of governmental administration, can bring these advantages back for his posterity, that they may begin their moral agency and fix their disposition and character under these favorable influences once offered for the race.

What Adam may now do under the new administration of Grace, can go only for himself. If there come repentance, and faith, and return to allegiance, and thus to communion again with God, this can be for himself alone, and only through the mediation of the new covenant. He and the individuals of his posterity must each hereafter stand upon the responsibilities of personal agency. His first trial, from the necessity of the case, was as public head of humanity; and thus in itself representative and determinative of the forming conditions of character for all, settling once and forever how his posterity must begin their spiritual agency, and under what conditions they must form their permanent disposition; and now no other act of his can reverse the first trial, or begin any new trial for them.

2. *Fallen humanity will perpetuate depravity through the race.* — Man's trial has been the most favorable for virtuous integrity possible, and the fact of his fall has left no other way open for a rising posterity but through a gracious provision of redemption, which puts man upon a new probation, where each person must be held liable for his own spiritual disposing. In all this there has been nothing arbitrary, but it is just what it should be to satisfy reason. To neither God nor man can any other way be so well, and yet in just this moral arrangement for the race, it will occur that, through human perversion of the best and most gracious provisions, depravity will be propagated through all generations. The first sinners, left to their own way, though with capacities and under obligation to reform and restore the spirit to its rightful rule over sense, yet will never accomplish it. In their lapsed disposition is the will reluctating against the return to spirituality, and which perpetuates the depravity in them; and such lapse of the spirit under the dominion of the flesh has given the sense an ascendency and advantage, and has so aggravated and intensified its habitual control, that the physical propagation of the sense in the descendants will carry its inordinate carnal influences along

with it. These will be of sufficient prevalent impulse in every descendant, on the first originating of moral agency, to induce the spirit to yield to the sense, and fix the assenting disposition on the ends of the fleshly gratification, to the rejection of spiritual integrity. The first agency in moral personality will thus be as certainly perverse in the posterity, as the subsequent acts of the first sinner in the fallen ancestor will continue carnally apostate. The moving impulses of the vitiated sensibility will be alike in the sinning progenitor and the new offspring, the state of the spirit alone being different.

With the sinning parent, the flesh has its aggravated lusts, and moreover the spirit has already consented and bowed beneath its bondage, and the disposed will has nothing in it for reversing the depraved disposition; with the propagated descendant, the flesh has all the aggravated lusting impulses of the fallen parent, but the superinduced reason, as personal spirit, has not yet succumbed to the domination of appetite, and become perverted spirit. This spiritual disposition the child must first set within itself ere it shall take the sinful character of the fallen parent; and thus it is true of every descendant of fallen Adam, that it is his own disposing which fixes in him the carnal disposition of Adam, while his intensated sense impulses follow the law of social liabilities in physical propagation. The appetites have the aggravations of the fallen parent, but the rational spirit must consent to be in servitude to them, before the character can become sinfully apostate, as is that of the sinning parent.

In this way it is true that every descendant of Adam has his own trial, and fixes his own disposition in his own consent to carnal servitude; yet the necessary consequences of the trial and fall of the first sinner of the race make this free and responsible disposing a matter of certainty, that it will be a perverse disposing. The aggravated appetites follow natural law in physical generation, and the spiritual disposing which might be, and ought to be, in subjecting sense with all its aggravated lusting, yet certainly will be in basely yielding to sensual indulgence. A vitiated constitutional propensity to pilfer, known as *kleptomania,* sometimes manifests itself as with great difficulty restrained and subjected; a child of a confirmed inebriate sometimes inherits the vitiated impulse known as *oinomania,* which makes a life of sobriety hardly attainable; still in each case the propensity can be restrained by a virtuous resolution; so the vitiated sensibility diffused from Adam through humanity goes down to the children through the flesh, and not through the rational spirit, and in this case we learn both from revelation and experience, that all begotten of Adam, to a certainty, give the spirit over in bondage to this carnal lusting, if left of God to their own disposing.

This sense-pravity is *vitium,* and not *peccatum;* but

as it originated in the personal disposing of the spirit in bondage to sense by our first parents, and the vitiation beginning in them is perpetuated through their posterity, and is now in human nature, not as created, but as perverted in the first transgression, it is truly *originale vitium;* while the original sinning act, from which the *vitium* sprang, is *originale peccatum.* When, in theology, we speak of *original sin*, we must distinguish between *vitium* and *peccatum*, and apply sinful desert to the forming disposition which in each descendant follows his originally vitiated sensibility. While, then, a natural ability for disposing the spirit to the firm suppression and control of the vitiated sense, is still with the spirit itself, and the obligation rests upon every descendant of Adam so to do, yet the pravity of sense following the first sin gives certainty, that what might be and should be done will yet not be done, in any case, by self-movement. All are naturally *liable* to the necessary consequences of the progenitor's vitiated sensuality, but each is *responsible* morally only for his perversion of his own spirit. Here is no semi-pelagianism, as if the connection of the first sin and all subsequent sin were cut half in twain; nor any necessity for action in a pre-existing state to save personal freedom; but a connection of certainty in freedom, that as Adam vitiated sense, so all his posterity will deprave their disposition, and "go astray as soon as they be born.

3. *Redemption assumes this universal certainty of a sinning race.* — What the plan of Redemption is we shall further on better see; but we can here know that all prospective dealing in mercy with the race is on the assured ground that all will need the gracious interposition. To God, at the first, this was certain so soon as Adam sinned, and that the recovery of none could be effected but by grace, and their allegiance confirmed anew but by a divine redemption. The first Promise that the seed of the woman should bruise the serpent's head, while the seed of the serpent should bruise the heel only of humanity, was applicable to all, and carried in it the divine testimony that the consequences of the fall went down to coming ages, parallel with that deliverance which was designed to reach all ages. And so, also, the curses upon man and woman, spoken originally to Adam and Eve, were yet inclusive of all their descendants, inasmuch as the certainty of their sinning would involve their certain desert as truly as in the case of the first transgressors. The posterity did not actually sin in Adam's sin, but they take naturally and necessarily Adam's vitiated sensibility, and under this comes the certain voluntary disposing of the spirit in subjection to the flesh. They have no personal responsibilities for his act, but as natural descendants they have all the liabilities to the natural consequences of such act, and must of necessity dispose their spirit and fix their own character under the consequent conditions of Adam's act. The as-

sumption of the certainty of their sinning is not that they are made sinners by any other, and only the fore-affirming of the fact, that through the aggravations of the vitiated sense they will all make themselves to be sinners. The *vitium* is natural, the *peccatum* is moral and personal.

4. *The first trial failing, a remedial system must stand on "better promises."* — Paternal kindness seeks deliverance for lost humanity, and changes the mode of administering discipline to the race, and this mode must have advantages over the former, and include stronger influences for virtue, in order to justify its introduction. Why even divine pity attempt anything further, if there is not ground for higher encouragement than in the failing administration? God must uphold the integrity of his own character, in having arranged a mode of trial which has failed, and must find weightier motives on the side of a spiritual disposing and control over sense, than the first arrangement offered; in which case nothing will hinder his fatherly love in changing his dealings with man from the demands of equity to the solicitations of compassion.

Inasmuch as we find the race perpetuated and multiplying its generations over the earth, and as we find patience prolonged and grace sparing the convicted and condemned, we are obliged to conclude that God has in some way vindicated his name and authority, and put intenser impulses at work to bring the spirit over the flesh, and therein finally justifying himself to every conscience, in his wonderful, and wholly otherwise unprecedented, remedial measures for lost man's redemption. This remedial administration immediately supervened upon the first apostasy, and a history thence opens full of hope for man, and of interest and astonishment for other orders of spirits; and which, in fact, must reveal the secret counsel and purpose of God in peopling our earth, and settling upon it a race of flesh and blood, and yet endowed with the prerogatives of rationality. We know, at the start, that this history must bring out God's vindication of wisdom and righteousness in his way of saving the lost; and we shall not better comprehend how this can be, than by noting the long providential interpositions, which have taught the nations how God has put his hand into human history, for the redemption of the race from sensuality, to pure spiritual integrity and dignity. The degradation of mankind is so deep, that long centuries of discipline and instruction scarcely suffice to bring the race to know and choose the only method of recovery. We are to study the history as God's development of his own plan of salvation for man.

CHAPTER II.

THE REDEEMER MUST PREPARE HUMANITY FOR HIS COMING INCARNATION.

THE fall of man has left him in a state of degradation and ruin, from which there is nothing in humanity to effect deliverance. The carnal mind will never from itself return to its spiritual subjection, nor can the human spirit ever atone for its wilful sensuality. Another than man must come to men, and work out their deliverance, and the moving spring and efficient execution for this can nowhere be found, but in the abhorrence for sin and pity for the sinner which is in God himself. We have seen already the necessity for a threefold conscious voluntariness in Absolute Reason, that he may be known in Creation, and in governmental Administration; and equally is tri-personality necessary to know God in Redemption. The original eternal plan is of the Father; the manifesting this in human flesh is of the Son; and the execution of it, in the human heart and the universal church, is of the Holy Ghost. The same Reason which creates also redeems, and the One Absolute Reason can be known in human redemption only in this distinctive being and working of threefold consciousness and will. Essence, in pure simplicity, can be conceived neither as creative nor redemptive.

The first promise to fallen man assured him that a Conqueror of his tempter should come, as in some way the seed of the woman; but this promise in later scripture is shown as resting upon an earlier transaction in the counsels of the Godhead. The reference before made to the fifty-third chapter of Isaiah shows that this Conqueror was to be a suffering Saviour, since "it pleased the Lord to bruise him;" and that "he shall see of the travail of his soul and be satisfied;" and in these divine counsels, before all time, the pledge was given that this suffering Saviour was to be a victorious Sovereign, having a spiritual seed to serve him. And in Psalms we have the announcement of this eternal pledge and counsel, "I will declare the decree; the Lord hath said unto me, Thou art my Son; this day have I begotten thee."[1] It might have been anticipated, as in these revealed eternal counsels it is found to be, that the Logos as the second Person, or expressive manifester of the Father, would be the Redeemer of lost humanity, and that antecedent to his coming into humanity, he would prepare the race for his utterly unexampled mission. In Creation there is declared the glory of God, but in Redemption the divine wisdom and majesty are even more profoundly glorious. The race must be first disciplined and trained before they can receive the great mystery of God manifest in the flesh. We

[1] Psalm ii. 7.

need not, then, wonder at the intervening thousands of years between the promise and the coming; but in all the long history before the Christian era, we shall find the Logos, Jehovah himself, working in and upon the nations to prepare them for his successful coming and teaching as their Redeemer. The same divine Personality which enters human flesh, enters beforehand into human history, and integrates himself with the race, that he may bring them up to apprehend the meaning and the mercy of his incarnation. His human living and dying will be in vain, without his previous moulding and educating of the humanity he redeems.

SECTION I.

SPECIAL PROVIDENCES CURBING IN THE STRONG TENDENCIES TO IMPIETY AND VIOLENCE.

MAN, fallen under the control of sensuality, did not like to retain God in his knowledge, and the first tendencies of depraved humanity were towards irreligion and open atheism. The excited appetites prompted passionately to gratification, and in the selfishness of each, the weak were made the prey of the strong, and the quick result was the spread of violence and crime. "All flesh corrupted his way upon the earth," and the imagination, thought, and plan of the race became evil continually. The carnal mind was darkened, and the selfish heart was hardened. The ordinances and institutions of Paradise tending to purity and piety were overborne and perverted, and what would have been his safeguard in virtue became the provocative to all licentiousness in his depravity. God had said to the first pair in their innocence, "Be fruitful and multiply, and replenish the earth;" designing the propagation of the race under the restraints of marriage, and the genial sympathies of the family, but which was early prostituted to practices of polygamy, adultery, and promiscuous licentiousness. In the early vigor of the race and the unchecked indulgence of sexual passion, the earth was over-rapidly peopled by exorbitant births and prodigious longevity, so that communities and tribes, multiplying and enlarging faster than they could be socially disciplined and civilized, and seeking their territorial habitations at their own pleasure, interfered with and encroached upon each other, and at once opened in the savage practices of rapine, war, and enslavement of captives. The Sabbath had been instituted in the period of man's unsinning communion with God; and immediately upon the fall the way of sacrificial worship had been instituted, resting all access to God by the sinner upon the mediation of the coming expiatory death of the Saviour; but the growing masses of mankind carried their apostasy to utter rejection of all forms of religious devotion. Abel offered his acceptable sacrifice "by faith" in coming atoning blood; Seth and his posterity "called on the name of the Lord;" and Enoch "walked with God," and was translated; but the multitude discarded God, and wrought wickedness. The First-born among men slew the first Brother that was begotten, out of spite to God's regard for his expiatory offering; and so onward, infidelity towards God and crime towards man increasingly abounded, till "it repented the Lord that he had made man upon the earth," so hopeless of all reformation had the corrupt race made themselves before him.

Such general incorrigible impiety and vice demanded an interposing rebuke, as signally and widely indicative of God's displeasure and determination to arrest and restrain it. The first ebullitions of depraved sensuality were the most violent, and the correcting restraints were proportionally severe. Successive applications of discipline correct the growing generations, and curb the varied modes of outbreaking sensuality, till at length the ages come to such a measure of culture, that the Redeemer may enter into humanity, and penetrate, and purify it with a new spiritual life. His corrections are always equal and appropriate to the enormity of the offences.

1. The World overwhelmed by the Flood. — As in the first trial, so in the first peopling of the earth, God put man in the most favoring circumstances for the ends in view, and left the issue to man's responsi-

bility. But one family only of all the tribes of the human race had maintained the knowledge and worship of the true God, while the universal irreligion and profligacy of the rest of the world had made it manifest that fallen man would pervert those favoring circumstances, and that no discipline of ordinary providences would prepare humanity to profit by the introduction of the designed plan of redemption. Present wickedness, and the warning of coming generations, demanded a terrible judgment. God thus forewarned the race that "the end of all flesh had come;" and that he would "destroy them with the earth." One hundred and thirty years he delayed the desolating flood, while Noah preached righteousness to that generation, and prepared the Ark for the salvation of his family. But none heeded the warning, nor repented of their sins, and God's patience found its limit. "The windows of heaven were opened, and the fountains of the great deep were broken up;" "and the flood came and took them all away;" "and all flesh died that moved upon the earth." "And Noah only remained alive, and they that were with him in the Ark." Noah and wife, and his three sons, Shem, Ham, and Japheth, and their wives, were saved to begin a new peopling of the earth, under the more encouraging circumstances which the dreadful judgment had induced.

In many respects, the second spread of human population upon the earth was more favorable than when immediately from the first fallen pair. The terrible example of human wickedness and God's dealing with it were before the eyes of men; the mercy in the covenant that such destruction would not be repeated, and which the natural bow upon the rain-cloud was made to symbolize; and the religious order and control prevalent in the godly families saved over from the old world; and the manifestly greater carefulness in fixing the dwelling-places of the growing tribes and nations for mutual safety and general advantage and friendship, — all tended to individual improvement and public peace and harmony. In their separate journeyings and colonizing, they still strove to keep up monuments of common interest, and bonds for persistent communion in towers and public edifices.

2. The Shortening of Human Life in its Successive Generations. — An average duration of human life before the flood, following Hebrew chronology, had been about nine hundred years. Noah lived six hundred years before the flood, and three hundred and fifty years after it. But immediately after the deluge the ages of men upon the earth were gradually shortened to the time of Moses. We have the record of those in the direct line from Shem to Abraham, and these may be taken as fair examples of the longevity of other Shemitic families, as well as those descending from Ham and Japheth. The life of Shem was continued to six hundred years, being one third shorter than the average antediluvian life. Arphaxad lived four hundred and thirty-eight years, and from

him to Nahor, the father of Terah, and grandfather of Abraham, were six generations, by which time we have for his life one hundred and forty-eight years. His son Terah lived longer, to two hundred and five years, but Abraham's life was one hundred and seventy-five years; and thence to Moses, we have his own life of one hundred and twenty years; but in Psalm xc., referred to the time of Moses, the set time for the age of man is seventy years, and, in cases of more vigorous constitution, eighty years, at which point it has since remained through human generations.

Whatever may have been the proximate physiological tendency to diminished longevity, the great moral reason is to be seen in its influence on the government and discipline of the race. The long antediluvian ages were ministering occasions to the great wickedness of the old world. Sensuality had room to mature and execute its selfish schemes in the broadest manner, and the distance of anticipated death emboldened in indulgence and confirmed in habits of licentious excess and wanton iniquities. The death of the body, as the curse for the fall, was a merciful mitigation of the original penalty of eternal death for sin, and designed to hold the race under perpetual admonition of God's great displeasure against the transgression of the first pair, and a salutary restraint of controlling sensuality in coming ages. But this deferring the return of man to dust, through long centuries, had only eventuated in his fully setting his heart to do evil. The experience proved that a race of sinners, living a thousand years on the earth, could not be brought by any ordinary moral discipline to such a state of moral preparation that the promised Redeemer could come to them with any expectation of their acceptance of his salvation. But this cutting short of human life by nine tenths of its duration was a most powerful and largely successful means of bridling human lust and passion, and forcing a depraved race to feel their need of the coming of a gracious Deliverer. That the early postdiluvian generations might more rapidly repeople the desolated world, this contraction of the life of man was graduated through several centuries; yet by the tenth and twelfth generations, the old nearly thousand years of human probation had been shortened to threescore years and ten. By thus heavily pressing the fact of mortality constantly upon human conviction, there has been a continual gracious influence in keeping up a seed to serve the Lord

3. Guarding Human Life from Violence by Capital Punishment. — In connection with the permission to man to eat animal flesh as food after the flood, was the caution to abstain from eating the blood. All flesh was delivered into the hand of man; but as preventive of all wanton cruelty, and a guard from savage ferocity, blood, as the representative of life, was marked with special sanctity. And then, more effectually to restrain the violence between man and man, which had been so prevalent before the flood, God

took occasion from this prohibiting the use of animal blood, to require capital punishment for the malicious shedding of human blood. "At the hand of every man's brother will I require the life of man. Whoso sheddeth man's blood, by man shall his blood be shed; for in the image of God made he man."[1] Governmental execution of capital punishment, properly administered, will not deprave public sentiment, but impress upon it salutary awe and veneration, while the withholding of the punishment of death by civil process, in case of murder, tends to provoke the excited neighborhood to sudden vengeance by their own hands. The death-penalty should be most carefully and solemnly administered, but the forfeited life of the murderer should be taken lawfully, when outraged public sentiment is endangered to bloody vindication without law. If public sentiment may be so cultivated and elevated as to hold itself calm and orderly under milder forms of penal execution, capital punishment may then be abolished. But from the flood till now, humanity in no community has seemed to rise above the terrible necessity of legally exacting life for life.

In view of the sad experience of the old world from incorrigible crime and violence, it cannot be soberly doubted that the introduction of capital punishment by divine requisition was salutary and benevolent. It did not exclude all malice prepense from issuing in murder, but it did check much maliciousness, and hold back from many murders. It could not

[1] Gen. ix. 5, 6.

again be said, in any generation of Noah's descendants guarded by this legal sanction, as it was true of the old world, that "the earth was filled with violence." Combined civil authority restrained individual malignity.

4. Confounding their Language. — Under these restraining and remedial influences, the descendants of Noah, through his sons, Shem, Ham, and Japheth, multiplied in the earth, and lived in harmony among themselves. The salutary dread from the remembered deluge, and traditionary accounts and long perpetuated traces of it, kept alive the recognition of God and reverence for his authority. The multiplying families kept much in company, though roving from place to place. This continued through two or three centuries, all of one speech and preserving kindred cordiality and friendship; a great improvement in social life from that of the old world, but yet tending to evils of another kind and in the opposite direction. They chose to keep together, and thus would preclude many benefits from agriculture, enterprise, and separate national interests. It became necessary that there should be a special interposition for diffusing the population abroad into separate communities. This took place in the time of Peleg, as it is noted that "in his days was the earth divided."

Peleg was born ninety-seven years after the flood, and he lived two hundred and thirty-nine years; so that at least within about three centuries from the flood the families of man were again spreading wide abroad in the earth. The general history is thus given by inspiration: They were journeying all together "from the east," and came to "a plain in the land of Shinar." Here seemed a convenient place for their common abode, and they found abundant materials for the brick and mortar with which to build a city. To make the city a more important monument of common renown, and hold the people from scattering abroad, they built also a tower, whose top, in exaggerated speech, they meant "should reach unto heaven." Scattered tribes of common speech ere long make changes in the language, beyond the capability of mutual conversation; but here the problem was, to get the people of common speech in separate communities. They took determined means to hold themselves together. Jehovah, in his power and wisdom, reversed the natural process, and made their speech unintelligible among themselves, and thus obliged them to separate into different clans, according to their capability of using a common dialect. So were they necessarily sundered, and the different portions of the earth inhabited, and the common city and tower in the plain of Shinar deserted of at least the most of their builders. This gave the name Babel — confusion — to the tower in subsequent generations. So all the varied descendants of Japheth, and Ham, and Shem, "every one of them after his tongue," were divided in their countries and nations. Nimrod, "a mighty hunter from the Lord," had his kingdom from

Babel, and comprising many other cities which he built; Ashur built Nineveh on the Tigris, and other towns; and so Canaan, and Philistia, and Egypt, and the wide "isles of the Gentiles," were inhabited.

All these nations were now in their forming state, and the elements of the coming great Assyrian empire were gathering; and when at length these and other independent kingdoms emerge into the light of history, they are found with settled laws and established institutions, recognizing civil rights and religious obligations. The atheism and savage violence prevalent at the time of the flood were superseded, and a more elevated and cultivated population had been secured by the special and providential interpositions of the Lord; and yet their civilization was but little removed from barbarism, and their religion was superstitious and idolatrous. Polytheism generally prevailed, and among the tribes of Shem, who more conservatively retained the faith of monotheism, even here, universally, so far as appears, the believers in one God were so far degenerated and paganized, that they joined in the general practices of idolatry. Even Terah, Abraham's father, and his contemporaries, "served other gods."[1] Some new method of discipline must cure this idolatry.

[1] Josh. xxiv. 2.

SECTION II.

THE CALL OF ABRAHAM.

HUMANITY had attained the age and condition when general providences and special interpositions of judgment and mercy applied to all, or occurring promiscuously amid the varied families and nations of the earth, would not preserve the race from continued degeneracy in sensuality and false religion. If its sensuality tolerate any religion, it must be such as submits to be subservient to the flesh. The very gods it worships will have the passions and practices which itself delights to cherish. It will not recognize deity as a spirit, and worship him in spirit, but will have sensual media obscuring his pure spirituality, and ultimately tolerating the thought that God is such a one as itself. It is the age of idolatry, and in that point and period of its cultivation and experience, humanity will everywhere tend to nature-worship, hero-worship, or image-worship, and all connected cruel and debasing superstitions.

The wise expedient divinely taken is, to concentrate special instruction and influence upon one nation, which shall secure their acknowledgment and worship of the true God, and set this peculiar people conspicuously among the nations as a missionary people for the world. But no one race or nation can at the time be found distinctively spiritual and godly enough to set forth as the teacher of the world; and the necessary process is to begin with one Man, and lay accumulating influences enough on him and his rising descendants to make and keep them a special people for the Lord. The end in view is the elevation of the race, and not partiality and favoritism for the chosen people; and for the sake of the whole, that man must be taken which omniscience shall see shall secure the end best and surest for all.

In making such selection God designated Abram, a son of Terah, the eighth in descent from Shem, the son of Noah. The native place of Terah was in Ur of the Chaldees; but on removing from Chaldea to go into the land of Canaan, he journeyed so far as to the north-western border of Mesopotamia, and built a city for his followers, calling it Haran, after a son, who had died and been buried in Chaldea. This was his subsequent residence and burial-place, and the early home of Abram and country of his kinsmen. Here, when Abram was seventy-five years old, the Lord said to him, "Get thee out of thy country, and from thy kindred, and from thy father's house, unto a land that I shall tell thee. And I will make of thee a great nation, and I will bless thee, and make thy name great, and thou shalt be a blessing; and I will bless them that bless thee, and curse him that curseth thee; and in thee shall all the families of the earth be blessed."[1] Abram obeyed, and with his family and substance carried out his father's old intention of removing to Canaan; and upon his arrival at Sychem, in the land of Canaan, the Lord again appeared to him, and promised to give the land in which he was to his seed.[2] After having journeyed in different directions in the land with his family and substance, and Lot, his brother's son, and built altars to God where he rested; and having also, on occasion of a famine, been down to Egypt, and returned again to Canaan with great wealth, and when Lot had separated from him to dwell in the plain of the Jordan; Jehovah again promised him the land for his seed with greater particularity. "Lift up now thine eyes, and look from the place where thou art, northward and southward, and eastward and westward; for all the land which thou seest, to thee will I give it, and to thy seed forever. And I will make thy seed as the dust of the earth; so that if a man can number the dust of the earth, then shall thy seed also be numbered."[3]

The import of this Abrahamic promise needs to be carefully noted. It was in substance repeated to him, and subsequently to his son Isaac, and again to Jacob, and through following centuries was the basis of religious life and Christian expectation. The Old Testament church rested upon it, and the New Testament church is in fulfilment of it. In one part, it was an enlarged repetition of the promise to Adam

[1] Gen. xii. 1-3. [2] Gen. xii. 7. [3] Gen. xiii. 14-16.

after his fall, and renewed to Noah through Shem after the flood, that some great deliverer from the curse of sin should come in the seed of Eve. Here, to Abram, who had descended from Shem, it was particularized that the deliverance should be from his seed, and for all the nations of the earth. And another part promised a national possession of Canaan, and an innumerable posterity. The last national part was preparatóry and subsidiary to the universal spiritual part. The national part was clear and full; the spiritual part made the first promise at the fall more clear and full, but no one was yet able to see in it what the apostle Paul drew from it — "He saith not, And to seeds, as of many, but, Unto thy seed, which is Christ."[1] Besides frequent repetitions of the promise, there were significant interpositions and institutions in connection with it, giving prominence to the importance with which God regarded it; once, by instituting a special sacrifice, and giving a remarkable signal of his presence;[2] again, by changing his name Abram to Abraham;[3] and then, again, by the ordinance of circumcision.[4] On this promise the hope of a lost world rested.

1. Means for securing Abraham's Faith and Devotion to God. — As the ancestor of the chosen nation, Abraham must be made eminently a man of God. He had already been taken away from the

[1] Gal. iii. 16.
[2] Gen. xv. 9-17.
[3] Gen. xvii. 5.
[4] Gen. xvii. 9-14.

idolatries of Haran, and made to be a pilgrim and stranger in Canaan, and had thus been thrown upon the sole protection of God, who had intimately befriended him; and this pilgrimage life was perpetuated to the end of his days. The land was promised to his seed, but he had no possessions in it, save the purchased burial-place of the cave of Machpelah. He was greatly prospered in flocks, and herds, and numerous servants, but he constantly wandered from place to place.[1] And then there was the long deferring of children, apparently inducing the expectation that the heirship must come by adoption.[2] Then Ishmael is born, and Abraham would have God accept him, for Sarah has been barren, and is now aged. Then Isaac is promised of Sarah,[3] and again the time of his birth is foretold,[4] and at the set time he is born, Abraham a hundred and Sarah ninety years old. And then, at the destruction of Sodom for the great wickedness of the people, God communes with Abraham, and hears his requests and conditions for sparing the place if at length ten righteous persons could be found in it; and saves Lot from the overthrow; and more signally tries his faith, by demanding the sacrifice of Isaac; and further confirms it, by substituting a ram providentially supplied as the sacrificial victim.[5] The result of all God's discipline was, notwithstanding manifest faults in Abraham's life a steady-growing confidence in God

[1] Acts vii. 5. [2] Gen. xv. 2-4. [3] Gen. xvii. 19.
[4] Gen. xviii. 10. [5] Gen. xxii. 13.

and fidelity in his service, to the attainment of that eminence in piety which made him worthy to be known as "the father of the faithful."

2. Influences on Abraham's Descendants in the Line of the Promise. — Patriarchal government had continued from Noah to Abraham, whereby the authority and influence of the ancestors largely moulded the character and conduct of the descendants. To secure the piety of Abraham was thus to secure a patriarchal blessing upon his posterity. God strongly depended on this to prepare the way of Covenant descent in holiness. He says, "For I know him, that he will command his household and his children after him, and they shall keep the way of the Lord to do justice and judgment, that the Lord may bring upon Abraham that which he hath spoken of him."[1] Accordingly, in addition to the pious nurture and education of Isaac, care was taken for his marriage connection in the family of Nahor, Abraham's brother, by which Rebekah more favorably came within the privileges and under the obligations of the Covenant than could have been anticipated from any of the daughters of the Canaanites. To pious patriarchal government was added such a providential arrangement as made the progress towards a nation gradual, and very slow in the early generations of the patriarchs. The bearing of this upon the virtue of the national stock becomes strikingly apparent.

[1] Gen. xviii. 19.

Abraham had been called in Covenant at seventy-five years of age, and remained for years childless; and when Ishmael is born he is rejected from the promise, and Isaac is not born and taken into the Covenant till Abraham is one hundred years old. All this, we have seen, tried and ultimately strengthened the faith of the first heir of the promise. And the like delay still continues. Of the children of Isaac, Esau is rejected, and Jacob designated as the heir to the Covenant. For about one hundred years no multiplication is made of the Covenant descendants. Isaac singly perpetuates the line to Jacob, and Jacob stands alone till his children succeed, and from him all the posterity are reckoned. Why not push on this national arrangement more rapidly? To human view it might seem needful to hasten, but here, as often, it is manifest that God does not make haste, and the reason appears in the connected events. The Ishmaelites and the various tribes descended from Abraham by Keturah all soon forget the God of their father, and become idolaters. Esau's posterity all degenerate, and become absorbed in the general pagan superstitions. The great design in the Abrahamic Covenant matures as fast as the depravity of humanity in this age of the world will allow. By concentrating special influences upon Abraham, he is made strong in righteousness; by giving Isaac ease and peace, and kindly nurture all his life, he becomes a single link in the pious succession; and by throwing Jacob into exile, and making him pass through constant trials, and endure hardness all his days, he is made an appropriate stock, in which the twelve tribes of Israel branch off, and begin their hastening to the promised "great nation." And how certain does it now appear, that the multiplication is as rapid as the race will bear! How hardly does the expanded surface hold the strain of the inward depravity! Iniquity comes in to the chosen people like a flood. Reuben commits incest with Bilhah, and Judah with Tamar; Dinah gives herself up in fornication with Shechem, a Canaanitish prince; Simeon and Levi treacherously slay all the Shechemites, and plunder their substance; and all the brethren join in hatred to Joseph, and conspire to sell him to the Ishmaelites, and deceive Jacob to believe that he had been slain by a wild beast. The chosen stock cannot endure further growth, but it must have further purging and pruning.

SECTION III.

EGYPT, AND THE GOING DOWN OF THE ISRAELITES INTO IT.

Beside the dangers to the Covenant people from their own augmenting depravity, it is difficult to see how, without perpetual miraculous interpositions, they could be preserved to grow up to a nation among the

Canaanites. God's purpose concerning them was publicly known, and both on their own account and as a warning and means of instruction to the Gentile nations, the great Abrahamic promise must be kept prominent and often referred to. This would necessarily subject them to the jealousy and exterminating hatred of the doomed nation. The spirit which subsequently instigated Herod to slay the male children of Bethlehem would be excited, and in order to defeat the purpose would destroy the chosen people in their weakness. The way divine wisdom secured the result was to make a lodgment of the Hebrew family within the protection of the most powerful kingdom of the earth. Egypt was too strong to permit any or all the Canaanite nations to disturb Israel, and the interest of the Egyptians would secure the growing people from external or internal injury. From their long abode in Egypt it will be needful somewhat minutely to describe it.

There are so many monuments of the earlier ages still existing in the land of Egypt, so much interest has been awakened by the at least quite extensive deciphering of their old hieroglyphical inscriptions, and such learned and careful explorations have been made with the modern facilities for tourists to visit the tombs and temples of the Nile, that there is now little difficulty, connected with the accounts of old geographers and historians, in attaining much satisfactory knowledge of this oldest and strongest empire of its day in our world, though still more of its ancient history and internal experience has been irrecoverably lost from any modern research.

1. The Settlement and Growth of Egypt. — Egypt is known in Scripture as "the land of Ham." It cannot be certainly, nor perhaps probably, said that Ham ever entered the Egyptian valley; but his second son, Mizraim, with his descendants after their tongues, went there from the plain of Shinar, immediately after the confusion of language at Babel. In ancient historic notices Egypt is acknowledged as the land of Mizraim, which name Syncellus writes *Mestraim*, and which, as first king of Egypt, Herodotus, Manetho, and Diodorus write *Menes*. These old historians, and especially Herodotus, have generally increasing modern credit, and are confirmed by general accordance in their representations with the Bible history.

Herodotus says Menes built Memphis, after having reclaimed its site from the river by artificial embankments. The river is first known in history as Egyptus, and upon reaching it in their westward migration through the isthmus on the east, Mizraim and his followers passed upwards to this more elevated part of the valley, and built here their first permanent dwellings. In a few years the best situations on each side of the river would naturally become thriving towns, and soon some would be populous cities. Thus with On eastward and Memphis westward of the river, the former given in Grecian history as Heliopolis, or City of the Sun, and both retaining monumental proofs of similar early antiquity. As the first patriarch gave name to the whole land, so the sub-patriarchs of the tribes which settled in different directions gave their names to their portions of the country. The region from Memphis upwards to a considerable distance was the land of Noph, from Naphtuhim; the lower part and the Delta was the land of Zoan, or Zanam, from Anamim; and the Thebaid, or upper Egypt, was the land of Paphros, from Pathrusim. These were three sons of Mizraim;[1] and another son, Casluhim, had Philistim, who settled the south-eastern shore of the Mediterranean, stopping on the way of the family-migration, or going up as a later colony from Egypt.

Such sub-patriarchal divisions gave many separate chieftains, who became each the king of his tribe; and thus came the early dynasties, with their several kings, which are found in later descriptions of the Egyptian government. Such consecutive dynasties, and the aggregate number and years of the particular kings, as these records present, can find no consistency in any acknowledged chronology; but if, as above, they were only partially successive to, and frequently concurrent with, each other, their dynastic history is readily explicable. The list of separate kings is given quite variously by different authors, such as Herodotus, Diodorus, Manetho, the Old Chronicle, and Eratosthenes, partially conforming in some names, yet in no way can they be made entirely con-

[1] Gen. x. 13, 14.

sistent together. They agree in Menes, which is Mizraim, as the first king, but are widely discordant in later reigns. Reference is most frequently had to the dynasties of Manetho, an Egyptian priest of Sebennytus, two hundred and eighty years before the Christian era, and near one hundred years after the last or thirtieth dynasty had run out in Nectanebes II., when followed the Persian conquest of Egypt by Ochus, known as Artaxerxes III. The dynasties of Manetho are numbered, and mostly give particular names, and the years they reigned; but in the earlier instances many names are omitted, and not unfrequently the dynasty has only the aggregate years of all, with no name specified. The deciphered hieroglyphical names of Egyptian monarchs on the monuments are, however, so frequently like the names of the kings in Manetho's dynasties, that the monuments add credit to the historic record, and the two become somewhat mutually explanatory and confirmatory.

Bunsen (Egypt's Place in History) puts with great positiveness the settlement and civilization of Egypt at a much earlier date than Menes. He assumes to rely on "Egyptian monuments, records, and traditions" for proof that the valley of the Nile was peopled as early as 10,000 B. C.; and Lepsius before him had assigned an earlier period still; and Renan has recently put the age of Egypt even yet further back; all alleging the necessity of a longer time than the Hebrew chronology, or ordinary history, allows for so great national development as is evinced in the building of the pyramids and Egyptian monuments. From Noah to Abraham in Hebrew chronology is but about four hundred years; but the Greek chronology of the Septuagint gives about thirteen hundred years. These chronologies must have been in accordance in the age of Christ, since the Saviour and evangelists quote from the Septuagint, and Luke's genealogy follows the Septuagint peculiarities, in open communication with the Jews. One must since have been lengthened, or the other shortened; and much the most probable is it that the old Rabbis shortened the Hebrew chronology, that thereby they might disparage the claims of Christ as the Messiah.[1]

This Septuagint chronology gives all needed time, if even the Hebrew is deemed insufficient. No period is reliable as assumed without monumental confirmation, and the oldest royal names yet found are the last of the third and the first two of the fourth dynasties. On the rocks in the Sinaitic peninsula are found the royal ovals of Sephuris, Soris, and Suphis, tallying, as above, with Manetho's dynasties. In the great pyramid, the oldest human structure in the world, a way has been forced through the solid masonry, above the ceiling of the kings' chamber, into open interstices between the granite blocks that sustain the superincumbent pressure, and in this hidden recess there appear, on the rough faces of the limestone blocks, the quarry-marks of the workmen hastily sketched in red pigment, and among them the name,

[1] See Seyffarth's Summary, *passim*.

in the royal oval, of Soofo, or Suphis; thus seeming to fix the author and period as that of the second king of the fourth dynasty, and who must have been the same as Cheops, given by Herodotus. Wilkinson (Manners and Customs of Ancient Egyptians) puts the time of Suphis 2123 B. C. C. Piazzi Smyth (Life and Works at Great Pyramid) makes the design in building it to have been a fixed standard of weights and measures, quite ingeniously if not profoundly; and by an astronomical calculation he fixes its date at 2170 B. C.

No monumental inscriptions yet found date further back, and in Hebrew chronology this will give three hundred, or in Greek more than one thousand, years for Egypt's settlement before building the first pyramid. The ancestors of its builders participated in erecting the famous Tower of Babel, and all the cultivation of the old world had come across the flood, and no attained civilization of that age need ask for higher antiquity to have secured its cultivation.

The hill of lime-rock, on which the pyramids of Memphis are built, was a place of royal and noble sepulture for successive generations, and the region is filled with tombs, elaborately cut in the solid stone, and opening into separate vaults and more spacious chambers. Perfectly preserved paintings freshly present these old Egyptians in all the varied scenes and employments of their times; their dress, manners and customs, and national peculiarities. The great man of the tomb is represented of large size, his rod of power and punishment in hand, his scribe taking an inventory of his possessions, his flocks and herds around him, and his laborers under their task-masters at their varied employments. The Egyptian society had nothing of free communion and equal fellowship, but was everywhere the austere master and servile dependants; and even the family group was the lordly patriarch and submissively obedient wife and children. The tomb of Shaffre, the name so compounded as to be expressive of the second Suphis, or son of Suphis, has recently been disclosed at the south-east direction from the second pyramid, of which he was the builder, and abundantly testifies to the power, population, and wealth to which the kingdom had then attained; and the tombs of other great men of the time show that their occupants announced themselves as the priests of Suphis, or of Shaffre.

The ancient monuments and the improved engraving in granite manifest that population and culture spread from Memphis up the river, settling and building up the Faioum on the west, and Benihassan on the east of the river; and the improvement is persistently manifest upwards, till it culminates in Thebes and Luxor; and then shows its inferiority, as beyond the centre of cultivated art, towards Syene and the cataracts. All here is less perfect and sooner decayed. When Abraham visited Egypt, Suphis and Shaffre had already reigned, and builded, and died, and the nation in its power and prestige was tending upwards towards the Thebaid; and this had become a source of jealousy and dissension, that had ripened into revolt and rebellion before the coming of Joseph. In the twelfth dynasty, a king, by Manetho named Sesostris, a Diospolite or Theban ruler, had carried his arms around the Mediterranean into Europe, and left his emblems inscribed on the rocks in the countries he conquered; but in the subsequent dynasties till the eighteenth, there is continual change and consequent confusion, showing that the government was divided, and parts of the country had its different kings. Some are Diospolite, Xoite, or Zoan kings of the Delta; Shepherd kings; foreign Phenician kings; and Hellenic shepherd kings; mostly without names being given. The monuments give equal evidence of commotions and dissensions. Names have been violently obliterated, and in some of the tombs the paintings have been defaced and desecrated by hostile hands.

The earliest catholic forms of the worship of Osiris may well be taken as designed to check this spreading alienation. It represented the collecting of the scattered members and limbs of the god into one place, and the union of his votaries in common worship at his temple; as if designed to unite all Egyptians in fellowship and devotion at the shrine of their common patriarch Mizraim. The varied forms of the myth of Osiris, as in some way presenting the dying and reviving of nature by the falling and overflowing of the Nile, were later inventions. But the well-meant efforts at religious reconciliation and national union found their internal hostilities too strong to be so overcome. Different dynasties of kings reigned at the same time in different places, and were hostile to each other. Lower Egypt was peculiarly adapted to the feeding of flocks and herds, and the shepherds of Arabia, Canaan, and Phenicia removed, just as Abraham had done, their large flocks and herds to its rich pastures, and returned to their homes greatly enriched and prospered. The employment of the shepherd was then no peaceful Acadian life, but a perpetual strife with wild beasts and robbers, as in the experience of the young shepherd David. No men were so readily transferred to warriors and captains. They naturally made common cause with the Egyptian dissentients of their own region, and powerfully assisted them in their conflicts, and afterwards participated in the benefits of their victories. The kings of the lower and middle Egypt at first, and for a long time, triumphed over the old Diospolitans, and drove them into, and at one time, at least, beyond, the Thebaid, and had authority over all Egypt. But at length the patriotism, prowess, and boldness of the old Thebans prevailed, and drove the hated shepherd-assisted armies back to Memphis, to On, to Xois, and finally out of Zoan and Egypt itself, and recovered the entire kingdom, under the complete sway of the kings of the eighteenth dynasty. It is not necessary to look abroad for an invading empire strong enough to come in and conquer Egypt. All the circumstances best comport with the belief, that all the kings of

Egypt were still native Egyptians, and helped by foreign emigrant shepherds and traders, and that the causes of dissension and revolt were internal conflicting interests and superstitions, and not national foreign invasions. So long possession by a foreign nation must have left deeper traces of the exotic language and manners, if any such invasion had been.

Wilkinson finds the name of Osirtassen I. on the broken columns of a temple at Karnak; on two obelisks which belonged to Heliopolis below, and the Faioum above, Memphis; and in the rock-chambers at Beni-hassen; showing that he had carried his arms and made captives among the Asiatic tribes. His name .does not appear in any of the dynasties of Manetho, and is doubtless one of a dynasty of which he gives the aggregate years of the individual reigns, but not the kings' names. Wilkinson puts this Osirtassen at the year 1740 B. C., and deems him contemporary with the sale of Joseph to Potiphar, and begins from him what he considers authentic place and date in history. Because he had carried his arms beyond the Red Sea, Wilkinson deems that he could not have been in the times of the Shepherd dynasties; but as on the obelisks, and at Karnak, he has the ensign of "the lord of the upper and lower country," and might thus have reigned when the Thebaid kings were driven towards Ethiopia, in such case nothing would prevent that he should have had collisions with Arabians, and even Assyrians. All best agrees with the supposition that he was in the zenith of the sway of the Shepherd dynasties, if he was the king contemporary with Joseph.

2. THE GOVERNMENT OF EGYPT. — Its beginning was patriarchal. No descendant wished to dispute the authority of Mizraim, who was ruler and priest in one. Naturally the civil and sacerdotal authority became united in one person, and as long as this first patriarch lived, he was a monarch ruling in the place and with the sanction of God. Other sub-patriarchs stood to their particular tribes in a similar but subordinate position; and when the older patriarch died, the advantages of union kept the kindred clans voluntarily submissive to some venerable chieftain, whose rule was accepted as under the same divine sanction. Patriarchal government naturally merged in theocratic government. Old polytheistic nations were universally not monarchical only, but theocratic; and besides that it came up from the patriarchal state in course, it had the great recommendation that it promoted royal majesty and popular loyalty. The human king had the credit of being the vicegerent of the tutelar god while he lived, and if his reign had been specially acceptable and venerable, it was easy to set him among the gods when he died.

Where the government blended civil and religious authority, the priests were in consequence a power in the state, and though not direct participants in the sovereignty, as the accredited messengers of the gods they were the legitimate advisers of the sovereign, and must have special distinction and peculiar prerogatives. They must have their badges, and revenues, and spiritual functions, as a separate class in the community. The king communes with the gods directly through the priesthood. Herodotus so represents the position of the Egyptian priests.[1] "Those of Heliopolis were the most learned of any in all Egypt. The office was confined to men; and while in other nations priests usually wear the hair long, in Egypt they cut it short, except on occasions of great mourning. They observe great cleanliness, bathe twice a day, and practise religious ceremonies with great exactness. They have one kind of dress of linen, and their shoes were of the byblus. They do not spend their own incomes, but live of the sacrifices, a portion of which was assigned them ready dressed, and wine, but they may not eat of fish. Every deity has his priests and a chief priest, and at death a son succeeds."

The royal hieroglyph was the sun, or the hawk and globe; and the name for the sun was Phre, pronounced Phrah, which is the Hebrew spelling for Pharaoh, the common title of Egyptian monarchs. So, as sun-devoted, we have Poti-phar, Poti-pherah, Ho-phrah, &c., as human alliances with the patron deity.

3. THE RELIGION OF EGYPT. — Very soon after the flood, as already noticed, polytheism became univer-

[1] Euterpe, sec. 3, 35-37.

sal. Monotheism, as a faith and worship, lingered in few cases, as that of Melchisedek, king of Salem, and among the descendants of Shem; but at the call of Abraham idolatrous practices everywhere abounded. The Egyptian colony was superstitious and idolatrous from the first, and very early their peculiar religious *cultus* began its development. It may be deemed that the worship of the heavenly bodies, as the emblems of the true God, marked the first departure from the monotheistic faith in the family of Noah, and consequential upon this, polytheism and idolatry were sure. Herodotus supposes this to have been the first worship, as he deems society to have begun in paganism. "The original deities men adore are the sun, moon, earth, fire, &c." Clio, sec. 131. And Diodorus Siculus, lib. 1, says, "The ancients looking up to the heavens and universal nature, and wondering, received as the first eternal deities the sun and the moon." From what has been above noticed of the Egyptians, it has been evident that the sun was made their supreme deity. Their first king, Menes, the patriarch Mizraim, ruled in the place of this chief god, and was himself worshipped after his death, as Osiris, in the gathering of all relics of him that had been scattered, into one place, to unite all the people in one common superstition. With Osiris was connected the worship of Isis, the representative of the moon, as the former had been. through the king, the representative of the sun; and here was involved what was peculiar to the Egyptian religion. Some marked characteristic of animal or plant rendered the object sacred, proper to be dedicated to the deity, and induced its mark or name to become the standing hieroglyphical sign of the god. So the bull, as Apis, representing the fertilizing power of solar light and heat, was sacred to Osiris, as the heifer was to Isis. The Egyptian hawk, from his keen sight, represented the omniscience and wisdom of Thoth; the crocodile was terrible and tongueless, representing the certain, though silent, retributions of the deity; and thus with the goat, cat, ibis, and lotus and papyrus plants. The cat, from the peculiar fire of its eye in the dark, was a proper representation of the moon in the sun's absence, and so the cat was sacred to Isis. Particular animals of the kind were dedicated to the god, and henceforth the priest cherished and fed them as sacred. To kill such sacred animal was a capital offence, with no reprieve; and when they died they were embalmed, and carried to their sacred depositories in their assigned cities; and myriads of sacred cats, crocodiles, ibises, &c., lie embalmed in their assigned cemeteries.

These sacred animals, as dedicated to the god, were not always of the kind which might be sacrificed in its city, and as matter of fact, the sacrificial animals were of very limited variety. Herodotus[1] gives a minute account. The swine, though an unclean animal to an Egyptian, was yet sacrificed to Isis at the time of full moon only. In the Thebaid, goats, but

[1] Euterpe, sec. 41 and onward.

not sheep, were sacrificed, except at an annual festival they kill a ram and cast its skin over the image of the god; but at Mendes they sacrificed sheep and abstained from goats. Bulls and young male calves were sacrificed to Isis; but cows and young heifers were not reciprocated in sacrifice to Osiris. So scrupulous were the Egyptians about the blood of the sacred heifer, that they never used a knife or cooking utensil of another people, lest these should have touched the blood or flesh of the sacred animal. No other fowl but geese were offered in sacrifice. Herodotus[1] says expressly that swine, bulls, and male calves, and geese were all that were sacrificed, though from former statement he should have added goats at Thebes, and sheep at Mendes.

The great sacrifice was that of the sacred bull to Isis. Isis was represented as a woman, with the horns of the new moon upon her head. The preparation for the sacrifice was a careful examination of the animal by the designated priest. He must be wholly white, and a single black hair would tarnish his purity. When found unblemished, the priest affixes the sacred signet to his horns, and he is led with great solemnity to the altar. A fire is kindled, libations of wine poured out, the goddess is invoked, and the victim slain. The skin is then flayed, the head separated from the body, and imprecations heaped upon it to avert all divine anger from the worshippers, and then sold to a stranger or cast in the river. No Egyptian

[1] Sec. 45.

will feed from the head of any sacrificed bullock. The body is afterwards dismembered, carefully examined, and then burned with various ceremonies. Other sacrifices had their own peculiarities. There were also prescribed forms of divination in the consulting of the sacred oracles; and that of the great deity at Thebes was the parent of all subsequent Grecian and Roman oracles.

Some peculiar doctrines were much more elaborated in their teaching, and inculcated by national practices and customs. Such were especially the immortality of the soul, and rewards and punishments after death. The doctrine of metempsychosis, or varied transmigrations of the soul, was one form of Egyptian belief; and out of it grew the practice of embalming and careful preservation of the body in its mummy-state, that at the long period of the soul's return it might find and again inhabit its old tenement.

And so the representations in their tombs of the funeral procession over the river, the arraignment of the dead before Osiris, and his approving or disapproving sentence on the former life, and the disposal of the body under the sanction of the divine approbation, gave rise to similar mystic forms in their secret orgies, and which were the source of the famed mysteries in imitation at Eleusina, and Thrace, and other Grecian cities, and which mystic rites were continued from Greece to the Romans. The practice of embalming was a religious rite, and more perfect in later than in earlier times, when they had found and applied the most effectual bitumen to secure the most complete preservation of the mummy. The method need not be specified, as the mummy-pits are so abundantly open to modern inspection. The civil authority had its hand on all these religious rites, inasmuch as it used religious fears and hopes where it could not apply civil pains and penalties.

These may not have had their full development, as given by the Greek historians, in the time of Joseph; yet the principle and form of the Egyptian state regulations were early established, and the Hebrew people were now to be introduced into, and become familiar with, these Egyptian peculiarities.

4. THE GOING DOWN OF THE ISRAELITES INTO EGYPT. — From the call of Abraham to the going into Egypt had been two hundred and fifteen years, during which period the progress of the chosen people towards a national existence had been most remarkably slow, having increased in all to only seventy individuals. Their continuance in Egypt was precisely for the same period of two hundred and fifteen years, but in this latter period the accumulation of Abraham's posterity had been as remarkably rapid, numbering one year after their exodus six hundred and three thousand five hundred and fifty men above twenty years of age able to bear arms.[1] The tribe of Levi was excepted in this enumeration, as pertaining to the sacerdotal office, and not subject to military service. The

[1] Num. i. 45, 46.

addition of those, together with the aged, the children, and the women, could have made the entire population scarcely less than two million souls. So effective had been the divine arrangement for their safety and prosperity during their national minority.

Joseph, the oldest son of Rachel, and the favorite of Jacob, was already in Egypt, having, through the jealousy and hatred of his brethren, been sold by them to Midianitish merchants, who had again sold him to Potiphar, captain of Pharaoh's guard. Soon after, from the false charge of his licentious mistress, Joseph was imprisoned in Egypt; but both under Potiphar and in prison, the favor of God was with him, and all he did prospered. The spirit of prophecy imparted to him enabled him to interpret the dreams of two state prisoners with him according to subsequent fact, and this opened the way for his introduction to Pharaoh, and interpretation of two remarkable successive dreams, indicating seven years of great plenty in the land, to be followed by seven years of famine. He was in consequence at once set at the head of the national administration, allied in marriage to the priesthood, which was the highest order in the state, and managed all things during the years of plenty in provision for the succeeding years of famine. This famine reached the land of Canaan, and the family of Jacob became dependent upon the granaries of Egypt; and after the affecting trial of his brethren for Benjamin's sake, Joseph made himself known to them, and by Pharaoh's invitation, the whole patriarchal family went to Egypt, and were settled, by order of the king, in Goshen, the most fertile province of the realm.

Their early abode in Egypt was, on Joseph's account, under great royal favor. If, as we have before noticed, this Pharaoh was the Osirtassen I. found on the earliest monuments, and also one of Manetho's Sixteenth Dynasty of Shepherd Kings, who now reigned over all Egypt, the circumstances connected with the chosen race in Egypt find a natural and ready explanation. When Jacob and the family first came to Egypt, Joseph certainly designed to ingratiate the king towards them, and he tells Pharaoh that they were shepherds, and yet it was then true that "every shepherd was an abomination to the Egyptians." If the king was one of the old Theban monarchs, or of any regular Egyptian dynasty, such a course would seem inexplicable, and directly calculated to subvert Joseph's intention. But if he was of the Shepherd dynasty, as helped in power by foreign immigrants, whose retainers were as many each, and as warlike, as the trained servants of Abraham, nothing could have been more in accordance with the promptness and tact of Joseph. The king puts the Hebrew strangers at once in the midst of Egypt's choicest pastures, and directs that the most skilful of them be set over the royal flocks and herds. During this dynasty, Israel would be fostered and prospered. Joseph might have been, probably, thirty years of age at this time, and he lived to one hundred and ten years; and at least so long the favor and fostering care of Pharaoh would be sure to his brethren and their posterity.

In the mean time, Jacob had given the patriarchal and prophetic blessing to his children, died, been embalmed, and carried to his own burying-place in Canaan; Joseph had quieted all fears of retaliation, and pledged his brethren that he would nourish and protect their children after Jacob's death; his own family had largely increased, and the third generation of his children had grown up about him; and then on for a season after Joseph's death and all his brethren, the Hebrews remained still prosperous, so that emphatically it is said of them, "they were fruitful and increased abundantly, and multiplied and waxed exceeding mighty, and the land was filled with them."

But such constant and long-continued favor had its dangers. It tended to luxurious effeminacy and degeneracy; to forget their covenant, and undervalue its promises; to be satisfied with their state, and both unable and unwilling to meet the necessary hardships which must be passed through in taking possession of their promised inheritance. After this prosperity had lasted more than a century, God, in his providence, greatly changed their condition. The old Theban princes and captains renewed their courage and conflict, and recovered their government of the nation. Their insurgent enemies were gradually expelled, and the Hebrews, so much in favor with them, were sure to feel the jealousy and distrust of the embittered conquerors. As they forced the kings of the shepherd dynasties from Thebes, and then from Memphis, and down into the Delta, and took the rule of upper and middle Egypt, and pressed upon their retreating and enfeebled enemies utterly to subdue them, we have the coming in of the eighteenth dynasty, and the "new king arose who knew not Joseph."[1] These old insurgents might again make fight, and such a multitude of foreign people were dangerous.[2] "So they set over them task-masters, and made their lives bitter with hard bondage in mortar, and in brick, and in all manner of service in the field;" and when, notwithstanding this vigorous oppression, "the more they afflicted them, the more they multiplied and grew," this new king commanded the midwives to save alive only the female births and make way with all the male children. While this edict was in force, Moses was born; hid three months by his parents, and then exposed in a cradle of rushes on the brink of the river. The child was here found by the king's daughter, adopted by her as her own, and brought up in the palace, and became "learned in all the wisdom of the Egyptians." This prepared him so far for the post of captain and lawgiver to the chosen nation. The time had come, and God had made his oppressed people ready and willing to assume their independence, and go out to the conquest of their inheritance.

[1] Ex. i. 8. [2] Ex. i. 10.

SECTION IV.

THE EXODUS OF ISRAEL, AND ESTABLISHMENT OF A GOVERNMENT.

MOSES was forty years at the Court of Egypt. He still maintained his loyalty to his national Covenant with Jehovah, and his patriotic attachment to his people. By taking part with his brethren, and hastily slaying an Egyptian, an oppressor, he was forced to flee to Arabia, and became a shepherd in the land of Midian, married a daughter of Jethro, and kept his flocks in the valleys of the mountainous region about Sinai, and has here the very different discipline for his future work through the next forty years, and which future work was to occupy the last forty years of Moses' life in its execution. In this wild region about Sinai, he sees a bush in a flame while the bush itself is not burned, and a voice from it proclaimed the presence of the God of his fathers, and gave to him a commission to lead his people from bondage to their free inheritance in Canaan. After a series of most desolating judgments upon Egypt, which evinced the power of Israel's God above all the gods of Egypt, the stubborn opposition of Pharaoh was subdued, and he assented to Israel's departure. All being ready, the whole nation, old and young, left Egypt, and journeyed eastward to the western gulf at the northern extremity of the Red Sea. Here was the miracle of the divided waters for Israel's passage, and their returning flood for the destruction of the pursuing Egyptians, thus spreading wide among the nations of the earth the knowledge of the true God, whose power and authority above all gods it was the special mission of the seed of Abraham to publish and establish. Moses led the people on into the opening wilderness; God made the manna to fall about their encampments, and the stream to flow from the rock smitten by Moses' rod; and the attacking Midianites were overthrown, as the supported hands of Moses lift the rod all day towards heaven: and at length, in a three months' march from their leaving Egypt, they came to the place where God, from the burning bush, had ordered Moses to put the shoes from his feet because the place where he stood was holy ground; and here they pitched their tents, and prepared for a long encampment, at the foot of Mount Sinai. All disturbing enemies were overthrown, and all necessary sustenance was provided, and here the essential and difficult work of organizing the fugitive people, and establishing a stable constitution, and opening the administration of a national form of government, was to be accomplished.

1. Their Character and Tendencies from their Education in Egypt. — Their fathers had died in

Egypt, and they had all been born and nurtured there, and there will all their recollections and early associations turn the current of their thoughts and sympathies; and thus the influence of their abode in Egypt must be expected to characterize the temper and habit of the Israelites for the present, and manifest its tendencies for many ages. They had hence derived all their notions of social life, municipal and civil regulations, rights of property, and modes of agriculture, architecture, manufacture, and military training, and had been constantly under the influence of Egyptian religious doctrines and practices. They had preserved their Hebrew peculiarities, and by living mainly together had retained the habits induced by their education from the patriarchs, and especially their distinction from all other peoples in their Covenant and promise from God to their fathers; and many of them, under the discipline of their hard bondage, had doubtless imbibed the true spirit of their fathers' faith, and scrupulously conformed to their fathers' worship and piety; yet in many ways, it is manifest that the mass of the Hebrews had largely conformed in feeling and practice to Egyptian habits.

Their heavy burdens had not weaned their attachments from their old homes, nor kept them from falling in with the superstitions and idolatries of their oppressors. They desired more a relief from bondage in Egypt than a final departure from Egypt. Moses had early thought it easy to arouse them to their deliverance,[1] but a wider acquaintance with the spirit of his people had apparently made him hopeless of their ever waking up to independence and freedom, and he long resisted the taking upon himself God's commission to emancipate them.[2] At every rising difficulty and hardship, or special danger, in their way up from Egypt to Canaan, they murmur, are discouraged, and fill their minds with remembrances of the good things left behind them, and long to return to their enjoyment.[3] Even here before Sinai, while God is giving them their law, and Moses is withdrawn a few days from them in communion with the Divine Lawgiver, with the glory of Jehovah's presence bright before them, they make their golden calf, after the worship of the Egyptian sacred Bull, and cry, "These be thy gods, O Israel." And onward into their future history, Egyptian superstitions and idolatrious observances easily and repeatedly lead the people off from their Covenant; so deeply had they become Egyptianized in their early experience.

With the inward tendencies of fallen humanity to idolatry, and the universal influence from the practice of all surrounding nations, in connection with this early imbuing of the Hebrew mind with the idolatrous system matured and all-controlling in the valley of the Nile, it is very manifest that the strongest

[1] Ex. ii. 11–14. Confer Acts vii. 25.
[2] Ex. iii. 11, iv. 1, v. 20–23, vi. 12.
[3] Ex. xvi. 3, xvii. 3; Num. xi. 4–6, xiv. 3, 4.

guards and the most controlling and stringent regulations must be applied to Israel, or the very design of Abraham's Call, and the end of God's promise to his seed, must be lost in their apostasy and general impiety. To this end must we look for the peculiarities of God's dealings with the chosen people; and especially now, in their formal organization as an independent government and free state, should we anticipate the most comprehensive and profoundly wise adaptations and institutions inspired by Jehovah, and embodied in the constitution and code of laws which, under the divine direction and through the medium of Moses, are here to be proposed to the nation, and adopted by them. The Israelites staid in this safe and convenient encampment nearly a year; and in many respects, both to Israel and the human race, it is among the most important of any year of the world's history. More is done here to settle in human recognition the principles of God's gracious purposes of redemption, than in any other year will occur till the coming of the Messiah.

2. TO THIS CONDITION A THEOCRACY WAS EMINENTLY ADAPTED AND ADOPTED BOTH BY GOD AND THE PEOPLE. — The Egyptian government was a Theocracy, having the sun as the chief Deity, and worshipped as Ammun, Noph, Ra, Phrah, Osiris, &c., and from whom was assumed to come all civil and religious authority. He made the laws, and inspired the king and priesthood to apprehend, interpret, and apply his will, in all

legislation and administration of government. The civil power, on this principle, had the right to bind conscience and legislate on religion, for the king was the vicegerent of God, and ruled only under his direction and approbation. And not only in Egypt; the governments of all the early great nations of the earth were theocratic from principle and policy. The Patriarch of the family was the Ruler and Priest of the family and tribe, from the very constitution of the family by God. The descendants felt constrained to submit to the authority of the Patriarch as the ordinance of God, and to look to him as the constituted medium of addressing God in prayer and sacrifice; and as the family enlarged to a tribe, and a nation of tribes, so the king of the nation stood as the Patriarchal Ruler and religious functionary for all the people of the realm. And the policy perpetuated the application of the principle. For no matter how wise and powerful the monarch, nor how large and vigilant his official police, there must still be many crimes he could not detect, and some wrong-doers so strong that he could not punish; but nothing could be hidden from the gods, and none so powerful as to escape divine justice. The civil power in this way had at its use all the rewards and punishments of the future world.

Such form of government was highly expedient for the chosen people in all respects. They had become accustomed to government in that light; Moses had been instructed in all its principles and their Egyptian application; it was the common and almost necessary expedient for all idolatrous nations to call in to their help the presence of some god as their patron-deity, both as against vicious subjects and hostile enemies, and thus example favored such government for Israel; but still more appropriate was it for them, in the end of God's design, to bring them off from all idolatrous tendencies, and confirm their perpetual attachment to the one true Jehovah. By taking Jehovah as the national king and patron God, and thus establishing a true Theocracy, the whole government stood on right and solid principle, and secured the highest veneration and respect for the official authority, and the fullest protection and freedom for the subject. A Theocracy with a pagan god must be superstitious and delusive, and will surely become tyrannical and oppressive. The monarch and the priest will use the presence and the power of the false god for their own ambitious and selfish ends, but the presence and power of the true God will control alike prince and people, priest and worshipper. In such a true application of a theocracy, church and state rightly go together, and the source for civil pains and penalties is also the source for righteous control over conscience, and the application of spiritual blessings and divine judgments. Besides this, the true Jehovah had called Abraham, and chosen his seed to be a people through whom all nations of the earth should be blessed. The very end of their existence as an independent people was their salutary influence upon humanity, and that through them truth and righteousness should be spread over all people. Who shall prepare them for their mission, and govern and guide them in all their way, so legitimately and successfully as Jehovah himself, who has so benevolently raised them up and brought them to their present position? Neither they nor the world can be served so well as by God's direct government and legislation for them.

3. God's Institution and Establishment of a True Theocracy. — The general principles of early governments were theocratic; but inasmuch as the god was false, the government was unrighteous and always oppressive. Only one nation was ever in position for the righteous application of the theocratic principle, and only the government of the Hebrew Commonwealth was a righteous, legitimate theocracy. It is richer in instruction in all the principles of free, and firm, and salutary civil jurisprudence, and more worthy of deep study, than any other national government, ancient or modern. Besides its direct bearing on the preparation of humanity for the application of the promised redemption, even for purposes of civil sovereignty only, we can better dispense with all other lessons of history and philosophical treatises of law and polity, than to disregard or mistake the divine teaching in God's own government over this one prominent nation of antiquity, whose theocratic rule had its practical manifestation in the world for

fifteen hundred years; and the scattered people, still acknowledging its authority, live on under the changing forms of other governments, amid the rise and fall of nations, even to the present age.

A mere outline of the method of the divine institution of the Hebrew Theocracy is here given.

The Israelites were encamped upon the plain at the base of Sinai, and the manifestation of God's presence was in clouds and smoke on the mount, and God called Moses upward thither, and in communion with him he gives the preliminary conditions of all further proceeding, and requires him to go down to the people and make the divine proposition fairly understood, and get their free assent. "Ye have seen what I did unto the Egyptians, and how I bare you on eagles' wings, and brought you unto myself. Now therefore, if ye will obey my voice indeed, and keep my covenant, then ye shall be a peculiar treasure unto me above all people, for all the earth is mine; and ye shall be to me a kingdom of priests and a holy nation."[1] Moses obeyed, went down to the plain, made known to the people the distinct proposition through the elders; and then all the people intelligently and freely respond, "All that the Lord hath spoken we will do."[2] Moses then returned to Jehovah in the mount with their unanimous assent, and God accepted the full surrender, and bade Moses so to inform the people, and prepare themselves, by special sanctification and cleansing, to receive the formal

[1] Ex. xix. 4–6. [2] Ex. xix. 8.

ratification on the third day from that time; "and it came to pass, on the third day in the morning, that there were thunders, and lightnings, and a thick cloud upon the mount, and the voice of the trumpet exceeding loud, so that all the people that was in the camp trembled." "Moses speaks and God answers him by a voice." Thus in the audience of all the people God announces the ten commandments. In their terror, the people cried to Moses, "Speak thou with us, and we will hear; but let not God speak with us, lest we die."

God then gave to Moses in the mount the general regulations contained in chapters 21, 22, and 23; and he returned and rehearsed them to the people, and they again responded, "All the words which the Lord hath said will we do." After this verbal assent, Moses built an altar and made sacrifice, and formally wrote out the words of this general constitution now agreed upon, and read them again in full assembly; and this third time the people unanimously assent: "All that the Lord hath spoken will we do, and be obedient." Then Moses took the blood of the sacrifice and sprinkled with it the Book and all the people," saying, "Behold the blood of the covenant which the Lord hath made with you concerning all these words." The ten commandments were afterwards written upon two stone tablets, as fundamental and immutable moral obligations; and these, with the Book of the Constitution now ratified, and the whole code of legislation afterwards divinely announced in accordance with the constitution, were at length put for permanent preservation in the Ark of the Covenant,[1] and these were every seven years, at the year of release, to be read to the great convocation; and the last act of Moses' public official work was the calling attention anew, and assent of the nation, to these words of life and death for them.[2]

So God himself has respect to the right of a people to choose their king and adopt their form of government, and by such consent he becomes their civil Ruler as well as Patron Deity. It would have been another sin to have refused the divine proposal; but having accepted and ratified the covenant, henceforth all idolatry and participation in pagan superstitions became rebellion, and all open resistance to God's legislation was treason. Provision was at once made for the local abode and visible presence of their divine king within the nation. The Tabernacle, in the wilderness and for the first years of their possession in Canaan, was God's national dwelling-place; afterwards the costly temple by Solomon was substituted; and here the Shechina, or cloud of the Lord's presence, perpetually abode. Here the people came for counsel, brought their offerings, and through the High Priest received the sovereign responses. Here was his perpetual Table with the Shew-bread, the golden candlestick, and the constant smoke of incense; and the entire tribe of Levi

[1] Ex. xxv. 16. [2] Deut. xxxi. 15-20.

was assigned to be religious ministers and civil servants of his household; and a perpetual revenue was required in the tithes and offerings of first fruits and portions of the sacrifices.

Among the most remarkable manifestations of his presence and authority was the stated application of *special providences* in rewards and punishments. It was openly assumed and declared, that God would so deal with them as with no other people, and directly suit his providences to their conduct. No enemy should molest them in their faithful keeping of Sabbath days and the sabbatical year; the land was every seventh year neither to be sowed nor eared, and at the Jubilee, two years together was the land to be left fallow, and yet it was spontaneously to produce all that should be needed; and all needed good is theirs provided they maintain their loyalty and devotion. But all evil is threatened if rebellious. So their law speaks; so their prophets preach; so their sacred Psalms teach them; and even in some marked cases the retribution for parental disloyalty went down to the third and fourth generation. This liability to retributions in the posterity of the sinner was a prerogative of God as their king, but withholden expressly from the human magistrates.[1] A true Theocracy may so establish civil sanctions in this life, leaving each soul to bear his own iniquity for the future state,[2] for the true God can exactly discriminate and infallibly execute; but no false god

[1] Deut. xxiv. 16; 2 Chron. xxv. 3, 4. [2] Ezek. xviii.

can sustain such assumption, nor could Moses have afforded this legislation but as he was the Lawgiver in a true Theocracy.

While Jehovah was thus their chosen king, and the legitimate civil sovereignty was vested in him, and all captains, judges, and kings, that afterwards administered the government of Israel, were vicegerents of him, yet in the great transactions and changes of the administration, the people had an acknowledged and legitimate voice, and were recognized as the source of supreme power in the state which they had now voluntarily committed to a theocratic administration.[1] So far as left to human administration, the Hebrew Commonwealth was a Republic. In many respects the different Tribes were independent, and sovereign in their own jurisdiction, and yet all the tribes for national purposes were one sovereignty, and no one tribe could be permitted to withdraw from the rest in separate nationality but as revolutionary and rebellious. While Egypt and all surrounding nations were Absolute Despotisms, assuming divine right to rule, and maintaining their oppression by mythological delusions, the Hebrew theocracy kept prominent the liberty of the people, and recognized the rights of the citizen. They assent to the true God to be their king, and the true God can never administer an oppressive rule. "He is the freeman whom the truth makes free, and all are

[1] See Josh. ix. 18-21; 1 Sam. x. 24, xi. 14, 15.

slaves beside." "If the truth make you free, you shall be free indeed."

God took a *name* distinguishing him from all other gods, in which name he was publicly to be known as *their* patron-deity; and in this was another method of establishing a true theocracy. When God gave Moses his commission at the burning bush, he first announced himself as the God of Abraham, Isaac, and Jacob, and in this as peculiarly the covenant God of the Israelites. Moses was despondent that the people could be roused by references to the patriarchal faith, and felt from his past experience that they had succumbed to Egyptian influences too far to be readily restored to Hebrew loyalty, unless through some further sign and pledge of God's distinctive approbation and protection. "Moses said unto God, Behold, when I come unto the children of Israel, and shall say unto them, The God of your fathers hath sent me unto you, and they shall say unto me, What is his name? what shall I say unto them?" The Egyptian patron-god is known by name as peculiarly Egypt's protector and ruler; Israel will need a distinct deity, and an appropriated appellation attaching the nation to him as distinguishingly theirs. God assented to the reasonableness of Moses' proposal, and took the occasion to give himself a new name as the special protector of the chosen people. "And God said unto Moses, I am that I AM" — "say unto the children of Israel, I AM hath sent me unto you."[1]

[1] Ex. iii. 13, 14.

This name imports independent being, self-existence, and is expressed in the Hebrew language by JEHOVAH, as the God who only has underived being, and from whom all existence comes; and this is now first appropriated in connection with Israel's national deliverance. "And God spake unto Moses, and said unto him, I am Jehovah; and I appeared unto Abraham, unto Isaac, and unto Jacob, by the name of God Almighty, but by my name Jehovah was I not known unto them."[1] Of all the many names before applied to God, here comes first the appellation of the *living God*, distinguishing him especially from all national false gods, in whom is no life; and thus as holding all being in himself. JEHOVAH is Israel's full and exhaustless source of all good. This name was to a Hebrew the most sacred possible, and by superstitious veneration became the *ineffable* name, which was not to be uttered by human lips.

Now, all the responsibilities as well as immunities and privileges derived from a theocratic form of government, and immediate national alliance with the deity, were fully known to Israel, and a common acknowledgment of the people of all neighboring kingdoms. The people must obey, and worship, and everywhere acknowledge allegiance to their own patron-deity. Thus, as in Deuteronomy,[2] so in many other places, it is assumed that the nations Israel had conquered will each have their patron-god, and that Israel will be in danger of going after them as the

[1] Ex. vi. 3. [2] Deut. xii. 29–32.

gods locally, as well as nationally, of the countries conquered; and they are admonished not to have any regard to these old gods of the place, for Jehovah their God is Universal Lord, and all nations, all lands, all worlds are his. So the Amorites claimed the land Israel had taken from them, but Jephtha at once appealed to the common national right of appropriating the power of their own patron-deity. "The Lord God of Israel hath dispossessed the Amorites from before his people Israel, and shouldest thou possess it? Wilt thou not possess that which Chemosh thy god giveth thee to possess? So, whomsoever the Lord our God shall drive out from before us, them will we possess."[1]

4. Special Ordinances separating Israel from Gentile Idolaters. — The tendency to idolatry was so strong, and the influence of pagan example so universal and constant to turn the chosen people from their true God, that at the expense of all the benefits of national sympathy and communion between different kingdoms, it was necessary to keep Israel separate, and institute ordinances and ceremonial practices which should prove a separating wall between Jew and Gentile. Incidental evils might occur, and national pride and presumption be fostered, in Israel by perverting these remedial measures against Gentile superstitions; but the dan-

[1] Judges xi. 23, 24. See also 1 Sam. xxvi. 19, 1 Kings xx. 23, and 2 Kings xvii. 24–33.

ger from public example was so imminent, that, for the time, seclusion and non-intercourse were the only safe expedients. When Israel shall have been weaned from idolatry, and the world made ready, in the Mediator's coming, for universal brotherhood, then must such a separating-wall between distinctive peoples be broken down.

Among such Ordinances was that relative to ceremonial *uncleanness from the dead.* The touching of a dead body, a bone, or any human relic, defiled the person, and excluded him from communion with the congregation for seven days.[1] The Egyptian doctrine of the metempsychosis with its resulting practice of embalming and preserving the dead was sacred, and thus in Egypt dead bodies and perpetual contact with them abounded; and with such an ordinance among the Hebrews, nothing could more effectually separate the two communities. What was sacred to one was abominable profaneness to another. And then, the method of an Israelite's *cleansing from uncleanness* by touching the dead still very much more strengthened the partition-wall between the nations. The heifer was sacred to Isis, and to an Egyptian one who had shed the blood or eaten the flesh of a red heifer was an abomination. They would not use a knife or any cooking utensil of a foreigner, nor by any means eat with strangers, lest they should come in contact with that which had become desecrated by violating the sanctity of Isis.

[1] See Lev. xxi. 2 and 11; Num. ix. 6–14, xix. 11–16.

But God instituted the very blood of the Egyptians' sacred red heifer to cleanse an Israelite from his defilement by the dead. A red heifer must be slain, the carcass burned, the ashes collected and mingled with water; and this was preserved in readiness, and called "the water of separation," by which the unclean was to be sprinkled, and if he came abroad without such ceremonial cleansing, he was to be cut off from the congregation.[1] A pious Hebrew and an idolatrous Egyptian must hold each other in abomination, and such could not dwell together but by their conversion to a common faith and practice.

So, also, the ordinance of *clean and unclean meats.* Nothing is unclean of itself, but for purposes of discipline, God made to an Israelite certain animals ceremonially unclean; and the law of unclean meats had manifestly one design of separating Israel from idolaters. With an Egyptian, swine, dogs, cats, mice, lizards and serpents, the crocodile, and among fowls, the hawk, owl, and bat were sacred; dedicated to their gods, and eaten for food. The Hebrew Law for clean and unclean animals[2] would necessarily separate them from the Egyptians, and in a similar way from the idolatrous nations of Canaan, when they should enter their inheritance.[3]

Still further with the ordinance of *marriage.* An Israelite was forbidden from all intermarriage with the heathen nations;[4] and the reason given is, "lest

[1] Num. xix.
[2] Lev. xi.; Deut. xiv.
[3] Lev. xx. 24-26.
[4] Deut. vii. 3, 4; Josh. xxiii. 12, 13.

they draw you away after their gods." The violation of this law always evinced the expediency of its enactment by the deleterious consequences of its rejection.[1] The Captivity in Babylon, and the strict and severe execution of this law of intermarriage by Ezra on their return, finally eradicated the Israelitish tendency to idols.[2]

Then there was the distinct prohibition of *several leading idolatrous superstitions.* Spencer[3] says it was a custom with idolatrous nations of antiquity to stand over the sepulchres or bodies of the dead, and pluck out or shave off the hair of the head or the beard, letting it fall upon the corpse or into the tomb, as a devoted peace-offering to the departed spirit, or to evil demons. So the prohibition to Israel of "cutting the hair, marring the corners of the beard, and cutting and scarring the flesh for the dead,"[4] had a direct intent to exclude heathenish superstition. So, again, Spencer,[5] referring to the Mosaic prohibitions of sowing a vineyard with different seeds, ploughing with an ox and an ass together, wearing garments of mingled linen and woollen, and inducing different species of cattle to engender together,[6] says "idolaters designed to signify by these mixtures and conjunctures, that husbandmen and shepherds were under obligation to the favoring influences of the planets, because they thought that the plenty of wool on the

[1] Num. xxv. 1-9; 1 Kings xi. 4.
[2] Ezra ix. and x.
[3] Leg. Heb. B. II. chap. xii.
[4] Lev. xix. 27, 28.
[5] Leg. Heb. B. II. chap. xxi.
[6] Lev. xix. 19; Deut. xxii. 9-11.

animal, and of linen in the fields, were from the favor of the stars." And quoting from another author in the same place, "All these mixtures are prohibited in detestation of idolatry, because the Egyptians, in veneration of the stars, made divers commixtures of seeds, and animals, and in their garments, thus representing different conjunctions of the planets." And to the same purport is the prohibition to seethe a kid in its mother's milk.[1] Bishop Patrick, com. *in loco*, says, "Rabbi Abarbinel affirms, the ancient idolaters were accustomed, when they gathered the fruits of the earth, to seethe a kid in his mother's milk, that the gods might be propititious to them." And Cudworth, on the Lord's Supper,[2] quotes a Karaite Jew as saying, "It was a custom of the ancient heathen, when they had gathered in all their fruits, to take a kid and boil it in the dam's milk, and then, in a magical way, to go about and besprinkle with it all their trees, fields, gardens, and orchards, thinking by this means they should make them fructify more abundantly the following year." Thus what might seem trifling, and even supersitious, legislation, is seen to have a serious and direct bearing against all superstition, as then insnaringly abounding.

To all the above may be finally added the solemn prohibition to "*pass through the fire to Moloch.*"[3] Rabbi Maimonides, Mor. Nev. Part III. c. 37: "This was one great artifice of idolatrous priests to work

[1] Ex. xxiii. 19, xxxiv. 26; Deut. xiv. 21. [2] Chap. ii.
[3] Lev. xviii. 21, xx. 1-5; Deut. xviii. 10.

upon the superstitious temper of weak men. They knew that they feared nothing more than the loss of their children, and thus the worshippers of fire taught, that if they did not make their sons and daughters pass through the fire, all their children would die." And Lowman[1] says, "Such purifications were well understood to be an act of consecration to Moloch, the son, or prince, of the heavenly host. Subsequently, they not only passed *through* the fire as devoted to the idol, but were literally burnt as an offering to the god."

SECTION V.

SPECIAL TRUTHS OF REDEMPTION TAUGHT UNDER A DOUBLE-SENSE.

THE Theocracy was a form of civil government for the nation, and in the conditions of the Hebrew people was the form most expedient for their freedom and prosperity; but it looked much further than their national freedom and power, and was indeed itself wholly subservient to a higher spiritual design. It was best adapted to make and keep the people to be worshippers of the one true God, and to spread the knowledge and worship of Jehovah among other

[1] Rationale of Heb. Rit. p. 232.

nations; and still spiritual in a further sense than teaching the doctrine and service of one true God, even the doctrine of the promised redemption of humanity from the curse consequent upon the fall and depravity of the race. The Hebrew nation was to be free and powerful, and also worshippers of the one true God, for the further end that they might be taught, and then might teach others, the mystery of God's plan for recovering a fallen race again to holiness and heaven. Inasmuch as God is civil-Ruler not only, but also patron-Deity, we should anticipate that his legislation will include institutions directly bearing upon Israel's needed preparation for the Redeemer's coming, and in their preparation as a chosen people thereby making the world ready for the coming of its promised deliverer.

Their Egyptian experience had accustomed them to be taught spiritual doctrines by divinely appointed ceremonies, as well as civil duties by direct divine enactments. There were the common funeral ceremonies and sacrificial observances, to which all had access, and where were taught the *exoteric* or public doctrine of the gods; and there were the higher mysteries, to which statesmen, priests, and philosophers were initiated, and in which the *esoteric* or hidden and profoundly speculative teachings were presented; and in each, appointed and arranged rites and significant representations were exhibited. And so we shall find in God's legislation for Israel sacrificial rites and ceremonial observances, required from all the people as national institutions and ordinances, and which are directly calculated to subserve order and national liberty, and to exclude idolatry and promote true piety; while they reach much further, and teach the truths yet little comprehended of God's wonderful plan of redemption. Both the lower and the higher ends are contained in the same required observances, and the serious and thoughtful performance, by one who sees only the lower design, will tend directly to bring him up to the apprehension and adoption of the higher. The divinely appointed forms are significant of real things, and foreshadow coming substances, and a devout, habitual observance opens the mind to expect, and prepares it to embrace, the reality at the time of its manifestation. It was a wise and effective system of national education, bringing the people gradually up from sensual apprehension to spiritual discernment. The Mosaic Ritual, as an entire system, is thus a schoolmaster to bring the nation to the coming Messiah; but we need now to allude only to some more prominent instances of its mode of teaching as specimens of the whole.

1. The Passover Feast. — The meaning designed as the most direct and obvious in the Passover was a memorial of God's gracious interposition in delivering the Hebrews from their Egyptian bondage; and as this was so signal and effective at the opening of their national independence, it was ever after held as one of the most prominent of Hebrew observances.

It was instituted by God at the time of the last judgment upon Pharaoh and the Egyptians in the slaying of their first-born, and which for the time subdued the stubbornness of Israel's oppressors. All the forms observed were minutely appropriate to such memorial. The sprinkling of the blood of the paschal-lamb; eating the flesh with bitter herbs; doing it in haste, and with loins girt, and shoes on, and staves in hand; and the exclusion of all leaven, — all commemorated their bitter bondage, the discriminating favor of the destroying angel, and their speedy remove from the land of their oppressors, as given in full in Exodus.[1] It was made a perpetual monition of the supremacy of Jehovah, their God, over all the gods of Egypt.

Here was, however, but its lower application. The same ceremony was comprehensive of a higher meaning. It was designed as truly for a type of human redemption as for a memorial of Hebrew deliverance. The Paschal Lamb foretokened "the Lamb of God slain from the foundation of the world," and the necessity that "Christ our Passover should be sacrificed for us," as intentionally by God, as it recalled the sparing of Israel's first-born when in Egyptian families "there was not a house wherein was not one dead." It was subsequently ordered in divine providence, that Christ's crucifixion occurred at the day and hour in the year for the killing of the Passover victim according to the Hebrew Ritual.[2] And the

[1] Ex. xii. and xiii.
[2] See Matt. xxvii. 62; Luke xxii. 7–20; John xix. 14.

Lord's Supper then was made the memorial of Christ's death, instead of the Passover as typical of it. The hidden meaning of the Passover came more and more fully out, to the pious and thoughtful Israelite, till the nation and the world became ready for the redemption sacrifice of the Lamb of God.

2. THE CEREMONY OF THE SCAPE-GOAT. — This was included in the complex ceremony of the sin-offering, which involved both a sacrifice and a sign of remission. A bullock was to be slain, and the blood sprinkled before the holy-place, and put upon the horns of the altar. Two young goats were then selected, one of which was slain, and the blood sprinkled like that of the bullock, while the other was let go alive into the wilderness, after the formal laying of the high priest's hands on the head, and confessing over it the sins of the people. Both the high priest and all connected in this transaction were made unclean by it, and the parts of the victims were carried without the camp and burned with fire; signifying the impurity of the sinner as abominable to God, and transferring his uncleanness to all communing with him. To a common Israelite this lower national defilement and its removal by ceremonial substitution were all that he apprehended. But in God's design, in addition to this there was a deeper meaning. It typified the expiation of human guilt by the substitution of Christ's atoning sacrifice, and led the thoughtful mind to look to more precious blood than that of

bulls and goats, which could only ceremonially, and not literally and eternally, take away sin. Hence Christ is termed a sin-offering,[1] and is said to have "suffered without the gate;"[2] and his sacrifice is the "taking away" of the sins of the world.[3]

3. THE CONSTRUCTION OF THE TABERNACLE AND TEMPLE, AND SERVICES CONNECTED WITH THEM. — In their common and primary intent, their construction and use manifested the presence and power of Jehovah, their God and King, in the midst of them, and confirming the national allegiance to him. The ceremonial services were national atonements, and legal purifications, propitiatory towards their tutelar-deity, and standing to them as a civil community in distinction from the idolatrous temples and altars peculiar respectively to other organized communities about them. But a much higher end was to be attained, and a deeper meaning was put into the tabernacle and temple service. Hence the precision with which Moses was required to fashion every part, and to "see that he made all things according to the pattern shown in the mount."[4] An extended explanation of this is given by the author of the Hebrews, especially in the fifth, eighth, ninth, and tenth chapters. The temple is taken as a figure, a hieroglyphical representation of the coming Gospel Kingdom. The High Priest is the Lord Jesus Christ, and the blood of the

[1] 2 Cor. v. 21.
[2] Heb. xiii. 11, 12.
[3] John i. 29.
[4] Ex. xxv. 40.

sacrifices is for his atoning blood; the holy of holies is heaven, into which this High Priest has entered, forever making intercession; and the entire ritual stands as the shadow of realities that are coming. They could better be understood after Christ had come, and died, and risen again; but the very shadows taught the studious Israelite much, and made the nation and the world anticipate largely the truths of Christ's redemption before he came and substantially fulfilled them.

In addition, thus, to the promises more and more full from time to time, and the prophecies more and more clear from age to age, and the provision of scribes, and priests, and schools of the nation for transcribing, and reading, and expounding the divine law, there was a prepared system of symbols and ceremonies with a common meaning for all, and a deeper and more important meaning for those capable of spiritual discernment.

4. This Method of Instruction by Double-meaning requires careful Discrimination. — Many words are used with different meanings, and sometimes the same word has directly opposite meanings. The words *life* and *death* may have a large variety of significations, and a careful attention to the connection can alone, in some cases, distinguish which is there the true meaning. The word *let* may mean to permit or to hinder; and the word *prevent*, which primarily means a fore-going, may be applied in the opposite senses of going before to block up, or to open the

way. One may studiously use these ambiguous words with intent to perplex, and make his speech a riddle; or with intent to deceive, and make his speech mendacious. The first is trifling, the second is lying; and by no such "paltering in a double sense" can direct instruction be given. The Mosaic ritual employs nothing of this form of double-meaning.

There is, further, an assumed form of interpreting any scripture, by taking its plain, literal facts and incidents as of no account in themselves, and affording no historic nor narrated instruction, but as a corresponding spiritual meaning is made out from them. "A system of correspondencies" is invented, and all plain statement and historic narrative is void of all meaning, except as the suggested spiritual truth is attained. To a lively fancy, such spiritualizing of all plain speech may be very captivating, and taken also to be very pious, but no solid instruction can be so imparted or received, for nothing determines whether the writer and the interpreter have the same spiritual meaning in common. This can hardly be known as double-sense, for one sense only is of any importance, and the unimportant sense is too empty to be made a medium for any reliable spiritual communication. Not thus does God, in any part of his Word, allow us to presume that we have truly caught his intentional spiritual meaning.

Certain acts may be so plainly representative of certain other events, that the former may intentionally be made use of to express and teach the latter. Such methods of communication God not unfrequently employs. By divine direction, Isaiah walks three years, naked and barefoot, to warn Egypt of the coming invasion and captivity of the Assyrians.[1] Jeremiah hides his girdle in a rock until it is marred, to teach that destruction is imminent for Judah.[2] Ezekiel portrays the siege of a city upon a tile, sets up an iron pan as a wall of defence, &c., representing the coming siege of Jerusalem.[3] And by representative acts, Christ taught humility and kindness by washing the disciples' feet.[4] And Agabus warned Paul of coming persecution by binding himself with Paul's girdle.[5] The act is made intelligently expressive of the intent, and so truly teaches the intended lesson; and such teaching by *signs* is frequent, legitimate, and emphatic. It is, however, hardly double-sense; for the representation, though striking, has but one meaning, and the sign truly communicates that meaning only.

There may be such use of language as intentionally to convey an obvious meaning to one class of minds, and at the same time have another meaning designed to be apprehended by another class, or by the first class in another stage of improvement. There are truly two meanings, one apprehended by some, and both apprehended by others, and God may use language designed for the communication of such form of double-meaning. So in relation to the trial and temptation of our first parents. The agency of

[1] Isa. xx. 2–4. [2] Jer. xiii. 1–11. [3] Ezek. iv. 1–17.
[4] John xiii. 4–19. [5] Acts xxi. 11.

the serpent was designed to be expressed, and this was at once apprehended; but just as certainly was the agency of the devil meant to be included, though not apprehended till a later generation.[1] So also *the rest in Canaan* was one meaning of Psalm xcv. 11, but this included also the meaning of *the rest of the Sabbath* and *the rest of heaven.*[2] Psalm lxix. has primary reference to David, but it was so expressed as also to include the sufferings of Christ and the treachery of his enemies.[3] And especially predictions of future events are not seldom given in a double-meaning. Psalm lxxii. applies directly to Solomon, but has its adequate fulfilment only in Christ; and Joel, i. and ii., has intentionally the two meanings of an army of locusts and of the Assyrian army; and the foretelling of the destruction of Jerusalem[4] also includes the prediction of the end of the world and the final judgment. In a rhetorical figure, or the use of a parable, only one meaning is given; but here two distinct meanings are contained, and designed, by some minds at some time, to be both distinctly understood.

And this use of a double-sense is still more directly employed in teaching higher truths in connection with a lower and more familiar meaning, by what is properly typical representation. A *type* differs from a *sign* in that it has two senses, and the sign but one intended meaning. The Passover, as a sign, meant

[1] Gen. iii. Cf. John viii. 44; Heb. ii. 14, 15; 1 John iii. 8; Rev. xii. 9.

[2] Heb. iii. and iv.

[3] Cf. John xix. 28, 29; Acts i. 20.

[4] Matt. xxiv.

only Israel's deliverance,[1] but as a type, it included Christ's redemption; [2] and this, in common with many other typical ceremonies, God extensively and successfully used in the instruction of his chosen people. One common meaning, studied and followed out in its leading direction, opened fairly into higher light and more important truth. Nothing was deceptive or delusive, much less false or contradictory; both meanings were true, desirable to be apprehended; but the last was best attained by coming to it through the study and practice of the first.

5. The Theocratic Ritual demanded a Spiritual Observance. — We have not unfrequently, but very superficially, the derogatory assumption that the Hebrew ritual was a mere system of sensible, formal observances, tending rather to superstition than spirituality, and cherishing self-righteousness rather than inward holiness. And the reproach is often extended to the whole Old Testament, as the sacred oracles of the Israelites, that they present God as severe, vindictive, an object of fear rather than of trust and love; and the religion inculcated to be a gross and selfish servility towards God, and supercilious contempt and hate towards other nations. But with the world as it was, and humanity as it had developed itself in that age, and the idolatry and cruelty and sensuality everywhere abounding, and the necessity that the true Theocracy should take the chosen seed

[1] Ex. xii. 14–27. [2] 1 Cor. v. 7.

as it was in itself, and with its surrounding influences; and the plain truth is, that the adaptation of the whole Hebrew government, in its civil enactments and religious ordinances, to civilize and spiritualize the rising generations of Israel, is so direct and wise, and in its results so effective and successful, that it proves its superhuman origin, and has no lower source than the infinite wisdom, and power, and goodness of Jehovah. The grace of the gospel could not have been reached by the generations of man, and the plan of redemption could not have found an age ready that its wonders should have been wrought in it, except through just such an intervention as the call of Abraham, and the legislation of Moses, and the subsequent teaching of divine prophecy and providence secured.

The Theocracy taught that God was one; was a spirit that could not have any material likeness; and that, though the heaven of heavens could not contain him, yet that, in very deed, he dwelt with men; and though he did by no means clear the guilty, yet was he the "Lord God, merciful and gracious, long-suffering, and abundant in goodness and truth, keeping mercy for thousands, and forgiving iniquity, transgression, and sin." No formal obedience alone could be acceptable, and the very formality of the divinely instituted ritual demanded, and was designed to secure, a pure service of the heart.[1] No language can more fully or forcibly enjoin a hearty service, or show

[1] See Ex. xxxiv. 7; Lev. xix. 1, 2; Deut. x. 12-19, xxx. 6; 1 Sam. xvi. 7; Ps. xv. 1-3, li. 1-17; Isa. i. 10-20, lxvi. 2; Joel ii. 12, 13.

the law more completely written on and filling the heart, than such expressions and the experiences recorded by the Psalmist.[1]

So with the civil and religious polity of Israel: the grand design was the establishment of a free and powerful nation; to cultivate them in the arts of peace, and inculcate pure morality and national piety; and though necessarily, in their ignorance and darkness, appealing to sense, yet in such a way as most effectually to reach, elevate, and purify the spirit. While all the other peoples of the world continued in their idolatry and polytheistic superstitions, the Hebrew people, with frequent lapses and many apostasies, still preserved the faith and worship of the true God, and taught the nations to expect the advent of a Divine Prince and Saviour.

SECTION VI.

ADMINISTRATION OF THE THEOCRACY TO THE BABYLONIAN CAPTIVITY.

THE encampment of Israel at Sinai continued about eleven months, during which period the law was given and the tabernacle made and furnished according to minutely specific directions; and henceforth the established form of worship was maintained,

[1] Ps. xix., lxiii., lxxxiv., cxix., &c.

sacrifices offered, and ceremonies observed according to the directions of the inspired Ritual. The Shechina, or bright appearance of God's presence and glory, was perpetually with the nation, and gave to them the direction of their future movements by peculiar indications when to move and where to encamp.[1] God was thus manifestly in the midst of them, and known by them as Jehovah, their national King and patron-Deity. It was, however, convenient and expedient that a human ruler should be interposed between the divine king and people, and it was the prerogative of God to indicate his will in the determination of whom it should be that they were to acknowledge as his vicegerent in the government. While the transactions at Sinai had been in progress, the will of God had been fully manifested that Moses was his lawgiver and constituted leader.[2] When, afterwards, Moses' authority was questioned and resisted, God vindicated it terribly and effectually.[3]

1. THE THEOCRACY UNDER MOSES. — Just thirteen months and twenty days from the exodus,[4] the Israelites, by the command of Moses from the Lord, took their departure from Sinai, and the cloud of the Lord was taken up from the tabernacle, and the tribes followed in their prescribed order, with their standards, officers, and people, and the cloud next rested

[1] Num. ix. 15–23.

[2] Ex. xxiv. 9–18, xxxii. 33, 34, xxxiii. 8–11, xxxiv. 29–35.

[3] Num. xii. 1–15, xvi. 1–35.

[4] Num. x. 11.

in the wilderness of Paran. So, journeying from day to day direct towards Canaan, they came in a short time to the borders of their promised possession, and a man from each tribe constituted a commission to go through the land and return a true report. Within forty days they return, and report in great praise of the country; but all except two, Joshua and Caleb, are terrified and utterly unmanned by the power of the people and the defence of their cities. "We be not able to go against this people." "We were in our own sight as grasshoppers, and so we were in their sight."[1]

With this report the timid Israelites were overwhelmed with despair, and evince how little they are prepared to conquer their promised inheritance, and take an independent place amid powerful nations. They murmur and clamorously rebel, and determine to make themselves "a captain and return to Egypt." The contradictory report of Joshua and Caleb, and the interposed persuasion of Aaron, and the authority of Moses, avail nothing; they become furious and headstrong in their riotous purpose, and proceed to stone all opposed.[2] A more courageous and disciplined generation must come up, or the great designs of their fathers' covenant and promise must fail. In the midst of their turbulent frenzy and obstinacy, the glory of the Lord in the tabernacle suddenly manifested the divine displeasure, and in terrible majesty Jehovah declares that he is about to destroy them

[1] Num. xiii. 27-33. [2] Num. xiv. 1-10.

utterly and instantly. Moses interceded, and Jehovah spared, but announced that they should all turn back into the wilderness, and journey and die there in their wandering till another generation should be born and disciplined, worthy with Joshua and Caleb to go over Jordan and plant their divine institutions in the land. While this enunciation was being given, the ten cowardly spies died by a plague from the Lord, and the mutiny was hushed; but the spirit of the people was no more loyal than before. In spite of warnings and prohibitions, they desperately presumed to go against the Canaanites, and ascended "to the hill-top," where the Amalekites and Canaanites discomfit and destroy them.[1] There is no alternative to the survivors but to go back to the wilderness till "their carcasses fall there."

"After the number of the days in which ye searched the land, even forty days, each day for a year shall ye bear your iniquities, even forty years;"[2] so God threatened, and so God dealt by them, and effected the necessary training of a disciplined, hardy, courageous generation. In Numbers[3] is given the record of their wanderings and several encampments, and directly under Moses' leading and Jehovah's supervision they gained the confirmed habit of orderly conduct and prompt obedience. By removals and restings of the glory of his presence, the Lord controlled their marches and encampments.[4] And by

[1] Num. xiv. 10-45.
[2] Num. xiv. 34.
[3] Chap. xxxiii.
[4] Num. ix. 15-23.

precise arrangements and relative positions to each other and to the tabernacle, with their captains, Moses systematized all their movements with military exactness,[1] and thereby made them to become both good soldiers and good citizens. They learned subordination, precision, prompt execution; and from long slavery there came out a race of hardy and trusty freemen.

Aaron, Moses' brother and high priest, died at Mount Hor, and his son Eleazer was designated by God, and invested by Moses with the office of high priest;[2] and then, a short time after, when they made their second approach to Canaan, Moses ascended Mount Nebo by God's direction, and from the pinnacle of Pisgah looked westward over the Jordan, and saw the outspread hills and plains of Canaan, and died there alone with God in the mountain, "and the Lord buried him."[3] Besides particular transgressions of Aaron and Moses, by which they forfeited the favor of personally entering the promised inheritance of Israel, there was a national result to be attained in their successive deaths and the transmission of their offices to other incumbents. It accustomed the people to the necessary succession of magistrates, and habituated them to expect and respect the appointments of God in the places of the dead. Had Moses and Aaron lived to go over Jordan, and added the veneration and affection which would ensue from conquering the land for them to all the influence of their counsel and

[1] Num. x. 11-28. [2] Num. xx. 22-29. [3] Deut. xxxiv. 1-6.

command in the forty years' wanderings from the exodus, it would have been a more difficult matter to content the people with any successors of such eminent leaders; but by the removing of their rulers at different times, and dividing the glory of the grand events and achievements from Egypt to the possession of Canaan, the people readily learned submission and obedience to such as Jehovah should appoint for them.

2. THE ADMINISTRATION OF THE THEOCRACY UNDER JOSHUA. — All the generation which left Egypt were now dead, except Joshua and Caleb, the faithful commissioners who had spied the land thirty-nine years before; and thus, besides these two, all Israel's thousands were under sixty years of age, counting those then under twenty years who had not been numbered at Sinai.[1] Here, then, were a people in full vigor, hardy and independent, disciplined and taught by severe experiences to trust and obey their officers, and acknowledge Jehovah as their King and Lord. Joshua had already, by God, been invested with the office of chief captain in Moses' stead, and been specially commissioned to make full conquest of the land of Canaan, and promised the constant presence and counsel of Jehovah.[2] Within three days he roused the people to prepare for the expedition; made Reuben, Gad, and the half tribe of Manasseh, whose possessions had already been assigned them east of the Jordan, to join in the war of conquest; and sending two men to spy

[1] Num. xiv. 29. [2] Josh. i. 1-9.

the land, he marched, and made his military encampment on the east bank of the Jordan. Here again were three days' solemn preparation, and receiving divine directions for following the sacred ark, borne by the priests, in the miraculous passage of the river. Here began the series of divinely assisted successes, which much further disciplined and matured the chosen people for their great mission, in teaching to the idolatrous nations the power and supremacy of the one true God.

After the crossing of the Jordan there occurred the destruction of Jericho, whose walls fell to the ground with no human instrumentality, save the shout of the army and the blowing of the priests' trumpets; and then the manifestation of an omniscient watch which detected the sin of Achan, and the severe punishment which warned against all future appropriating of the accursed wealth of Canaan to private possession.[1] After which followed the perpetual victory of the army, in overcoming one Canaanitish city and people after another, for about seven years of uninterrupted conflict, conquest, and complete extirpation of the native population. The whole land was so brought into possession, that what of its inhabitants were not utterly exterminated, as had been required, were at least so subdued or terrified that they yielded unquestioning service and submission to their resistless invaders.

And here occurs the serious question of the moral

[1] Josh. vii.

right of Israel to invade and exterminate the Canaanites. To put it directly, as infidelity affirms it to have been, Was it not cruel, inhuman, and horribly wicked for this foreign people to come and slay old and young, and take permanent possession? If we look to nothing higher than humanity in those transactions, they could not be justified; they must be most sternly rebuked and condemned. No man, and no numbers of men, have the right so to invade and destroy their fellows. But this is not the light in which to put and judge these proceedings. It was not Joshua's command, and the people's ready execution, that stood ultimately responsible. Jehovah was their King and their God, and he commanded that "their eye should not pity, nor their hand spare."[1] And their God was also the God of all flesh, and thus the real question is, May God command one people to exterminate another, and may that people righteously execute such command? We do not look the truth directly in the face, till we question God's right to do what he will with his own. And here we may say, on both sides, reverently and unhesitatingly, that the right of God is not in his mere arbitrary will, nor in this that all flesh is his by creation and power; but it is in this, that God is Absolute Reason, and that he should fix his purpose and execute his will universally in the end of reason. We, who, as human, can only have a finite endowment of reason, may not always, now or ever, be competent to judge the Absolute in all cases; and yet, so far as

[1] Deut. vii. 16.

divine purposes and acts come within the sphere of human comprehension, we may judge the rightness of such purposes and acts. God himself permits it, and appeals to such reason within the sphere of its finite compass.[1]

The following considerations sustain the divine equity and benevolence in the transaction. God is the moral governor of all people, and he has in nature given sufficient light to read and know his being and authority.[2]

The nations of Canaan were notoriously wicked, and had been long spared by God, and were now ripe for judgment;[3] and he might have wholly exterminated them righteously by some providential judgment.

He commissioned Israel to be his authorized executioners,[4] and made this work a discipline for them and for their warning.[5] It showed to them and the nations God's abhorrence of idolatry. In this is enough to silence all questioning.

Joshua lived to make the conquest of Canaan, and settle the tribes in it according to their assigned portions, and faithfully and successfully administered the government for several years afterwards, while the people were at peace, cultivating the soil and building up the ruined cities. The tabernacle had been set up at Shechem, and there, when he had lived one hundred and ten years, Joshua summoned a full convocation of the people, and recounted before them the wonders

[1] Isa. i. 18, v. 3, 4; Ezek. xviii. 25–29.
[2] Rom. i. 19, 20, ii. 14, 15.
[3] Gen. xv. 16.
[4] Num. xxxiii. 50–56.
[5] Deut. vii.

of God to their fathers and to them, and gave them his solemn charge to be faithful to God and their national covenant, and then died, committing them to the care and protection of Jehovah.[1]

3. The Administration under the Judges. — For some time after Joshua's death, and while the elders who survived him remained, the people were peaceful, industrious, and obedient to the law, without any appointed head of the nation.[2] The prudence of Moses in their wanderings, and the prowess of Joshua in their wars, had made these chief captains necessary in their times; but the day for almost exclusive military training was past, and a more popular civil method of governing might be admitted. Instead of a single ruler, God designated the tribe of Judah to have the pre-eminence in counsel and leading measures;[3] and under the precedence of this tribe there were various successful expeditions against the uneasy remnants of some of the Canaanites, while some still held themselves in their strong places, notwithstanding all efforts made to dislodge them.[4]

Under the influence of these remaining idolaters, and the Hebrew tendency to relapse into superstition, the people, after the first generations passed away, began to forsake God and serve Balaam and Ashtaroth;[5] and God, according to his previous announcement to make his special providences conform

[1] Josh. xxiii., xxiv. [2] Josh. xxiv. 31.
[3] Judges i. 1-20. [4] Judges i. 22-36. [5] Judges ii. 13.

to their national fidelity or rejection of him, began to give their enemies power over them, and to oppress them with severe exactions.[1] Then came the administration of Judges, whom the Lord raised up for their deliverance.[2] These judges were a different order of magistracy from the chief ruler or captain, as in the case of Moses and Joshua, who had been permanent in their office through all changes. The judges were raised up for a special emergency, and on critical occasions. They were for the time in full authority as Jehovah's vicegerents, and held both judicial and executive power, declared war, headed the army, made peace, and often maintained their rule after the exigency which had called them out had passed by. But they exacted no annual revenue, kept no royal courts, had no badge of official dignity, and designated no successors.[3] Sometimes they judged all Israel; but in other cases their jurisdiction was partial, and in some cases two were contemporary. They grew at the last, under Eli and Samuel, to be more permanent, powerful, and dictatorial. In one case, Deborah, a woman, in connection with Barak, judged Israel forty years. Their appointment began with Othniel, on occasion of eight years' oppression of Chusan-rishathaim, of Mesopotamia, and in all, to Samuel, were fourteen in number, and the sum of their periods of office was four hundred and ninety years. There may have been intervals, and perhaps overlappings, and the exact time from Joshua's death to

[1] Judges ii. 14, 15. [2] Judges ii. 16–19. [3] Judges ii. 16–23.

Samuel's anointing Saul as king cannot well be determined, but will not have been far from five hundred years. Very special interpositions of Jehovah by some of the judges, particularly Deborah, Gideon, Jephtha, Samson, and Samuel, made conspicuous his power and protection of his people, and his rebuke for their backslidings; and the taking of the Ark of the Covenant by the Philistines under Eli not only rebuked Israel, but confounded the idols of the heathen in their own temples. So God kept his people together before the nations till the days of Samuel.

4. The Theocratic Administration under Kings. — In the old age of Samuel, he made his sons associates with him in the judge's office; but they became unjust and mercenary, "accepted bribes and perverted judgment." It was also a critical time with the nation, which was then dangerously beset with powerful enemies. The people were dissatisfied and alarmed, and the elders in concert repaired to Samuel at Ramah, and asked directly for a king to rule them, after the manner of other nations.[1] This request for a king displeased Samuel; but on inquiry of the Lord, the divine answer affirmed the request to be unrighteous, and yet directed Samuel to a compliance with their wish. Samuel prophetically announced to them the consequences of their choice, and the exactions and oppressions their kings would make upon the people, and the burdens the nation must bear to sup-

[1] 1 Sam. viii. 1-5.

port the royal state and dignity; but the elders, nevertheless, were persistent in their purpose, and by God's direction Samuel complied with their request, though holding it unreasonable, and sent them away with the understanding a king would be found and inaugurated.

Saul, a son of Kish, of the tribe of Benjamin, was hunting the strayed asses of his father; and becoming wearied and discouraged by a long search, he said to his servant that he would go to the city of Samuel and take counsel of the man of God. At the entrance of the city Samuel met them, and having been already directed by God, he privately there anointed Saul king over Israel. Soon after, a solemn convocation of the people at Mizpeh was made, and the lot was cast by the prophet, to determine before all the people who their king should be, first by tribes, then by families, and then man by man. First the lot fell to the tribe of Benjamin, then to the family of Matri; and ultimately among the individuals of the family, the lot fell to the very man whom Samuel had already prophetically and privately anointed. When found and presented, his great stature and comely form and features struck at once the popular favor, and by acclamation they acknowledge him their king. He was soon publicly inaugurated at Gilgal, and divinely invested with the regal authority.

Israel's sin in seeking a king was rather in the manner and motive than in the fact. Moses had in his day anticipated such a result, and had given such directions as permitted, and even encouraged, the nation to have a king.[1] Their motive in asking a king, though occasioned by the age of Samuel and the immorality of his sons, was the gratification of vanity and national glory, and too much after the custom of the heathen about them; for they said, after Samuel's prudential expostulations, "No, but we will have a king over us, that we also may be like all the nations, and that our king may judge us and fight our battles."[2] But most reprehensible was it that they forgot their theocratic allegiance, and desired a king incompatible with the claims of Jehovah. Says the Lord to Samuel, "They have not rejected thee, but they have rejected me, that I should not reign over them."[3] They had neither consulted God nor his prophets; they passed by the high priest and the Shechina; and of their own motion they demanded a king, to the exclusion of Jehovah, already their legitimate sovereign. God allowed their request, and made it the very means of punishing their sin, and disciplining their disloyalty to him. He maintained his supremacy, and held his constitutional authority, and in giving them a king as he pleased, he made the king to be his viceroy, and no independent monarch. The government was still a Theocracy, and the human king was God's vicegerent as truly as had been their chief captains and their judges. This peculiarity is to be recognized through all the kingly succession, that the human king acts

[1] Deut. xvii. 14-20. [2] 1 Sam. viii. 20. [3] 1 Sam. viii. 7.

in Jehovah's stead and by his authority. He regulated the religious arrangements of the courses of the priests' service, the orders of the singers, and the employments of the Levites under the prescribed ritual;[1] he could arrange and officer the army,[2] and he could appoint the civil magistrates for executing the laws through the land;[3] but he could originate no new laws or ceremonies not in execution of the divine statutes, except as committed to him by the divine Sovereign. Hence the rebukes and threatening of the prophets to disobedient kings were legitimate; they were Jehovah's accredited messengers calling delinquent vicegerents to account.

The first year of Saul's reign was without reproach, but after the second year he began to exhibit the truth of Samuel's forewarning. He raised a large body-guard of three thousand men, two thousand for himself, and one thousand he committed to the charge of his son Jonathan.[4] He offered sacrifices presumptuously, and was plainly told the kingdom would go from his family;[5] and some time after, for direct disobedience, Jehovah took the kingdom from him, and gave it in his own purpose to Saul's neighbor.[6] After this Samuel dropped all intercourse with Saul, and under the Lord's direction privately anointed the youthful son of Jesse to be the future king of Israel.[7] After this Saul became irritable, jealous, and reck-

[1] 1 Chron. xv., xvi., and xxiii.-xxvii. [2] 2 Sam. xxiii.; 1 Kings iv.
[3] 2 Chron. xix. [4] 1 Sam. xiii. 1, 2. [5] 1 Sam. xiii.
[6] 1 Sam. xv. [7] 1 Sam. xvi. 13.

less; and as the Lord had forsaken him, he applied, after Samuel's death, to the woman of Endor, who had a familiar spirit; and to the surprise of the woman and the confusion of Saul, the dead Samuel appeared, and announced his doom, that on the next day he should be with Samuel in the eternal world. In the morrow's battle with the Philistines on Mount Gilboa, his army was defeated; and as he was hard pressed by his enemies, he fell upon his own sword, and died, he and his armor-bearer.[1] Saul reigned forty years.

When David heard of the death of Saul, he inquired of God, who answered by sending him up from Ziklag to Hebron, in the tribe of Judah, and the men of Judah came to him and anointed him king over the house of Judah;[2] but Abner, Saul's chief captain, took Ishbosheth, a son of Saul, and made him king over all Israel beside Judah.[3] After seven years, Ishbosheth was slain, and all the tribes came to David in Hebron, and made him king over them all.[4]

David's reign was prosperous, and Israel became numerous and powerful, fighting many battles and overcoming their enemies, and maintaining the worship of the true God at the sanctuary. David greatly delighted in the holy-days' convocations at the tabernacle; arranged the order of the priests in their ministrations, and the singers; and wrote the larger portion of their devotional Psalms. But his generally

[1] 1 Sam. xxxi. 4, 5.
[2] 2 Sam. ii. 4.
[3] 2 Sam. ii. 8, 9.
[4] 2 Sam. v. 5.

holy life was dishonored by some outbreaking iniquities, as in the matter of Uriah; and the retributive judgments of God followed, marking before the nation and carrying to his own conscience the evidence of the divine displeasure. The revolt and death of Absalom, the incest of Amnon, and the destructive pestilence when he numbered the people of his own motion, officiously and vain-gloriously,—all chastened his spirit, and induced bitter repentance and deep humility. In his last days, his son Adonijah attempted to usurp the kingdom which God had intimated should descend to Solomon, and David sent at once Nathan the prophet, and the high priest, and the chief captain, and they anointed Solomon king; and David gave to him a special charge, and then died, having reigned, in all, forty years.[1]

The reign of Solomon was peaceful and long, and Israel rose to the height of national greatness and renown. The costly temple was built, and the Ark of God transferred to it from the tabernacle; and all the imposing ceremonial worship of the daily services and yearly solemnities brought the people before the Lord, advancing them in the knowledge of what the Covenant with their fathers and the theocratic reign of Jehovah meant to them as a people, and in preparation of the world for the Messiah's coming. And yet, with all this teaching, and in many persons learning, the will and work of the Lord, the long prosperity of Solomon's reign was more than fallen humanity

[1] 1 Kings ii. 10, 11.

could bear. Wealth flowed in on every side, luxuries abounded, and sensuality greatly overpowered the king and the nation. Solomon disobeyed the injunction against foreign marriages, and multiplied his wives from the heathen nations, and especially an Egyptian princess,[1] and made alliance with Pharaoh, and opened the way for all Egyptian superstitions and idolatries again to come in to the people. As Solomon grew old, he was in this way led into heathen practices, and set up altars and built high places over against Jerusalem.[2] This rapid religious degeneracy demanded an effectual check, and God convulsed and divided the kingdom, and brought out a lasting separation between the idolatrous and the true worshippers.

In the latter part of the reign of Solomon, Jeroboam became conspicuous as a man of enterprise and valor, and Solomon promoted him to be captain of the tribe of Joseph. The prophet Ahijah was commissioned by the Lord to announce to him that the nation should be rent in twain, and that ten tribes would come under his sway, because of the national idolatry, but that the consummation should be delayed during the life of Solomon. Owing probably to Jeroboam's insolence and to Solomon's jealousy, Solomon sought the life of Jeroboam, and the latter fled to Egypt, and was protected and favored by Shishak, the then reigning Pharaoh. Shishak was doubtless the first king of Manetho's twenty-second dynasty, known

[1] 1 Kings iii. 1. [2] 1 Kings xi. 1–8.

on the monuments as Sheshonk, and probably had gained his crown by violence or treachery from Solomon's father-in-law, as the last king of Manetho's twenty-first dynasty;[1] and thus Shishak was ready to foster the refugee from Solomon. So soon as Solomon died, having reigned forty years, Jeroboam returned, and was present when all Israel had gathered at Shechem to make Solomon's son, Rehoboam, king in the place of his father. At his instigation they demanded of Rehoboam a diminution of the taxes, which the old counsellors of Solomon advised him to make, but the young men advised him to assert his prerogative, and threaten stronger exactions. So Rehoboam haughtily answered; and at once, on the signal from Jeroboam, an uproar was made, the council was broken up, and the tribes, except those of Judah and Benjamin, went to their own homes. Rehoboam, in the same haughty spirit as his threat, sent his treasurer to collect their augmented taxes, whom they stoned to death, and stood out in open mutiny. Rehoboam cowered and fled in fear to the fortifications in Jerusalem, and the ten tribes made Jeroboam their king, while Rehoboam held the allegiance of the two tribes, Judah and Benjamin. An army of the two tribes was at once ready, with a hundred and fifty thousand men to fight the ten rebellious tribes into submission; but by the prophet Shemaiah, the Lord forbade Rehoboam to go out to battle, for this whole matter had been under his providential

[1] Wilkinson's Ancient Egyptians, Chapter II.

supervision. Henceforth the Hebrews were two kingdoms — that of Israel and that of Judah, Israelites and Jews. The Israelites made Samaria in the lot of Ephraim their capital, while the Jews kept the old capital at Jerusalem, which was nearly on the dividing line between the lot of Judah and of Benjamin. The one kingdom was often known also as that of Ephraim, as the other was that of Judah, from the tribal locality of the royal residence.

5. After the Division, to Israel's Dispersion and Judah's Babylonian Captivity. — The revolt of the ten tribes was of the Lord, in the sense that he overruled what he condemned as wrong, for the better fulfilment of his great purpose to fit the world for the promised Redeemer's coming. Their revolt was a rejection of God as their king, a rebellion against their legitimate sovereign, and alienation of themselves from the Abrahamic Covenant and Promise, and thus cutting themselves off from all the privileges and prerogatives of the theocratic state. Henceforth the history of Israel as a nation is of no more interest in the covenant institutions of Jehovah, than the history of any Gentile nation, except as their old connection and still close neighborhood with Judah had a more special influence upon the kingdom and people who remained in covenant. God continued his warnings by occasional prophets, and announcing his threatened judgments, and thus gave them opportunity for repentance and return to allegiance; but as

a kingdom, they rejected all warnings, and steadily departed further from the true worship till they became lost in history among the nations. We only outline their experience to their final dispersion.

Besides Jeroboam, with whom the revolt commenced, and who reigned twenty-two years, there were eighteen kings, and two periods of interregnum of twelve and of eight years respectively, and making for the duration of the separate kingdom of Israel two hundred and sixty years and seven months in all. Of all these successive kings it is specifically recorded that "they did evil in the sight of the Lord," and among them ten, at least, lost their lives by violence. At once it was manifest how dangerous to the permanent separation from Judah it would be to permit the Israelites so disposed to go up to Jerusalem at the yearly feasts and solemn convocation, and on consultation with his courtiers, Jeroboam made two golden images of the Egyptian Apis, known as "the golden calves," and placed one at Dan, in the tribe of Naphtali, at the northern extreme of the kingdom, and the other at Bethel, within the tribe of Ephraim, and at the southern portion of the kingdom, and erected temples and altars, and appointed priests not of the tribe of Levi, and established feast days, and thus introduced a superstitious and idolatrous worship after the Egyptian model. Some pious Israelites remained and refused to join in the idolatrous practices,[1] but the most of the nation became confirmed in pagan worship.

[1] 1 Kings xix. 18.

While Jeroboan was burning incense at his idolatrous altar at Bethel, a prophet from Judah announced to him the destruction of this altar and worship by a future king of Judah, Josiah by name, and Jeroboam in great anger stretched out his arm to arrest the prophet; but in the act the arm was paralyzed, and the altar burst asunder and scattered around the fire and ashes. The terrified king was humbled, and asked the prophet's intercession to God for his restoration, which was done, and his impotent arm healed; but in his perverseness he still clave to his idolatries, and multiplied profane priests, and kept his people from the Lord. His son Abijah was dangerously sick, and his judgment and conscience constrained him to inquire of the Lord, and not of his idols; but lest his people should recognize his want of confidence in his gods, he sent his wife secretly to Ahijah, at Shiloh, to make the inquiry. This old prophet, who in Solomon's reign had foretold Jeroboam of his coming elevation to the kingdom, was now blind; but forewarned of God, he announced who she was, and rebuked the hypocritical concealment, and uttered the curse of the Lord upon the house of Jeroboam for his wickedness. The child should die or ever she entered the capital city, and the only favor given was this natural death, for all the rest of the house should die by violence. "The Lord will smite Israel as a reed is shaken in the water, and he will root up Israel out of this good land which he gave to their fathers, and will scatter them beyond the river, because they have made their groves, provoking the Lord to anger."[1]

Jeroboam warred against Judah, and the battle was set in array, eight hundred thousand men of Israel against four hundred thousand men of Judah, in the days of Abijah, son and successor to Rehoboam. Standing on a mountain over against the army of Israel, Abijah reproved them for their idolatry and rebellion against the family of David, and would dissuade them from fighting against the people of the Lord God of their fathers. Jeroboam secretly directed an ambush to get in stealth behind the army of Judah, and when Abijah and Judah knew it, they put their trust in God, and shouted the battle-cry, and attacked and slew of Israel five hundred thousand men, took Bethel and many other cities, and so weakened and discouraged Israel, that Judah was left in peace of Jeroboam ever after. At length Jeroboam died of some divine judgment, for it is said, "The Lord struck him and he died."[2]

Then came treachery, and assassinations, and suicides among the kings of Israel, till Ahab took the throne, and with his heathen wife, Jezebel, filled Israel with abominations.[3] Elijah, the Lord's prophet, often rebuked and reproved him, tested the supremacy of Jehovah against Baal by the answer of fire from the Lord, and threatened him that the dogs should lick his blood in the vineyard of Naboth, which he had robbed by violence. Ahab was slain in battle with

[1] 1 Kings xiv. 15. [2] 2 Chron. xiii. [3] 1 Kings xvi.

the Syrians, and they washed the blood from his chariot, which the dogs licked up in this stolen vineyard. Jehu followed him in the kingdom, and with burning zeal for a time slew seventy of Ahab's sons, and Jezebel, Ahab's pagan wife, and the priests of Baal, and demolished this idol's temple and altars; but he left the Egyptian golden calves, and "took no heed to walk in the law of the Lord God." After Elijah there were the prophets Jonah, Amos, and Hosea, who continued the divine warnings till the kingdom was given over to destruction. The later kings reigned short and wickedly, and were violently destroyed till Hoshea took the throne. Shalmanezer, king of Assyria, conquered Israel, and subjected the nation to tribute, and when Hoshea made alliance with Egypt, and refused to pay the tribute, Shalmanezer again invaded Israel, and carried the people captive to Assyria, and put them in Halah, and in Habor, by the river Gozan, and in the cities of the Medes.[1]

Ere long the king of Assyria brought families from different provinces of his empire, and settled them in the vacated territories of the captive ten tribes. These blended the worship of Jehovah with that of their provincial gods, and were known in after generations as Samaritans with whom the Jews would have no dealings.[2] The ten tribes so dispersed in Persia and Media have become lost from all historic recognition, and only such as joined themselves with Judah

[1] 2 Kings xviii. 9-12. [2] John iv. 9.

previous to the dispersion have been retained within the circumscription of the Abrahamic Promise.

We return to take up the notice of the Theocracy under the kings, and follow the experiences of the kingdom of Judah from the division of the nation, which people were henceforth known as the Jews. Many pious Israelites joined themselves to Judah and the worship of Jehovah from the first, and at subsequent times the defection of the godly from Israel to the Jews was frequent and numerous, and almost universally the priests and Levites, who had no countenance from the Israelitish grovernment,[1] left their cities in Israel for those in Judah. The Theocratic government and Ritual service, together with the responses of the Oracle in the holy of holies, concentrated their influences upon this limited and better portion of the chosen people, and in connection with the national competition for superiority over the revolted tribes, their religious culture greatly elevated the Jewish character. There was more genuine piety and firm adherence to their Covenant than any former age had witnessed. So was it mainly with Judah till the time of the Israelites' dispersion, when the absence of national rivalry and the universal example of pagan idolatry allowed the strong under-current towards heathen superstitions to gain force, and finally over-flow in wide-spread pagan practices and rejection of covenant obligations.

Beginning with Rehoboam, who reigned seventeen

[1] 2 Chron. xi. 13, 14, xiii. 9.

years, there were to the Babylonian captivity twenty reigns, one of which was that of queen Athaliah, making in all the sum of three hundred and ninety-four years. The two hundred and sixty years and seven months of the Israelitish kingdom ran out in the sixth year of Hezekiah, king of Judah, and from thence to the Babylonian captivity was a period of one hundred and thirty-three years and six months, at the termination of the eleventh year of Zedekiah, king of Judah. Of the Jewish reigns before the dispersion, there were six whose influence was good, embracing a period of more than two hundred years; and there were also six whose influence was evil, but whose duration was so shortened that they embraced but about fifty years. After the dispersion of Israel the change was rapid and lamentable. Passing the remaining years of Hezekiah's reign, which were twenty-three, and all good, there were six evil kings, reigning in all eighty years, and only one godly reign, that of good Josiah, of thirty-one years' continuance. The lapse in iniquity and idolatry was fearful, making the visits of divine judgments a necessity, if the defection from God was to be arrested.

Manasseh's most wicked reign followed that of pious Hezekiah, and he filled the land with idolatry, setting up his images in the very temple, and wrought abomination in Judah more than any king before him. God, by his prophets, announced the coming destruction: "I will wipe Jerusalem as a man wipeth a dish, wiping it and turning it upside down."[1] Amon followed Manasseh, and also imitated his wickedness, but in two years was assassinated in his own palace. The prophets Nahum, Joel, and Habakkuk taught and warned in these evil times; yet would the kings and people not be reclaimed. The good reign of Josiah partially restored the defection and delayed the ruin; but it was only a respite, and not a deliverance, for there was no confirmed reformation. In his day were the prophets Zephaniah and Jeremiah, by whom God said he spared Judah for Josiah's sake, but that ultimately he would remove Judah as he had Israel from his sight, and reject Jerusalem as the place for his name.[2]

Jehoahaz followed in the kingdom, and "turned to work wickedness," and in three months the desolation began. The king of Egypt invaded and conquered the land, and carried him away captive, and put Jehoiakim in his place. He also wrought wickedness, and Nebuchadnezzar of Babylon invaded his kingdom, and subjected him to tribute. After three years, on Jehoiakim's refusal to pay the tribute, the Chaldeans again invaded the land, and oppressed the people, in the midst of which he died, and Jehoiachin took the throne; and in the third month Nebuchadnezzar came again, and carried the royal family, and mighty men, and skilled artisans to Babylon, and put Zedekiah on the throne as his own vassal. The prophet Ezekiel now lived, and was also carried captive with

[1] 2 Kings xxi. 13. [2] 2 Kings xxii., xxiii.

the chief men. In the ninth year of his reign Zedekiah rebelled, and Nebuchadnezzar came back and besieged Jerusalem, and after resisting the siege three years, and enduring famine and suffering, the Jews were forced to surrender, the walls of Jerusalem were broken down, the temple was burned, the holy vessels and costly ornaments of the temple plundered and carried to Babylon. The sons of Zedekiah were slain before his eyes, and then his own eyes were put out, and he in his blindness was carried a prisoner to Babylon. The poor and oppressed people left in the land were governed by rulers put over them by their conquerors. This captivity had repeatedly been foretold as determined by Jehovah, and that its continuance should be for seventy years; and this thorough execution of the desolation is fully narrated.[1]

Besides the terrible, and in the end effectual, discipline of Judah by these calamities, there was the throwing of the Jewish influence and knowledge of the true faith upon another and wider portion of humanity. Not Canaan, and Egypt, and Syria, as mainly hitherto, but the Assyrian empire over all Eastern Asia, was made acquainted with the institutions of Jehovah and the practices of his people. Their desolation purified the Jews, and they, in their recovered loyalty to God, taught the nations the promise of his coming redemption for the whole lost family of mankind.

[1] 2 Kings xxiv., xxv.

SECTION VII.

FROM THE BABYLONIAN CAPTIVITY TO THE COMING OF MESSIAH.

HENCEFORTH inspired Scripture ceases to direct our way in the history of God's dealing with humanity, till we come to the New Testament record, save the Books of Daniel and Esther, which give some occurrences in Babylon, and those of Ezra and Nehemiah, relating to events connected with the restoration from captivity. The captivity and experience in Babylon did much in fixing the Jews in loyalty to Jehovah, and the preparation for the advent of their promised Redeemer. They came out of that furnace greatly purified, and ever after abhorred idolatry as deeply as before they had been inclined to all pagan superstitions. The peculiarities of the Theocratic rule and ritual were henceforth less needful, and having mainly accomplished their end, the whole dispensation was wearing away. The captivity destroyed and lost many of their sacred symbols, which at their return were never restored. The ark of the covenant, with the original copy of the law. the golden pot of old manna, and the blossoming almond rod of Aaron, which had been laid up before the Lord, were all lost with the burning of the first temple; and more than all, the Shechina, or visible presence of Jehovah, passed away without any return to the second temple. The successive removals, to its final departure, are strikingly given in the visions of Ezekiel, step by step, just preceding the burning of the temple.[1] Jehovah's perpetual witness of himself in special providences also began its decline as less marked and constant, and the open entailment of judgments upon the children for the fathers' sins, in civil vindication, were prophetically announced as then ceasing.[2]

Still in its expiring light the old Theocracy does not cease its salutary teachings. Its eve is as important in its lessons to us as its morn or its midday splendor. It tells of God's work done by it, and marks the passing away of an important day in order that the more important scenes of a gospel day may open. And as the old passes away, we shall find its expiring light and influence thrown out wider and further upon the nations. The providence of God mingles his people more with mankind, and sets their faith and worship out on broader scenes than had before been exhibited. The Jews go to Babylon and make their impression on the Assyrian empire; the Assyrian is subverted by the Persian, this by the

[1] With Ezek. i. confer viii. 4, ix. 3, x. 4, 18, xi. 23, 24.
[2] Ezek. xviii. 2, 3.

Grecian, and then this by the Roman universal monarchies; and amid them all, the chosen people of Jehovah, and their persistent faith and worship, are kept constantly and most prominently conspicuous. These great transactions fulfil the divine prediction, "I will overturn, overturn, overturn it, and it shall be no more, until he cometh whose right it is, and I will give it him."[1] "Yet once, it is a little while, and I will shake the heavens and the earth, and the sea and the dry land; and I will shake all nations, and the Desire of all nations shall come."[2] No such mighty overturnings have taken place among the nations of the earth as those within the five hundred years preceding the advent of Christ, from the beginning until now; and yet this one people mingled in them all, shed its light upon them all, and stood unbroken through them all, till the Lord and Saviour of all came in the flesh and tabernacled with men.

We shall follow the history from the captivity to the advent of Christ, through the great monarchies with which the Jews were influentially familiar, and the marked epochs occurring in their experience.

1. The Jews as subject to the Assyrians. — There was a first and last invasion of Judea by Nebuchadnezzar, with an interval of eighteen years, and an intervening hostile visit, in all of which captive Jews, more or less, were taken to Babylon; and thus the

[1] Ezek. xxi. 27. [2] Hag. ii. 6, 7.

captivity, as one event, filled a period of eighteen years. Nebuchadnezzar was sent with an army against Egypt, through Palestine, by his father, Nabopolassar; and in this expedition he took Jerusalem, in the fourth year of Jehoiakim, and Daniel and his companions, with many chief families of the Jews, were sent to Babylon.[1] In profane history we learn that two years thereafter Nabopolassar died, and Nebuchadnezzar hastened back to Babylon to receive the kingdom. Jehoiakim soon refused paying tribute, and the armies from the subject Assyrian provinces overran Judea;[2] and in these troubles Jehoiakim died. In the third month of Jehoiachin, his successor's reign, Nebuchadnezzar a second time came, and carried away the royal family and many noble Jews back with him to Babylon, and made Zedekiah king.[3] Zedekiah soon rebelled, and Nebuchadnezzar a third time came and finished the work of desolation and captivity, and put Gedaliah as governor over the poor and miserable families which he left in the land.[4] This was the nineteenth year of Nebuchadnezzar,[5] i. e., from his commissioned expedition on his first visit to Jerusalem, but the seventeenth year from reigning alone.[6]

The beginning of the captivity we thus put at the fourth year of Jehoiakim, and first of Nebuchadnezzar's royal commission, and which was the year 606 B. C.

[1] 2 Kings xxiv. 1; Dan. i. 1-7.
[2] 2 Kings xxiv. 2.
[3] 2 Kings xxiv. 8-17.
[4] 2 Kings xxv.; Jer. xxix.
[5] 2 Kings xxv. 8.
[6] Prideaux, B. I.

The Jews were then in Babylon under Assyrian monarchs, as follows: —

	Years.	Months.
Nebuchadnezzar's reign, ...	44	—
Evil-merodach's reign, ...	2	—
Nerriglissor's reign, ...	4	—
Laborosoarchod's reign, ...		9
Nabonadius, or Belshazzar's reign, . .	17	—
Making in all, ...	67	9

During this period we may note the following occurrences and influences: —

Gedaliah, left by Nebuchadnezzar, at his first invasion of Judea, as governor, was mild and kind, and the dispersed families in the land gathered themselves readily under his rule; but within seven months he was treacherously slain by Ishmael, with all his attendants. Johanan then drove Ishmael away to the Ammonites, and he, with the remnant of Jews, removed to the southern border of Palestine, near to Egypt, in fear of the revenge which the Chaldeans might take for Ishmael's treachery and assassination. Jeremiah the prophet was with them, and when they inquired of him if they should pass over into Egypt, he, from the Lord, forbade such purpose. In defiance of this, they determined to go, and soon relapsed into the old Egyptian superstition, and worshipped the queen of heaven, joining in sacrifices to Isis. Jeremiah here denounced the exterminating judgment of the future coming of the king of Babylon.[1]

[1] Jer. xl. to xliv.

Those Jews who had been carried to Babylon were kindly treated, and Daniel was in high estimation, and raised to eminent civil authority; and when Evil-merodach took the kingdom, he freed Jehoiachin, and gave him royal support in his own palace.[1] During Nebuchadnezzar's reign his interpretation of the king's dreams, the deliverance of his three friends from the burning furnace, and the madness which, according to Daniel's prediction, came upon the king, when they drove him from the presence of men to be with the beasts,[2] — all this powerfully affected the Assyrian empire, and seems to have made Nebuchadnezzar, on his recovery, a humble worshipper of the true Jehovah.[3] The steadfast refusal of Shadrach, Meshech, and Abednego to bow to the king's golden image evinces how soon and strong the captivity had served to dissuade the Jews from idolatry. Their own sadness, while they wept by the rivers of Babylon, and hanged their harps on the willows, and the sympathy of their captors, who asked them to sing their songs of Zion,[4] all manifest how effectually God's dealings with them were working out his own counsels. The seventy years' duration of the captivity set by the prophet[5] was drawing near its close, and in the way of the destined deliverance, the Assyrian dynasty was overthrown by that of the Medes and Persians.

[1] 2 Kings xxv. 27. [2] Dan. iii. and iv. [3] Dan. iv. 34-37.
[4] Psalm cxxxvii. [5] Jer. xxv. 11, xxix. 10.

2. THE JEWS AS SUBJECT TO THE PERSIANS. — The last of the Assyrian monarchs was Belshazzar, an effeminate ruler, who, while Cyrus was besieging him in his capital, gave himself up to pleasure. At a voluptuous feast, in contempt of Jehovah, he ordered the sacred vessels of the Jerusalem temple to be used in his drunken revelry. The dread prodigy of a supernatural hand appeared writing on the wall, and left the ominous characters there legible. Daniel interpreted them plainly, and the interpretation was immediately fulfilled, in that the besiegers took the city that very night, slew Belshazzar, and Darius the Median took the kingdom.[1] Cyrus was the general who had taken Babylon, and while the power was in his hands, he left Darius, who was his uncle, and known as Cyaxares, to rule at Babylon, while he prosecuted his designs of further conquest. Darius died after about two years, when Cyrus took the kingdom in his own name. The Persian monarchy may be noted as beginning in the year 538 B. C.

Darius	reigned	2	years.
Cyrus	"	7	"
Cambyses, or Ahasuerus of Ezra iv. 6	"	7	"
Smerdis, or Artaxerxes of Ezra iv. 7	"	1	"
Darius Hystaspes	"	36	"
Xerxes the Great	"	21	"
Artaxerxes Longimanus, or Ahasuerus of Esther,	"	40	"
Xerxes II., known as Sogdianus, ...	"	1	"

[1] Dan. v. 31.

Darius Nothus	reigned	19 years.
Artaxerxes Mnemon	"	46 "
Darius Ochus	"	21 "
Darius Arses	"	2 "
Darius Codomanus	"	4 "
In all		207 "

With this new race of kings at Babylon, God at once began the exhibitions of his power in favor of his own chosen people. Daniel was elevated to great favor and power, for, as Darius divided his new kingdom into one hundred and twenty provinces, with their rulers, he put over these three presidents, the first of which presidencies was given to Daniel. He was envied and hated by the other officers, who conspired for his downfall. They knew his discretion and probity, and despaired of success in their cabal except through some intrigue in the matter of his religion. They artfully procured a decree, unalterable in law by any authority, prohibiting any petition to any god or man, save to the king, for thirty days. Daniel knew the decree, and the penalty of being cast into the den of lions; but he opened his window three times a day towards Jerusalem, and prayed to Jehovah aloud as beforetimes. The issue came, and for a whole night he lay in the lions' den; and when the anxious king called to him in the morning, he answered that his God, Jehovah, had shut the lions' mouths, and he was safe. Joyfully the king received and honored him, but put his accusers at once in his place with the lions, who immediately devoured them.

Daniel, and his people, and his religion, were now respected.[1]

The seventy years from Nebuchadnezzar's first carrying the Jews captive to Babylon terminated in the first year of Cyrus. Daniel had consulted the prophetic books and found the time, and prayed and confessed to Jehovah, and had been answered in reference to the time the Jews should be restored, and also the time that the promised Saviour should come for the world's redemption.[2] Among the books consulted, and which must have been laid before Cyrus by David, was the remarkable prediction in Isaiah,[3] in connection with the majesty and sublimity of the description of Jehovah's unity and power. That it was this which impressed and moved Cyrus to restore the Jews, is quite manifest from the decree he made to this end.[4] The leaders in the execution of this decree of Cyrus were Zerubbabel, the grandson of Jehoiakim, called in Babylon Sheshbazzar, and Joshua, grandson of the high priest Seraiah, who, with king Jehoiakim, had been among the first captives. These two leaders, with about fifty thousand Jews, went up from Babylon to Judea, with horses, and camels, and vessels of the temple, and much treasure, to build up their own houses, and their fathers' cities, and the walls and temple at Jerusalem.[5] The Samaritans desired to assist, but they were not Jews, and their offer was unacceptable.

[1] Dan. vi. [2] Dan. ix. [3] Isa. xliv. 28, xlv.
[4] Given in Ezra i. 1–4. [5] Ezra i. to iii.

On this account their real enmity in heart disclosed itself, and they immediately and persistently opposed the undertaking. They hindered as they could all through the reign of Cyrus; they wrote accusing letters of the Jews to his successor, Ahasuerus; and especially to Artaxerxes Smerdis, and finally from him attained a command to make the Jews stop building, and they forced the Jews to cease from their work to the time of Darius Hystaspes.[1] Here was the same intervening number of years in the whole period of restoration, viz., eighteen years, that there had been between the first and last carrying into captivity. So that, from the beginning of captivity to beginning of restoration was seventy years, and from the finishing of captivity till the full return was seventy years, and from the beginning to the completion of each event of captivity and restoration was a period of eighteen years. This full restoration was in the second year of Darius's reign, whose decree confirmed that of Cyrus, and annulled all intervening hindering authorities.[2] After two years' earnest labor, the second temple was finished and dedicated on the feast of the Passover, with great solemnity and national thanksgiving; and Darius befriended the Jews through his long reign. He was followed by Xerxes the Great, whose famous Grecian expedition and warlike enterprises absorbed his attention, leaving Judea to its own way.

Artaxerxes Longimanus followed in a long reign of

[1] Ezra iv. [2] Ezra vi.

forty years. He is the Ahasuerus of the Book of Esther, and the occurrences in the life of this Jewish queen, the circumvention of Haman's design to extirpate the whole Jewish people through the realm by Esther's foster-father Mordecai, with the execution of Haman, and the Jews' complete deliverance, took place early in his reign. The temple service and general Jewish ordinances had now been restored and regularly observed in Judea for fifty-eight years, but the walls of the city were yet unfinished, and many disorders were introduced and tolerated. In the seventh year of this king, Ezra, who was a scribe and direct descendant from Aaron, and of great repute and influence, was sent with a royal commission to redress all disorders, and complete and establish the work of Jewish polity and prosperity. By him the canon of Jewish Scripture was collected and settled, the ceremonial services orderly arranged, and especially the great disorder from foreign marriages was thoroughly corrected.[1]

Again, in the twentieth year of this king, Nehemiah, his captain, who was a Jew, heard of the still incomplete restoration and settlement of all matters at Jerusalem, and, at his request, the king gave him permission to go up to Judea and see what was its condition, and appointed him governor, with full authority to regulate all matters. He came and privately surveyed the still desolate breaches which had not been repaired, and set himself at once to rousing the

[1] Ezra vii. to x.

nation to their duty. He set the work of rebuilding immediately forward, resisted and overcame all the machinations of the old Samaritan opposers, finished the walls, redressed the oppressions of the strong over the poor, and in twelve years mainly accomplished his work, and returned to the king at Babylon. Shortly again he came back with new authority, redressed the Sabbath violations that had been introduced, and put the government and people in an orderly and prosperous condition.[1]

As the law had been found by Ezra, and read before the people, so out of this now began the practice of regularly reading it in smaller assemblies on the Sabbath; and thus was introduced the long-continued habit of synagogue worship, which was everywhere common among Jews in the time of Christ and his apostles. After Nehemiah, the province of Syria included Judea, and the Persian government of it was through the high priest, and thus the sacred office became much secularized and corrupted. It so remained for eighty years, till Alexander the Great conquered Persia.

3. The Jews as subject to Alexander and his Successors. — The empire of the world, attained by the conquests of Alexander, was at his death divided into four sovereignties, under four of his distinguished generals — Cassander over Macedon and Greece; Lysimachus over Thrace and the countries bordering

[1] Neh. throughout.

the Hellespont on the west and the Bosphorus on the east; Ptolemy over Egypt and Palestine; and Seleucus over Babylon and Syria. The Jews were immediately involved in the transactions of the two latter empires only. The conflicting interests and consequent contentions of these two made Judea, standing between them, the frequent battle-ground of their hostile armies. For several of the earlier reigns, Judea was directly subject to Egypt, and later in this period it was made a province of Syria, while for the whole time the Jews shared in the commotions of both, till their more independent state under the Maccabean heroes.

This period begins in the year 331 B. C.

Alexander,		8	years.
Egyptian.	Ptolemy Lagus,	39	"
"	Ptolemy Philadelphus,	38	"
"	Ptolemy Euergetes,	25	"
"	Ptolemy Philopator,	17	"
"	Ptolemy Epiphanes,	19	"
All Egyptian period,		146	
Syrian.	Seleucus Philopator,	11	"
"	Antiochus Epiphanes,	8	"
Whole period,		165	"

While in his conquests, Alexander the Great was besieging Tyre, he sent into the neighboring countries of Samaria and Judea, demanding supplies; but the Jews were subject to Persia, then ruled by Darius Codomanus, and fearing his displeasure, they refused the demand of Alexander. Immediately upon his conquest of Tyre, and offended by this refusal, Alexander marched with his army to Jerusalem, intending severe punishment for this Jewish slight. Jaddua, the Jewish high priest, met him on his coming, clothed with the holy vestments of his divine office, whom Alexander immediately received and saluted with profoundest veneration, saying that this very personage had appeared in a dream to him long before in Macedonia, and given him intimations and directions about his intended expedition, and that the deity of whom he was the priest must have inspired and directed his whole journey. Jaddua read to him the prophecy of Daniel,[1] concerning the destruction of Persia by a Grecian king, and applied the prophecy to Alexander himself, who was so favorably affected that he left Jerusalem safe, and conferred on the Jews many favors.[2]

After Alexander's death at Babylon, and the division of Egypt to Ptolemy, the latter determined to possess Judea and the neighboring region, as an intervening barrier between him and the Syrian empire of Seleucus at Babylon. The Jews resisted, and closed the gates of Jerusalem against him. Understanding that they would not fight on their Sabbath, Ptolemy attacked them on that day, routed them, and

[1] Dan. viii. 20, 21.

[2] Prideaux, anno 333 B. C. Stackhouse, Bible Hist. p. 749.

entered the city. The prophet[1] had ere this announced that special providences towards the nation should cease, and this is the first historic occurrence of a divinely undefended Sabbath for the chosen people. In this rule of Ptolemy lived Simon the Just, the eminent high priest who, the Jews say, completed their Scripture canon after Ezra.

Ptolemy Philadelphus succeeded Soter, and kept up the library and literary institutions the latter had fostered at Alexandria; and in his day the Septuagint translation of the Hebrew Scriptures into Greek was effected, and in this language the learned in all the nations of that age could read the history of the Hebrew Theocracy, and learn the doctrines and worship of the true religion. Philopator succeeded Philadelphus, and recovered Jerusalem, which had for a season been out of Egyptian control; he determined to enter the holy place in the temple spite of the protestations and warnings of the priests, and on his forcible approach to the holy of holies, he was mysteriously seized with a sudden fit of trembling and spiritual terror, that he became helpless, and was carried out by his attendants. When away, his fear subsided, and gave place to rage and cruel persecution of the Jews, and preparation for a general massacre of the people. He made his elephants drunk with wine, that they might in their frenzy trample the Jews to death; but they turned their fury upon his own men, and killed multitudes. His fear again re-

[1] Ezek. xviii. 2, 3.

turned, and he witnessed portents and prodigies in the sky, which induced the cessation of all Jewish persecution, and forced him to favor the nation he still hated.

Ptolemy Epiphanes succeeded Philopator; and in his nineteenth year, when Seleucus Philopator had succeeded his father, Antiochus the Great, in Babylon, Judea was made a province of Syria, and held by Seleucus, though Epiphanes reigned in Alexandria and Egypt five years longer. Seleucus treated at first the Jews kindly; but becoming satisfied that there were rich treasures in the temple, he determined on their possession, and sent his treasurer, Heliodorus, to rob the temple. On entering the temple, the treasurer was frightened by what he deemed a vision of angels, and he hastened out speechless and nearly senseless, giving up all notion of plunder. Antiochus Epiphanes succeeded Seleucus, and was a cruel persecutor of the Jews. He was persistent and unrelenting in applying torture and barbarous penalties to force the Jews into idolatry. But the superstitions to which the nation had before been so prone, had now become their abomination. They endured death in any form rather than sacrifice to an idol.[1] This persecution and oppression of Antiochus Epiphanes called out Jewish patriotism, piety, and courageous resistance.

Mattathias, a descendant from a renowned priest, Asmoneus, with five sons, began the heroic contest in

[1] 2 Mac. vi.

the place where they exiled themselves in the region of Dan, to avoid oppression. Here their tyrant attacked them, to force them to his idolatrous worship. Mattathias boldly stood the fight, and overcame and slew the king's messengers, and set himself upon the offensive, determined to drive the oppressive idolaters, by Jehovah's help, from the land. He fought with desperate valor in many battles, usually victorious, and died one hundred and forty-six years old, designating Judas, his eldest son, to succeed him in leading on the opposition.

4. THE JEWS UNDER THE MACCABEES. — The family of the Maccabees were called Asmoneans, from their eminent ancestor Asmoneus, but the origin of the name Maccabee is not so readily ascertained. One derives it from a Hebrew word for "cavern," from their early hiding-places against their persecutors; another from the first Hebrew letters of their adopted motto upon their ensign, "Who is like unto thee among the gods, O Jehovah!"[1] thus giving the spelling Maccabi. Antiochus continued his spite against the Jews and contempt for their religion after the death of Mattathias; he profaned the temple, entering the holy place and sacrificing swine's flesh on the great altar of burnt-offerings, and filled the temple with idols, devoting it to the worship of Jupiter Olympus; he forced the people to idolatry, or tortured them with every cruelty, and suppressed

[1] Ex. xv. 11.

all outward worship of Jehovah through the land. The sons of Mattathias resisted these edicts and efforts strenuously and boldly, and aroused and led on the people to the most courageous conflicts and signal victories.

166 B. C.

Judas Maccabeus,	8	years.
Jonathan "	14	"
Simon "	8	"
John Hyrcanus,	29	"
Aristobulus I.,	1	"
Alexander Janneus.	27	"
Alexandra, queen,	9	"
Aristobulus II.,	6	"
In all,	102	"

These were respectively high priests in their successions, as well as chief captains, except as queen Alexandra had Hyrcanus as high priest.

Judas Maccabeus, with a brave band of followers, went through the country from city to city, demolishing idols and their altars, and defeating the large armies which Antiochus repeatedly sent into Judea, under the successive generals, Apollonius, Seron, Ptolemy Macron, Nicanor, Gorgias, and Lysias; overthrowing them with great slaughter, and taking large booty. He rescued and purified the temple, and restored its worship and daily ministrations, and gave deliverance largely to the nation. Antiochus, greatly enraged by these defeats, set out himself from Babylon with his army, determined to make Judea one vast sepulchre. In his haste his chariot was overset, his bones broken, and his bruised body became ulcerated and mortified, and he died after great agony, and with spiritual horror at the consciousness of his cruelty and wickedness now avenged by deserved judgments.

The idolatrous nations south-east from Judea, Idumeans, Ammonites, and Syrian tribes, after this, confederated against the Jews, and Judas went against and attacked them, thoroughly routing all their forces. The Tyrians and Sidonians, also on the west, put themselves in hostility, against whom his brother Simon was sent with three thousand men, and overcame them. Antiochus Eupator, succeeding Epiphanes, kept up the old contest, and Judas continued his successful resistance till he was slain in battle, and Jonathan, his brother, took the lead after him. He overthrew the Syrian general Bachides, who had been sent against him, and kept up for life the successful contest. He was at length slain by the treachery of Demetrius, who afterwards became king of Syria. The brother Simon then led the patriot band of Jewish warriors, who obtained terms of peace and partial independence, and used his authority for the elevation of the Jews and the service of Jehovah. His son-in-law, through some secret spite, invited Simon and two of his sons, Judas and Mattathias, to an entertainment, and treacherously assassinated them. After this, Hyrcanus, the son of Simon, became high priest and ruler, as the Maccabean brothers had passed away. Early in their rule, or perhaps even in the days of Mattathias, a Jewish court had been instituted, consisting of seventy of the most dignity and veneration among the aged, and which became the great council of the nation, known as the Jewish Sanhedrim, and which was perpetuated till the destruction of Jerusalem by the Romans. The different sects of Pharisees and Sadducees were now being formed under the discussions growing out of the reviving of the study of the Hebrew law and ritual, the Pharisees being strict constructionists of the letter of the law, and the Sadducees giving a wider and more liberal interpretation. They became strongly opposing parties, and struggled hard for leading influence and power in the government.

Hyrcanus at first paid tribute to Syria, but at length attained deliverance and independent authority. He conquered their old enemies, the Samaritans, and destroyed the temple Sanballat had built on Mount Gerizim; subdued the Idumeans, and so proselyted them to the Jewish faith that they became incorporated with the nation. He further made alliance with the Romans, whose power was beginning to be felt in the politics of the great nations of the world. He found the Pharisees jealous and reproachful towards him, and he gave in his adhesion fully to the Sadducees, and took that sect under government patronage. He died in peace, and Aristobulus, who was high priest, took the government, and was the first Asmonean who assumed the title of king of Judea. He was a very cruel, wicked, desperate ruler, imprisoning and starving to death his mother, and slaying his brothers, and in one year dying in horror of conscience under awakened conviction of his crimes. Alexander Janneus followed in a stormy reign of many years, and kept Judea in perpetual foreign or civil commotions. He was often in conflict with his own subjects, besides his wars with foreign enemies, and with varied fortunes and often cruelties, he finished his reign and life by diseases his intemperance and prodigality had induced, without having benefited his country by his ceaseless struggles. He gave his wife counsel on his dying bed to make friends of the Pharisees, and she thus succeeded to the throne, and made Hyrcanus high priest. She, with the Pharisees so coming into power, persecuted the Sadducees with great vindictiveness. At her death there was fierce contention between the high priest Hyrcanus and his brother Aristobulus for the ascendency. Aristobulus was at first successful, and obliged Hyrcanus to abdicate his office of high priest in his favor, and he took the government. Subsequently, by the assistance of an Arabian king, Aretas, Hyrcanus opposed him, and on appeal to the Roman Pompey, Aristobulus was deposed, and Hyrcanus took the rule. But Judea was no longer independent. Pompey had conquered it, and Hyrcanus reigned only as tributary and subject to the Romans.

After all this mingling of Jewish experience and

influence with the great monarchies, Assyrian, Persian, and Grecian, following the early Egyptian, and all now decayed and subverted, the Jews begin their connection with the iron dynasty of Rome, the most peculiar power the world has known, and most peculiarly fitted to bear universal sway when the Messiah shall come and set up his spiritual kingdom. An Asmonean prince is on the throne of Judea, but only nominally a king, for his power is all from Rome, and he only a Roman vassal.

5. The Jews under the Romans.—Pompey, the Roman general, took Jerusalem, and put Hyrcanus in the government in the year 63 B. C.

Hyrcanus II. reigns	24 years.
Antigonus, "	2 "
Herod the Great till John came,	32 "
In all, ...	58 years, to birth of John Baptist.

Pompey went into the temple and took note of all its treasures, but he took nothing away, and left the sacred services to their regular performance. He established Hyrcanus in the high priest's office, and committed the government of Judea to him, but subjected him to tribute, and forbade his wearing a crown. The conflict between Pompey and Cæsar, at Rome, occasioned new contentions between Aristobulus and Hyrcanus at Jerusalem, till Aristobulus's death at Rome, by poison, and Cæsar's ascendency to power, when Cæsar again confirmed Hyrcanus in his sacred office, but put Antipater, an Idumean convert to Judaism, as procurator in Judea, under the counsel of Hyrcanus. Antipater had two sons, Phasael and Herod, and these he associated in the government with himself, the former at Jerusalem, and the latter in Galilee. Herod was ambitious, prompt, and bold, and ingratiated himself in the favor of Julius Cæsar, who added to his power and influence. An officer of Hyrcanus, named Malicus, poisoned Antipater, and Herod slew him in revenge for his father's death.

Marcus Brutus assassinated Julius Cæsar, and then Mark Antony and Cæsar Octavianus subdued Brutus and Cassius, and became arbiters of the Roman state. Antony came to Antioch, and while there confirmed Phasael and Herod in their authority as tetrarchs, and took to Rome fifteen hundred eminent Jewish citizens as hostages for the quiet of the province. Subsequently, on a sedition of turbulent Jews and their assault of Herod's retinue, Antony put these hostages all to death at Rome.

Antigonus, a son of Aristobulus, obtained help from the Parthians, invaded Judea, and took Jerusalem, with Hyrcanus and Phasael, and cut off the ears of Hyrcanus, that thus maimed he might be perpetually disqualified from the priesthood. Phasael, believing his death was determined, took his own life by poison. Herod fled to Rome, and informed his patron, Antony, of these occurrences in Judea; and he, with Octavianus, afterwards Cæsar Augustus, espoused Herod's cause, and gave him an army against Antigonus. With these Roman forces Herod returned to Judea, and after varied successes and reverses, took Jerusalem, which the Roman soldiery plundered against the will of Herod, and who bought the soldiers off only by giving a large ransom. Antigonus, who had been in the high priesthood for two years, was delivered to the Romans, and by them put to death; and with him terminated the priesthood and princes of the Asmonean family.

Herod was now established in Judea as the sole governor, and attained the title of king, but ordinarily known as Herod the Great. He began by putting down his enemies, among whom were many of the Sanhedrim, and other eminent Jews. He made Ananel, a man of mean birth, high priest, and then deposed him and put the brother of his wife Mariamne, named Aristobulus, in his place. Soon after Aristobulus was drowned by Herod's order, from jealousy of his influence and favor with the Jewish people. Herod's cruelty increased to the greatest excess, dooming his friends, his wife Mariamne, and then his children, to death, and in sudden passion executing his jealous malignity on any occasional victim. As the natural result, his own spirit was perpetually the prey to remorse and terrible apprehensions. All this, and especially the setting of the Roman eagle over one of the gates of the temple, exceedingly exasperated the Jews against him, whom he soon found it his necessary policy to pacify. To do this, and at the same time gratify his own ambition, he determined to build anew the temple at Jerusalem. This had now stood about five hundred years since its rebuilding by Zerubbabel, on the return from the Babylonian captivity, and had become sadly defaced and greatly decayed. Two years were given to collecting materials, and nine and one half years more in rebuilding so far that the daily services could again commence; but the work went on in various additions and embellishments till his death; and then still on to the days of Christ's ministry, the work was yet continued, and the temple still in building.[1] Some of the old foundations of Solomon's temple remained in the second rebuilding, so that "the house" was known as the same;[2] and in this third building, the foundations of the first, and much of the work of the second, were there; yet was the increase in additions, porches, columns, and adornments, so much as to change the appearance in proportion and style to a new building. The eyes of the nations were again turned to Judea and Jerusalem, and the last uttered voice of prophecy was on the eve of fulfilment, "Behold, I will send my messenger, and he shall prepare the way before me; and the Lord, whom ye seek, shall suddenly come to his temple, even the messenger of the covenant, whom ye delight in; behold, he shall come, saith the Lord of Hosts."[3]

On occasions of Roman peace, the Temple of Janus was shut. This had occurred first in the days of

[1] John ii. 20. [2] Hag. ii. 3, 7, 9. [3] Mal. iii. 1.

Numa; again, at the close of the first Punic war; the third, on Cassius's victory over Antony; the fourth, on Cæsar's return from the war in Spain; and now fifth, and for twelve years, in the thirty-third year of Herod, as the last, and a prelude to the advent of the Prince of Peace.

6. The Ministry of John the Baptist.—In the nature of the case, it is reasonable to anticipate that when God, in his providence and ordinances, has brought his chosen people to a state of knowledge and expectancy prepared for the Saviour's coming, and through them prepared also the great nations of the world for his advent, he should immediately precede that event by a special administration, designed to call attention to it as just at hand, and secure direct and personal readiness to receive him and his message. Prophecy had long since indicated that such was the divine purpose. Isaiah begins such announcement by a most inspiriting message to the Jewish church: "Speak ye comfortably to Jerusalem, and cry unto her that her warfare is accomplished, that her iniquity is pardoned; for she hath received at the Lord's hand double for all her sin." The prophet then gives a summary of the work and ministry of the Messiah's forerunner, under the figure of "the voice of one crying in the wilderness," and expresses the work to be done by the commission—"Prepare ye the way of the Lord; make straight in the desert a highway for our God. Every valley shall be exalted,

and every mountain and hill shall be made low, and the crooked shall be made straight, and the rough places plain; and the glory of the Lord shall be revealed, and all flesh together shall see it, for the mouth of the Lord hath spoken it."[1] John expressly applies this prophecy to himself, when the Jews sent messengers to him to inquire "who he was." He unequivocally answers, "I am the voice of one crying in the wilderness."[2] So Malachi announces, "Behold, I will send my messenger, and he shall prepare the way before me."[3] And again, "Behold, I will send you Elijah the prophet before the coming of the great and dreadful day of the Lord; and he shall turn the heart of the fathers to the children, and the heart of the children to their fathers, lest I come and smite the earth with a curse."[4] This was the prediction the Jews interpreted literally, in reference to Elijah's second coming; and so the messengers which the Sanhedrim sent to John asked him, "Art thou Elijah?" and in answer to their false meaning he replies, "I am not."[5] The paraphrase of Luke (i. 17) gives the true interpretation of this prediction: "He (John) shall go before him (Messiah) in the spirit and power of Elijah, to turn the hearts of the fathers to the children, and the disobedient to the wisdom of the just; to make ready a people prepared for the Lord." John came "in the spirit and power of Elijah" in his manner

[1] Isa. xl. 1-5.
[2] John i. 22, 23; also Matt. iii. 3; Mark i. 3; Luke iii. 4-6.
[3] Mal. iii. 1. [4] Mal. iv. 5, 6. [5] John i. 21.

of life, boldness of reproof, and earnestness of appeal; and to see how striking the parallel is, take for Elijah,[1] and then for John,[2] the subjoined references. And then we have our Lord's own declaration concerning the fulfilment of the prophecy, "If ye will receive it, this is Elijah who was to come."[3] And again, his declaration that "Elijah had already come," and the disciples understanding it of John the Baptist.[4] Besides these prophetic announcements of John as forerunner of Christ, there seems to have been a particular personal commission given to him according to John (i. 33): "He that *sent me* to baptize with water, the same said to me, Upon whom thou shalt see the Spirit descending and remaining on him, the same is he who baptizeth with the Holy Ghost." Also John iii. 28.

What was the exact design of John's commission?— 1. To apprise his nation that the Messiah was at the door, and to insist on their repentance and its fruits as demanded to meet his advent. Malachi had said, "But who may abide the day of his coming? and who shall stand when he appeareth?"[5] And still further,[6] "Behold, the day cometh that shall burn as an oven." They were on the very eve preceding such a day, and while God had for ages been teaching them, and had brought them to such a state that the Messiah could come and not actually lose his mission in the world,

[1] 1 Kings xvii. to xix., xxi. 17-24; 2 Kings ii. 1-11, and his dress, i. 8.
[2] Matt. iii., xiv. 4; John i. 19-36, iii. 23-36.
[3] Matt. xi. 14.
[4] Matt. xvii. 9-13.
[5] Mal. iii. 2, 3.
[6] Mal. iv. 1-5.

yet were there few souls ready and waiting for him. A great moral reformation and purification of life were essential to save them from finding his advent a curse to them. A baptism of the Holy Ghost and of fire was coming, and John's mission was to rouse the people to a spiritual apprehension of it. And he very largely effected it. "Then went out to him Jerusalem, and all Judea, and all the region about Jordan, confessing their sin."[1] Many of the Pharisees and Sadducees came to his baptism; and the great burden of his preaching was, "Repent, for the kingdom of heaven is at hand."

2. To baptize the Messiah himself, and point him out as the actual Redeemer of humanity. John not only preached repentance to the people, and baptized such as manifested their obedience, but he had also another end to accomplish — to distinguish who the Messiah was, and testify his personal presence to the people: "That he should be made manifest to Israel, therefore am I come baptizing with water."[2] John, though a relative, in the flesh, of the Saviour, had not an acquaintance with him, but he had a pre-appointed signal that, on his official administration of baptism to him, the Holy Ghost should visibly appear and remain upon him.[3] At the age of thirty, the Saviour came to John to be baptized of him, and the intimation to John that he was the Christ, led John to say, "I have need to be baptized of thee, and comest thou to me?"[4]

[1] Matt. iii. 5–7.
[2] John i. 31 and 33.
[3] John i. 31.
[4] Matt. iii. 14.

The Saviour let John know that he did not seek the baptism of repentance belonging to John's commission to the Jewish people, but a baptism that rightly consecrated all official sacred investitures, and was now to fulfil his part in his entrance upon his public Messiahship; and with such explanation John was satisfied. "Then he suffered him."[1] The sign of the descending and awhile-abiding form of the Holy Ghost was given,[2] and then John the Baptist "saw and bare record that this is the Son of God;" and as Jesus walked among them, John again points him out, saying, "Behold the Lamb of God!"[3]

These two parts filled John's mission, and when they were accomplished, his administration ceased. He continued his testimony while Christ remained for some length of time after his baptism in comparative obscurity, and then John was imprisoned, and his active mission ended.

What was the peculiar distinction of John's Baptism? — The Abrahamic covenant made provision for the admission of converts from any Gentile people. Whoever was so received and circumcised came at once into all the privileges of a Hebrew of the Hebrews. A mode of purification was established in connection with the rite of circumcision, and which became a formal application of water, and known in the traditions of the elders as proselyte baptism. Without further consideration of this, it is sufficient to say, that John's baptism was quite different from proselyte

[1] Matt. iii. 15. [2] Matt. iii. 16, 17. [3] John i. 34-36.

baptism. His work was not bringing converts to Judaism, but preparation of Jews for the advent of Messiah. The baptisms of the two were as distinct as the doctrines and duties they symbolized.

John's baptism also differed from that which Christ instituted. Christian baptism was instituted by himself, and by his authority stood as the sacramental sign of admission to his established church; but John's baptism was before Christ came and the Christian church was introduced, and for the end of introducing Christ himself. Christian baptism was in the name of the Father, Son, and Holy Ghost; but John's baptism left his disciples without hearing that there was any Holy Ghost.[1] John himself made a great distinction between the two baptisms; one was "unto repentance," the other unto life, purified "with the Holy Ghost and with fire."[2] Those whom John baptized were baptized over again on entering the Christian church; as the three thousand Pentecost converts were all baptized, though many, and probably most, had been baptized by John.[3] Christian baptism is noticed as baptism, eminently and unequalifiedly; but John's baptism is always qualified as distinctive, as "baptism of John," "baptism of water," "baptism of repentance," &c. And finally, the qualification for John's baptism was a practical faith that Christ was just coming; but of Christian baptism the prerequisite was a practical faith that he had come, suffered, risen,

[1] Acts xix. 2, 3. [2] Matt. iii. 11.
[3] Acts ii. 41, xix. 3, 5.

and ascended. John's disciple stood above the Old Testament saint, in that he had added the belief, and conduct accordingly, of Christ's immediate coming; but Christ's disciples had a faith and conduct fastening them to the one known Christ, as already revealed in the flesh. In John's day no man had lived that was greater than he; but the least in Christ's kingdom was greater than John.[1]

With this view of John's office and its administration, there needs to be added only a short statement of his life and time. Herod had reigned in Judea thirty-two years when John the Baptist was born, and his reign continued three years longer, covering the bloody transaction of slaying the children of Bethlehem, in order to the destruction of the infant Saviour. In this thirty-second year of Herod, the angel Gabriel appeared to Zacharias, a priest ministering in the temple, of the course of Abia, and told him that his hitherto barren wife Elisabeth should bear a son, whom he should name John, and who should "go before" the coming Lord "in the spirit and power of Elias."[2] The history of John's infancy, youth, and manhood is not given till his opening ministry at thirty years of age. He must have known the destination of his life from his father and mother, and have doubtless been directed in training and expectation preparatory to it; but when the time for his public ministry came, we have the abrupt announcement, "In those days came John the Baptist,

[1] Matt. xi. 11.

[2] Luke i. 5-25.

preaching in the wilderness of Judea."[1] Mark begins his Gospel with this preaching of the forerunner; but Luke is quite specific in noting the time of its occurrence. "In the fifteenth year of the reign of Tiberius Cæsar, Pontius Pilate being governor of Judea, and Herod being tetrarch of Galilee, Annas and Caiaphas being the high priests, the word of God came to John, the son of Zacharias, in the wilderness."[2]

In the forty-second year of the reign of Augustus Cæsar he took Tiberius Cæsar into partnership with him in the government, and assigned to him the Roman provinces. John was thirty years of age at this fifteenth year of Tiberius, and thus fifteen years of age at the beginning of Tiberius' reign, as above, and his birth the twenty-seventh year of Augustus, which was the thirty-third year of Herod the Great in the kingdom at Jerusalem. John was about six months the senior of Christ, and Herod died in his thirty-fourth year in the kingdom, and thus had just time for the slaughter of the children at Bethlehem after Christ's birth, before his own death. Valerius Gratus had been made procurator of Judea by Tiberius, after the death of Augustus, and in his own full reign; and this Gratus had deposed Annas from the high priest's office, and while Annas was yet living had made several successive high priests and removed them, and this very fifteenth year of Tiberius' reign had at last made Joseph, called Caia-

[1] Matt. iii. 1. [2] Luke iii. 1, 2.

phas, high priest, while Annas the old high priest still lived. Within this year of Caiaphas' appointment to the high priest's office, Gratus was himself recalled to Rome, and Pontius Pilate was put in his place in the government of Judea, and Herod Antipas was then tetrarch of Galilee; and thus all stood as Luke relates at John's opening ministry.

The reckoning of time from the Christian era commenced in the sixth century, and mistakingly began the date four years later than Christ's birth, and so this year of John's commencing ministry was according to the vulgar reckoning 26 A. D. About six months from its commencement, he baptized the Lord Jesus, and in the fulfilment of his dispensation in pointing him out as the Messiah already come, he must have occupied a much longer time, according to Prideaux' reckoning three years; and others make, some two years and some one year. He was then cast into prison by Herod Antipas for plainly rebuking his adulterous connection with Herodias, the wife of his brother Philip. Prideaux makes this imprisonment to have lasted a year, during which time John's disciples came to Christ, in doubt about fasting, while Christ's disciples did not fast.[1] And then, again, perhaps desponding at his hard lot, or, as may be, seeking an opportunity to strengthen his disciples' faith in Jesus' Messiahship beyond his own teaching, he sent two of them to Jesus to ask if he were "the Saviour that was to come, or if they were to expect another."[2]

[1] Matt. ix. 14-17. [2] Matt. xi. 2-6.

At the time of their presence, Jesus took occasion to work many miracles, and preach the truth plainly to the poor sufferers he healed, and then sent his disciples back to John to tell him what they had seen and heard in confirmation that he was the Christ, and to assure John of Christ's blessing if he held his confidence full to the testimony given.[1]

Soon after this, Herodias' daughter danced before Herod on a convivial occasion, and so pleased him that he promised, with an oath, to give her what she should ask. She, instructed by her mother, whose harbored spite towards John, for his reproof to Herod on her account, had made nothing to be so desirable to her as the death of the stern reprover, asked Herod to give to her John Baptist's head. By Herod's order, John was at once executed in prison, and his head brought to the daughter and mother in a charger.[2] His disciples took the headless body and buried it, and went and told Jesus.[3]

We now finish this chapter of the history of God's dealings with mankind, through long ages, to get the world ready for the Redeemer to come among men, and next open a chapter for the consideration of his advent, and establishment of his kingdom, and fulfilment of all his purpose and promise in saving the lost.

[1] Luke vii. 19–23. [2] Matt. xiv. 10, 11. [3] Matt. xiv. 12.

CHAPTER III.

THE INCARNATION, WITH THE WORK AND DOCTRINE OF REDEMPTION.

THE same person in the Godhead, who has created the worlds, and made man upon this earth, when man sinned has promised a way of redemption for him, and has been working upon the nations of the earth, through his chosen people, to prepare the way for the coming of the promised Deliverer; and now, with the preparation made, it is also the same second person of the Trinity who is to be Redeemer, and come and dwell among men, to open the door for the fallen to rise again into favor and communion with God. It is thus still the dispensation of the Logos that we further contemplate through this chapter; but not as tracing successive transactions and occurrences historically any more, we rather take the records the evangelists have given, and from them show who the Redeemer is, and what is the redemption he has wrought out for humanity.

What he has already done, in covenant connection with Abraham's seed, has put the race in condition for his alliance with it more intimately than before.

Iniquity and idolatry are still widely prevalent, but one nation has been cured of its pagan tendencies, and been brought formally to worship the one true Jehovah. They have, moreover, thrown so much light over the polytheistic world, that the idolatrous nations have been obliged to recognize in the Jehovah of Israel a Deity more powerful and pure than any of their patron gods. They have also been made to expect, through Hebrew ritual and prophecy, the speedy coming of a heavenly Messenger, who shall bring with him divine deliverance for sorrowing humanity. Most of his own covenant people will be found still too sensuous to receive him, and faith in his salvation will make but slow progress among the Gentiles; but so many hearts have been made open for him, that the great Redeemer may now come and live among men, and preach his new Gospel of Salvation to them, and the spiritual truths he shall reveal shall not fall on a soil wholly barren. The world's salvation will now be more rapidly hastened by his coming personally in it, than by any longer delay in preparation for him; "the fulness of time" has thus come, and the incarnation of Jehovah is at hand. He who made all things, and crowned his work on earth with man, is now to be made flesh and dwell with men.

SECTION I.

THE INCARNATION OF THE LOGOS.

SPECULATIVE Reason can walk alone here just as little as in determining the work of creating the heavens and the earth. Phenomenal facts must first be apprehended, and in them the insight of reason must read the traces of God's handiwork; and equally so in redemption; revealed facts must be the symbols in which reason shall read God's spiritual meaning. The facts are indeed a dead letter to sense, and all logical deductions from sense; but they have in them a living meaning to reason's insight, and which can by no possibility be brought into contemplation, except by reason alone. They contain spiritual truth, and this must be spiritually discerned, not sensibly perceived, nor logically deduced from any sense-perceptions. Yet while the spiritual eye may read, the insight can get no more truth than God has put within the record; all this contemplative reason may see, and boldly should strive to read all that the record contains.

1. THE REDEEMER IS BORN OF A VIRGIN. — Two evangelists only give the specific record of the facts

in the Redeemer's incarnation, viz., Matthew[1] and Luke.[2] John[3] states pre-existing truths, and teaches fundamental doctrine, beyond any other evangelist, about "the word made flesh;" but John records nothing concerning the birth from a human mother. The evangelical Epistles, also, communicate much valuable and valid doctrine of the coming of our Lord from heaven to earth, but do not say anything descriptive of the manner by which the Logos entered into humanity. We may take these teachings afterwards and interpret the historic narrative by them, but the first lesson to learn is in these distinct and particular records of the above two evangelists. There is doubtless more meaning here than the human mind has yet recognized; and all that is here God would have men carefully contemplate, and comprehensively appropriate. He designed here to communicate supernatural truths; and as he has given to man reason competent to discern supernatural truth, it cannot be to God's honor that any man should deem the sanctity of the mysteries forbids an honest and hopeful attempt to attain the supernatural communication. The danger is twofold; that some shall sink the whole in bald naturalism, or that others shall take the supernaturalism to be too profound for human comprehension.

The account in Luke has all that Matthew gives, and is the more explicit and particular. There is here, moreover, the advantage of having the account of John the Baptist's foretold birth and mission, paral-

[1] Matt. i. 18-25. [2] Luke i. 26-80. [3] John i.

lel with the account of the birth and mission of the Messiah; and the comparisons and contrasts in the two will greatly help in comprehending the truths belonging to the Redeemer's personality. We thus carefully note the record in the Gospel of Luke.

We have the account concerning John of the angel Gabriel appearing to the priest Zacharias in the temple, and foretelling, antecedently to his conception, the birth of his son, and that he should call his name John; that this son should be the Lord's forerunner, and should turn the faith of many in Israel to the Redeemer's advent. Beyond the angel's foresight, what was here supernatural was the quickening of Elisabeth from barreness; the making of the father dumb till the birth occurred, and then healing him, and the endowing of the child with unwonted spiritual power by the Holy Ghost. But this child, given under such supernatural conditions, was a human being only. Zacharias was his father, as Elisabeth was his mother; and John was a descendant of his parents by ordinary generation, just as they and he were natural descendants from the first man and woman.

Six months after, the same angel Gabriel appeared to the virgin Mary, and foretold the birth of a son from her, and that she should call his name Jesus; that he should have an endless kingdom, and be known as the Son of the Highest. Mary's conscious virginity induced the scrupulous inquiry how such an event could be. The answer was direct, and intentionally unequivocal and emphatic, that the conception should be miraculous. The living seed should be God's creation in a virgin ovarium, and the originated embryo should there grow to the birth; and that "the holy thing which shall be born of thee shall be called the Son of God." In this is the parallelism between John's and Jesus' birth, that they are both human and born of woman; and so Jesus is man as truly as John. But beyond the parallel, there springs a contrast, for while John is son of Zacharias, Jesus is Son of God.

And here, taking solely the evangelical narrative, perhaps it might be said, Adam was created man directly by God with no previous parentage, and tracing up the genealogy of Jesus to Adam, Luke says of Adam, "who was the son of God."[1] And now Adam, though truly human, was yet no more than human: may it not then be accepted that this is the whole meaning of the appellation "Son of God," and that of Jesus, this alone is true, he is a mere man immediately originated from God? Leaving here the narrative to be in other things interpreted as it may, in this there is no dispute — that it teaches Jesus was man, and originally, as was Adam, immediately from God. But from other authentic and inspired sources, we have the clear revelation —

2. Jesus was born more than human. — Admit that Adam and Jesus have their parallel in their direct divine origination; they find also their con-

[1] Luke iii. 38.

trast in that Adam then began while Jesus had pre-existence. "The Word was made flesh," but this "Word was in the beginning with God."[1] Of Jesus Christ, the apostle Paul declares, "who thought it not robbery to be equal with God, took upon himself the form of a servant, and was made in the likeness of sinful men."[2] And it is this contrast precisely which the same apostle affirms between Adam and Jesus Christ, when he says, "The first man is of the earth, earthy; the second man is the Lord from heaven."[3] While, then, it is plain that in this son of Mary we have a man in all respects like other men born of woman, except that his origin as man was immediately from God, as plain, also, is it that in this birth we have more than man — even that which did not then begin, but pre-existed from all beginning. Unlike any other being, in his full personality he is the one only living God-man.

We should presume too much on the cultivation of human reason to suppose that in this age the full comprehension of this strictly unique being might be attained by any man. Even angels desire to look deeper and see more.[4] Yet as the ages pass onward, the reason of humanity does advance in philosophic and theologic comprehension; and this deep mystery of godliness — God manifest in the flesh — is less a mystery, though no less in majesty and glory, than it was in earlier ages; and some things concerning it

[1] John i. 1–14.
[2] Phil. ii. 6, 7.
[3] 1 Cor. xv. 47.
[4] 1 Pet. i. 12.

are more adequately contemplated by us than they were by our fathers. And the more we may know of it, through our deep and reverent study, the more shall we profit man and please God.

Physical life propagates itself in sexual generation from age to age. In the vegetable, the life is mere unconscious instinct, spontaneously working itself out in successive flower and fruit from year to year. But something can never originate from nothing, and the product have more than was in the producer. Plant-life can never go over in fructification to the higher kingdom of animal life. The irritability of nerve and contractibility of muscle must first be, or animal sensation and locomotion cannot be. Bodily organs may be given in less or more varieties, but the organ first must be, or sense-perception can have no manifestation; and in sex-propagation, the mere plant-parentage can never beget an animal offspring. And so again, the animal can never pass into the sphere of the human, and use the insight of reason in philosophy, morals, and religion, from a mere sentient organism. There must be the human body for the human spirit, and the mere animal cannot beget the man. Sense must be an original superinduction upon plant-life, and then reason must be superinduced upon animal sense, and the higher life can alone work out the higher organism.

We know this to be reason's truth and reason's order, and hence we know it to be nature's necessity; and nowhere was nature ever found to step over this order of Absolute Reason in any kingdom of propagated successions. Any interchange of organic function in organic grades is at once known as supernatural; and it was as really a miraculous interposition which made the dumb ass to speak, as it would be to make trees walk, or plants hear. The exigency must demand the supernatural interposition, and then in nature will be given the manifestation. For the work of redemption there comes the need that humanity be exalted to the divine; that is, Deity must manifest himself in the experiences of humanity, and no sexually generated organism can be competent to the emergency. Even Adam's body, as he was first created man, would not, as a tabernacle, be fitting for the indwelling of Jehovah, and much less any body in sexual descent from him after the vitiation of his fall. There must here be the Lamb without spot; a sacrifice for sin which the blood of bulls and goats, and even the offering of a human first-born, cannot be made adequately to answer. Wherefore, when the divine Redeemer comes, it must be that in honest, hearty satisfaction he can say to the Father, "A body hast thou fitted for me."[1] It is not an angel form that he may assume, nor angelic experience into which he is consciously to enter, but as the seed of Abraham, and partaker of flesh and blood, so that between God and offending man he may stand as faithful high priest, making reconciliation with sovereignty on one side, and succoring the tempted on the other.[2] Hence, too,

[1] Heb. x. 5. [2] Heb. ii. 14-18.

when the Son is sent forth into the world of humanity, he must be "made of a woman, made under the law;"[1] and yet not in ordinary generation, as just seen, but he must be born of a virgin whom "the power of the Highest has overshadowed."[2] Here are the conditions which we may now see can alone consistently introduce the divine to participation with the human. So existing, the Messiah is truly "IMMANUEL — God with us."

3. THE REDEEMER, SO BEING, IS STILL ONE BEING. — The tree is one as truly as the stone is one. There is a force pervading the stone, which may be termed cohesion, or chemical combination, that holds all parts together and makes a whole. And in the tree there is a profounder bond pervading every part, and the one life everywhere grasps root and trunk and branch in unity, and makes the many still a single. This tree-life put upon mere force gives to us the tree as one, in a higher and more comprehensive sense than the force of cohesion gives to us the stone as one. Through the everywhere diffused life in which the parts grow together, we know the tree to be more a unit than the stone which has its parts only stuck together. And then, again, the animal has not only, as the tree, everywhere life diffused through it, but over and above life, there is everywhere sensation all-pervading. This one sense holds the animal in higher identity than the one life does the plant; and we

[1] Gal. iv. 4. [2] Luke i. 34, 35.

know the sense in every member and organ to be the same, and making the body one in its one feeling, in a profounder meaning than that the tree is one in its one life. As life is a deeper bond than force, so sense is a more sublimated connective than vitality. And then, when reason is put over sense in man, and gives him insight of phenomenal principles and laws, and enables him to guide his actions by science, taste, and conscience, it puts the whole man under self-control, and the one will is made regulative of all sense-experience. The man is then one in his personality in a higher sense than any plant or animal is one. The whole animal sense is taken in, and thoroughly suffused by, the superinduced rationality.

All this opens the light upon the unity of Jesus Christ's personality. His manhood is one, as with all men; but there is put upon the man the higher connective of the divine, and the very will and personality of Jehovah is integrated in the human reason, and lifts the man within the comprehensive sphere of divine intelligence and action. One divine will and consciousness holds sense and human reason in unity, and the oneness of the divine Redeemer is as superior to that of man, as Absolute Reason transcends the endowment of human rationality.

Now, in the Godhead, as Absolute Reason, there is the distinct will that plans, and has within itself the Ideal; and the separate will that objectifies, and gives Expression; and the still other will, that puts idea and object in consistent comprehensive Unity; and these three wills, in their discrimination, are three persons in their own conscious activities, and can be recognized in nothing so appropriate as respective personalities. And yet are the three not so many beings, for the being of all is in the one Absolute Reason. And the personality incarnated in the Redeemer is the second, known as Logos, or Word, i. e., the expresser, or outward manifester of the unseen Ideal. This Word originally was "with God," and "was God," and here is "made flesh;" entering truly into humanity. This complexity, as One in Jesus Christ the Redeemer, reconciles the many apparent paradoxical representations given of him in the Gospels. Thus, "he came down from heaven," and while on earth talking with his disciples he was also "in heaven."[1] He says also of himself, "I and my Father are one;"[2] and then again, "My Father is greater than I;"[3] and also, "He that hath seen me hath seen the Father."[4] And so, also, we have the representation, that this assuming of a human body and dwelling with men was a humbling condescension, involving much personal sacrifice. "He made himself of no reputation;" "he humbled himself, and became obedient."[5] "He became poor, that ye through his poverty might be rich."[6] His perfection, as Redeemer of men, is through suffering.[7] There must needs be occasion for speaking of the Redeemer

[1] John iii. 13. [2] John x. 30. [3] John xiv. 28.
[4] John xiv. 9. [5] Phil. ii. 7. [6] 2 Cor. viii. 9.
[7] Heb. ii. 10.

in all the phases of his complex being, viz., as God in Trinity, as man in the flesh, and as both God and man in his mediation. It would be impossible to fill out his record in redemption without giving more or less such paradoxical exhibitions of him. As Redeemer of men he is one, and yet not complete in his oneness, except as the divine takes up in its unity the animal sense and the human spirit, and makes *them* a unit in *its* absolute unity. This one virgin-birth raised humanity into the sphere of God-consciousness, and brought Deity into the sphere of human experience. While in the man-Jesus "dwelt all the fulness of the Godhead bodily,"[1] in the Jehovah-Jesus was the susceptibility to be "touched with the feeling of our infirmities."[2] So incarnated, Deity can be tempted; so exalted, humanity can endure any temptation without sin.

4. THIS ONE REDEEMER IS IN HIMSELF PROPHET, PRIEST, AND KING. — Not as offices conferred upon him, and into which he has been inaugurated by some separate authority, but in his own essence such offices already belong to him in the mode of his existence.

He is Prophet in the acceptation that the message he brings from above needs not to be first delivered to him, but stands already in his own omniscient consciousness. What Jesus communicates is just what God himself is. His truth is the truth in God. His

[1] Col. ii. 9. [2] Heb. iv. 15.

exhibited feeling is God's feeling; his will is God's will. He says of himself, "I do always those things that please the Father."[1] And the Father says of him, "This is my beloved Son, in whom I am well pleased."[2] His pleasure is God's pleasure, and seen through its expression in his life and daily action and conversation, we see directly into the heart and purpose of God. "He that hath seen me hath seen the Father." Jesus has Divinity; he is Deity; and in himself he expresses what the Godhead is.

And so, moreover, he is mediating High Priest, not as taking commissioned authority from superior sovereignty, and delegated representation from assenting subjects, and so acting by consent and sufferance of parties; but in what he is he already touches both parties, and has within himself the interests both of man and God. Essentially he is Mediator between the two, and he can no more renounce the wants of man than the claims of God. His intercession is humanity interceding, just as his pardoning and accepting is the valid justification by God. "I knew that thou hearest me always."[3]

His mediatorial Reign also is his essential prerogative. To be so born of a virgin gives inheritance to the sceptre of humanity. It is a dominion to which mere man could not be exalted, and one which, out of the flesh, God could not condescend to take. But the humbling of himself to be born of woman, and become obedient to the death of the cross, makes it

[1] John viii. 29. [2] Matt. iii. 17. [3] John xi. 42.

his right to be highly exalted as "King in Zion," and "head over all things to his church." His triumphant resurrection gives into his hand the "keys of Hell and of Death," and sets him on "the right hand of the Throne of Majesty in the Heavens."

In all these offices he bears, it is in virtue of what is essential in him that he determines how to execute them. It is his to say what he will reveal as Prophet, when he will intercede and when pronounce absolution as High Priest, and how legislate, and judge, and execute as Mediatorial Sovereign; and all he so does stands forever in the validity of Absolute Authority. The Absolute Reason, in redeeming a lost race, requires a second person for the manifestation of his secret plan and counsel, just as in the eternal Ideal of created worlds there must be the manifesting will that fixes them in objective steadfastness; and it is by the same second Person, as Son, God redeems humanity, that it was by whom also in the beginning "he made the worlds."[1]

[1] Heb. i. 2.

SECTION II

THE REDEMPTIVE WORK AS WROUGHT IN HUMAN FLESH.

THE coming of Christ in the flesh, and so taking humanity, was the great redeeming-work of God. This has in it all the virtue for salvation that any subsequent manifestation can bring out of it, and in itself, to the divine comprehension, expresses the length and breadth, the height and depth, of the love of God; and has in it, too, all the purpose and promise of the first announcement of redemption after the fall, when God said of the enmity between the seed of the woman and the seed of the serpent, "It shall bruise thy head, and thou shalt bruise his heel." But to finite spirits, and especially to human reason, this "mystery of godliness" will not have its hidden truth unfolded but through a life-and-death-experience, which shall carry out before them the very work of self-sacrifice which is essentially in the very incarnation itself. This has already been prefigured as plainly as ritual representations could effect it, in the sacrifice of the paschal lamb, and the sin-offering of the slain goat, and bearing-away-iniquity of the scape-goat; but though as clearly as humanity could then receive it, yet how inadequately can animal blood, anyhow shed, indicate the depth of abhorrence in God for human sin, and the intense pity in God for the human sinner! These both are fully set within the incarnate Word, in the fact of the incarnation itself, and no further exhibition is about to add anything to the essence of this expiation; but more vividly, and more truly, the life and death of Christ may show this to men, than has been, or ever can be, done by any ceremonial sacrifices. Prophecy had also done what it could in setting an incarnate redemption in expectancy before men; but now the life and death of Jesus may better manifest to men what God has already put into his incarnation; and his actual experience tell the story of his sin-hating and his soul-loving redemption, better than any combinations of ritual-foreshadowings and prophetic-announcings can accomplish. Already in the manger at Bethlehem is the essential self-sacrifice; and love to God and man, which is to reveal itself more clearly, is not to be any more really, in his ministry, or in Gethsemane, or on Calvary, than in his being "made of a woman."

By far the greatest number of years in the life of Jesus have little significance in opening the hidden meaning of his incarnation, except as the fact of his passing through them testifies to his humility in consenting to take "the form of a servant." He grew up through his childhood, youth, and into early manhood, as others of the human race, and the manly mind developed as the manly stature was matured.

There were continual indications, of the supernatural portent given in his miraculous conception, shining out through this early experience; and maternal interest and solicitude made Mary quick to note them, and "she hid all his sayings in her heart." His conference with the Sanhedrim at the Temple, in his twelfth year, astonished them by the wisdom of his questions and answers; and his answer to the affectionate rebuke of Mary, that his tarrying behind had made for father and mother hours of sorrowing search after him, was no less astonishing to his parents — "Wist ye not that I must be about my Father's business?" How surely gleams out here the perpetual inner consciousness, even of his childhood, that he was "the Word made flesh." Yet during the first thirty years of his life, Jesus kept his inner characteristics and communings of the human and divine mainly in his own bosom. He went back home with his parents from that talk with the doctors of the law in the Temple, and was subject to them, and wrought with his father at his daily occupation, and was known familiarly as "the carpenter's son." At thirty years of age he came to John, at the Jordan, to be baptized of him, and was thus formally, and by God's appearing and audible announcement authoritatively, inaugurated into his official Messiahship; and thence began the work of his redemption-administration.

1. The Work opened in a Private Personal Conflict with the first Deceiver. — We have the record

in Matt. iv. and Luke iv., and in a short statement by Mark i. 13. The significance of the conflict is, that there was a triumph of Jesus over the devil at the opening of his redemptive work. The first accomplishment was a victory over the flesh and Satan, evincing his perfect competency for the work of human redemption. The devil knew what his own agency and its success had been in the fall of humanity, and that in prospect was a redemptive work for man purposed and promised by God, and enough had been disclosed to make clear indication that Jesus Christ was this designed Redeemer. He had confronted Jehovah before as the Logos, or original manifester of the Father, and had been expelled from angelic communion, and Jesus had seen him "fall like lightning from heaven." But now the Word was made flesh, and accessible to temptation through sense, and the devil promptly seized this first offered occasion for tempting Deity. As Absolute Spirit, "God cannot be tempted of evil," for no other end can be of so high an inducement to action as that of satisfying his own reason, or, as the same thing, securing his honor and glory.

On the other hand, Jesus was as promptly intent to meet Satan. Immediately after his baptism, he was led by the Spirit into the wilderness beyond the Jordan for this very purpose, "to be tempted of the devil." He went, manifestly conscious that the scene of temptation in the flesh awaited him, and that it was a part of his redemptive work now to be accomplished. The devil's temptation was as subtle and artful towards Jesus as it had been towards Eve. There was the craving hunger from long fasting; and the insinuation was, that notwithstanding forty days' service of God in fasting, he was left of the Father to his own resources. If he were the Son of God, it was the proper time to put out his omnipotence in his own behalf, and make the stone to be bread. Jesus undervalued the life sustained by bread to the life which was nourished by the word of God. Then the temptation took the opposite form of rashly trusting the Father, and casting himself from the pinnacle of the Temple, expecting to be miraculously borne up; but Jesus would not trust the Father, even, irreverently and presumptuously. Then all that flesh could enjoy was offered to induce Jesus to forsake the worship of the Father altogether, and do homage to him who held the world in his gift; but to Jesus nothing was so pleasing as the worship and service of God only.

As truly man, Jesus felt the full force of these appeals to sense, and was as conscious of stimulated appetite and desire as any man might be; but as divine, though temptable, he was invincible. In his own experience, also, he felt the glow of conflict and the flush of victory. The conscious dignity of virtue satisfied his own approbation and self-respect, like other righteous men, when the devil left him and angels ministered to him.

2. General Outline of Christ's Public Ministry. —The grand end was to present his claims to the Messiahship, and gain their recognition and obedience among men. The Jewish nation were the covenant people, and through them the preparation had been secured for his coming in the flesh, and it was in course that the first application of Messianic truth and work should be made to the Jews, and as was appropriate, directly and immediately to the authorized rulers of the nation. Jesus Christ gave the government in official sovereignty the first opportunity, as it was their prime obligation, as theocratic magistrates, to acknowledge the coming of their long-promised Prince and Saviour. When the rulers rejected his claim with scorn and enmity, he turned to the people, and directed his ministry to them, and through them pushed his claims upon the nation to own their covenant King and Redeemer. And when still the rulers rejected and sought to kill him, notwithstanding the wide popularity, his doctrine and work gained, he turned specially to teach his disciples personally, and the apostles more eminently, to carry on the work of evangelization among Jews and Gentiles when he should have finished his own mission and gone back to the Father.

These three distinct steps in Jesus' ministry appear fully on a careful synopsis of the four evangelists. Matthew had in view more directly Jewish converts to Christ, and Mark and Luke, each in his several way, both Jewish and Gentile converts; but all three had reference to the bearing of Christ's ministry upon Christians and the Christian church, without any reference to peculiar Jewish privileges and obligations. John in his Gospel had specially in view the claims of Jesus to the Messiahship everywhere, and sought to represent the facts of his life and ministry as best to induce in all men belief in his One Salvation.[1] In this way it was divinely ordered that Christ's own intention in the prosecution of his work should be successively and distinctly disclosed. With their end in view, the first three evangelists had no use to make of the work of Christ, as intended for the rulers and national authority as such, and they all commence Jesus' public ministry with the facts occurring after John's imprisonment; but the evangelist John, for his purpose, wants the work of Christ directly to the rulers on his first announcement of his Messiahship, and hence we get many early transactions in his ministry the others have entirely passed by, as occurring during John the Baptist's life and active dispensation. So understood, we must begin to gather the facts of Christ's public ministry from the Gospel of John.

Immediately after the temptation, Jesus returned from the wilderness beyond, back to John at the Jordan, where he was still preaching to the multitudes and baptizing, and John at once pointed him out as the Lamb of God — the Saviour already come. This induced two of his disciples to follow Jesus, one of

[1] John xx. 30, 31.

whom was Andrew, and he led his brother Peter to Christ. Next day Jesus called Philip, who was here at the Jordan from the same city, Bethsaida, as Andrew and Peter; and Philip induces Nathanael to come, whom Christ receives as an Israelite in whom is no guile.[1] With these five disciples Jesus went from the valley of the Jordan to Cana of Galilee, and wrought his first miracle of changing water to wine; and thence for a few days to Capernaum with his mother, when the Passover occurred, and he went to Jerusalem, and openly assumed the authority of his Messiahship in cleansing the Temple and facing the rulers when they questioned his claim. His teaching and miracles convinced many at the Passover, but the rulers rejected, and Christ made no commitment of himself to gather them, though he knew them.[2] Nicodemus, a ruler, here came to Jesus secretly by night, and Jesus taught him the nature and necessity of the new birth; and afterwards he, with the five disciples, went out into the country of Judea preaching, and his disciples baptizing the converts. John the Baptist was then at Ænon, away from the Jordan, testifying of Christ, and rejoicing with no jealousy at Christ's success, though Christ was making converts faster than himself.[3]

To give John's ministry full success, and save all attempted disturbance by the rulers in provoking the envy of John or his disciples, Christ left Judea for Galilee, and passing through Samaria, he had his

[1] John i. 15-51. [2] John ii. [3] John iii.

conversation with the woman at the well, followed by the conversion of many Samaritans;[1] and then coming to Cana wrought there a second miracle by healing the nobleman's son sick at a distance in Capernaum.[2]

Again from Galilee Jesus returned to Jerusalem, and set out his claims before the Sanhedrim and ruling sect of the Pharisees at a public feast, probably the second Passover of his ministry; cured the impotent man at the pool of Bethesda on the Sabbath; and then boldly defended his claim, and sharply rebuked the Jews for their unbelief and rejection, and finished the part of his ministry that had reference to immediate governmental acknowledgment.[3] He had referred to John Baptist's testimony as a past transaction,[4] evincing that John was now imprisoned; and here we come to the point, when the other evangelists begin their account of the Messiah's work after his temptation.[5] During this last visit to Jerusalem in this part of his ministry, Jesus seems to have been alone, and the five disciples to have gone to their homes.

From hence we must make a synopsis from all the Evangelists. On going to Galilee he preaches at Nazareth in the synagogue, and supernaturally escapes their malice;[6] and then went to Capernaum as a residence for some time, making that a central point for many circuits in his Messianic ministry. Here he calls back his former disciples, and adds to them others,

[1] John iv. 1-43. [2] John iv. 43-54. [3] John v. [4] John v. 33-35.
[5] Matt. iv. 12-17; Mark i. 14, 15; Luke iv. 14, 15.
[6] Luke iv. 16-30.

making twelve apostles; preaches and works miracles through all the region, and his open ministry to the people commences, and is for a time continued without further attention to the national rulers, who rejected him utterly, and would have killed him. Multitudes follow him, and we have the sermon on the mount;[1] John Baptist sending two disciples to him from his prison;[2] teaching, at another time, John's disciples why his own disciples do not fast;[3] and extensively spreading his fame and influence by repeated journeys and miracles through all Galilee, till on sending out his apostles also to preach his doctrine and work miracles, he hears of the death of John Baptist.[4]

Jesus has now very much finished his direct work to the people, and has his highest measure of public attention. Many believe in him as the true Messiah, and many more wonder, admire, deem him a great prophet, but are not ready to commit themselves to him; while others follow him only from wonder, or interest; and many more, with the scribes and rulers, reject, despise, and hate his humbling doctrines and spiritual requirements. He has come to his own, and his own receiveth him not. Enough has been given power to become the sons of God, and believe on his name, to constitute a seed to serve him, and insure a church against which the gates of hell shall not prevail; but the Jews, as a nation and

[1] Matt. v., vi., vii.
[2] Luke vii. 19–23.
[3] Matt. ix. 14–17.
[4] Mark vi. 14–30.

people, prove themselves degenerate from their covenant, and must be broken off as dry branches, fruitless and reprobate. Henceforth the grand work of Jesus is specially with the disciples and apostles; to confirm their faith, enlighten their piety, teach them the way of his suffering death and their coming persecutions, and harden them to the burden and task they are to endure when he shall be taken from them. From this point onward, this is manifestly the increasing urgency of his Messianic mission. He withdraws more from the public, talks more plainly and tenderly with his disciples; at length leaves Galilee, and goes up boldly to Judea to confront his enemies, and warn and rebuke them more sharply, and meet the sacrificial death appointed, and triumph in it and by it.

It cannot be shown from any historic data how long John's ministry lasted; how long he was in prison before his execution; nor how long Jesus' public ministration continued, and when his crucifixion occurred. He was baptized by John at about thirty years of age, the twenty-sixth year of the common Christian era. There were, at least, three intervening passovers, and there will have been four if the "feast" of John[1] was the paschal feast, and there may have been more which Jesus did not attend, and are not mentioned, while he was in Galilee; but several facts restrict the furthest computation to the passover of A. D. 33 for his death, and while nearly all years between A. D. 33 and 28 have their advocates, the

[1] John v. 1.

longest period is more probable than the shortest; yet among recent writers on the topic, the most names probably will be found meeting in A. D. 30 for the time of our Lord's crucifixion.

3. THE COMPREHENSIVE IMPORT OF HIS TEACHING.—While the first grand requisition for all was the hearty reception of himself as the only Saviour, and that the soul be wholly trusted to his grace, the manifestation and proof of this was to be found in complete newness of life and godly conversation. The controlling principle was the subjection of sense in all cases to the rule of the spirit. The old disposition of sense-gratification and selfish indulgence must be utterly renounced, and the purity and integrity of the spirit be the steadfast purpose. This is the burden of long discourses, like the sermon on the mount; of striking parables, like the prodigal son, the sower, and the rich man and Lazarus; and is condensed in innumerable terse expressions and stringent requisitions. "A man's life consisteth not in the abundance of the things he possesseth," for these are not his when God taketh away the soul.[1] "Life is more than meat, and the body than raiment." "Seek first the kingdom of God and his righteousness."[2] "Fear not them which kill the body, but are not able to kill the soul; but rather fear him which is able to destroy both soul and body in hell."[3] "What shall it profit a man if he shall gain the whole world and lose his own

[1] Luke xii. 13-21. [2] Matt. vi. 24-34. [3] Matt. x. 28.

soul? and what shall a man give in exchange for his soul?"[1] and even more intensely, "If thy foot or hand offend thee, cut them off; if thine eye offend thee, pluck it out; better enter into life halt or maimed, or with one eye, rather than that the whole body be cast into hell, where the worm dieth not, and the fire is not qnenched."[2]

4. JESUS' LIFE AND EXAMPLE WERE LIKE HIS TEACHING. — "He came down from heaven not to do his own will, but the will of him that sent him;"[3] and while he went about doing good,[4] "ministering to others, not others to him,"[5] and submitted to the devil's temptation as evincing that he is the more ready to succor us in our temptations; and when his hour was come, he steadfastly set his face to Jerusalem as "straitened till his baptism was accomplished;" there are yet two special instances of the most striking magnanimity in holding his flesh to the endurance of what the spirit claimed in finishing his work for us.

The first is, when his hour has come,[6] and he says, "Now is my soul troubled, and what shall I say? Father, save me from this hour; but for this cause came I unto this hour. Father, glorify thy name." He was here in full view of the terrible experiences of the coming three days, and his sentient soul was appalled and amazed. What shall I say? Yield to the shrink-

[1] Mark viii. 34–38. [2] Mark ix. 43–50. [3] John vi. 38.
[4] Matt. iv. 23, ix. 35. [5] Matt. xx. 28. [6] John xii. 27, 28.

ing sense, and cry, Save me from this hour? But that will be to desert the very end of my mission. I came from heaven to meet this very crisis. The flesh must be held to its endurance, and the fixed resolve comes, "Father, glorify thy name;" and the response, as in thunder, was, "I have both glorified it, and will glorify it again."

The second case is the agony in Gethsemane.[1] The tender scene of the last passover was ended, the sacramental supper had been instituted, and the last parting hymn sung; and the Master and disciples go over the brook Kedron to the oft-visited garden. He knew the malice of Jewish rulers, the treachery of Judas, the timid love and faith of his disciples, and that he must meet and bear his burdens alone; and his sensitive nature was overwhelmingly distressed and dismayed. The whole weight of incarnate humiliation was concentrated in that hour of agony, and he went away alone to give vent to his distressed soul in prayer, and the sweat, as drops of blood, fell from his body on the ground. "Father, all things are possible to thee; take away this cup from me." So sorrowful, even unto death, was he, that he repeats the prayer three times, and then the angel comes from heaven to strengthen him. The bitter cup he was then drinking was not that of the anticipated crucifixion, but a present inward grief and anguish. Of this very scene it is said in Hebrews,[2] "who, in the days of his flesh, when he had offered up prayers

[1] Mark xiv. Luke xxii. [2] Heb. v. 7.

and supplications, with strong crying and tears, unto him that was able to save him from death, and was heard in that which he feared." The agony he feared was more than he could sustain with life, and yet the unflinching spirit says, "O, my Father, if this cup may not pass from me except I drink it, thy will be done."

5. Jesus rose from the Sepulchre on the Third Day. — The preceding agony, the dying on the cross, the pale, still corpse in Joseph's tomb, were the last manifestations of mediatorial suffering and reproach. Henceforth he appears a conqueror in triumph. And the manifestations of victory are as necessary to redemption as the bowing of his head in death. He must be a reigning as well as an atoning Mediator. His resurrection is as important in the ends of the incarnation as his flowing blood. As humanity pervaded by deity, he could both lay down his life and take it again, and he is declared to be the Son of God with power according to the Spirit of holiness, by the resurrection from the dead.[1]

The evidence of his resurrection is as convincing as that of his death; and after his resurrection he further taught his disciples about his coming kingdom, commissioned the apostles to their work, promised the Spirit for which they were to wait at Jerusalem, and then led them to Bethany; and while his hands were lifted in blessing, he was carried up, and

[1] Rom. i. 4.

a cloud intercepted all further sight. Two heavenly messengers told the gazing people, "This same Jesus shall come in like manner as ye have seen him go into heaven."[1]

This second coming is more fully spoken of in the Epistles and Revelation, as the closing up of the mediatorial work. Meantime he is at the right hand of power, and the Holy Spirit has authoritative dispensation in the church on earth.[2]

SECTION III.

THE DOCTRINE OF REDEMPTION IN THE DIVINE INCARNATION.

REDEMPTION from sin includes deliverance from penal consequences, and restoration to divine favor. How "the Word made flesh" avails to this can be made intelligible only in view of the relation in which the sinner stands to God. On the creation of man as sense and spirit, it behooved God at once to put him under appropriate conditions for trial, and such form of trial we have already sufficiently considered. The test given was a law imposed, and the wilful departure from the test was an overt violation of law, and put

[1] Luke xxiv.; Acts i.

[2] Luke xxiv. 49; John xiv. 16, 17, xvi. 7–14; Acts i. 8, ii. 2–4.

the authority and honor of God directly in the way of the man's peaceful communion with God. As Lawgiver and law-violator, there was conflict between them. And in this light we attain the true meaning of the strong phraseology, which divine revelation uses to set forth the disagreement between God and fallen man. On the part of man, there is represented to be hatred, scorn, enmity; and on the part of God, wrath, fury, vengeance. And yet on man's part the hatred is from forbidden gratification, and not because there is anything in God obnoxious to the sinner's reason and conscience; and on the part of God, the wrath is the deep disapprobation of sin, and not any exclusion of tender compassion for the sinner. The sinner hates while he still justifies God, and God punishes while he still pities the guilty.

Standing face to face with such feeling, as God and man did after the fall, all peaceful communion was impossible. If the sinner continue a rebellion which he cannot justify, as left to himself he will, the compassion of God cannot be allowed to repress his vindication of authority by applying penalty. Even while he pities, he must execute the legal sanction. Both self-reproach and open dishonor must come from a compassion that overrides reason. And so also, if God, self-moved, arrange a way for remission, he must both uphold his own honor and require returning loyalty from the pardoned. A sinner could not be at peace with himself, nor have respect for God, if his pardon was against his reason. If such provision be wholly impracticable, then must all reconciliation be utterly impossible; and very probable is it, that to all finite spirits such a way of deliverance must have seemed impossible, and thus the sinner's condemnation irremediable. Only when God has opened the way will finite reason come to comprehend it. And this way is opened through the incarnation, life, and death of the Lord Jesus Christ. It is known as Redemption in that it is a price equivalent to the penal claim, and opens deliverance from bondage;[1] yet the captive must come out cordially confiding, or the redeeming price is not available for him. It is also known as Atonement, in that it covers guilt, and appeases offence,[2] and thus opens reconciliation; yet the sinner must penitently take the atoning offering, or the expiation cannot cover his iniquities.[3]

Redemption and Atonement, thus, both mean the same thing, and differ only as the direction of view changes the aspect. How, then, through "the Word made flesh," is the price of redemption paid, or the expiation of an atonement effected?

1. Not in any Way of Legal Justice. — The sinner is condemned by law, and cannot in any way be saved by law. He can never stand reconciled to God, in either his own or others' estimation, on any legal footing. No one can do anything that can give peace between the sinner and God in the eye of law. Legal justice must ever stand in this attitude to man, —

[1] 1 Peter i. 18, 19. [2] Rom. v. 10, 11. [3] Heb. x. 14.

"Give to law sinless obedience, and I approve; give sinful disobedience, and I condemn," — and once having fallen in sin, there is in the case itself guilt which justice can never cleanse. Sinless obedience in all else is but just what should have been, and this sinful disobedience is just what should not have been; and the former can make no just amends for the latter. Any legal substitution is in the case itself impossible. The obedience should have been the sinner's, and not that of another; and for the disobedience of the sinner, the just punishment must be his, and not that of any other for him. Justice can never permit the innocent legally to be punished for the guilty. Even if willing, the suffering of another cannot be vicarious penalty; for penal suffering must have conscious demerit, and should the innocent suffer with full consent, justice could not take that as penal, and legally absolve the guilty. In the sight of reason, Absolute or finite, that would not be justice. Such remission, if made, could not make peace between man and God legally, for the reason of both man and God must see a fallacy in it.

It may, however, here be objected, that Scripture represents the sinless Saviour as suffering for the guilty. Prophetically it was said, "He was wounded for our transgressions; he was bruised for our iniquities; the chastisement of our peace was upon him, and with his stripes we are healed."[1] And in the New Testament it is said, "He died for our sins."[2] Christ

[1] Isa. liii. 5. [2] 1 Cor. xv. 3.

"hath once suffered for us, the just for the unjust, that he might bring us to God."[1] To this it need only be here answered, that Jesus' suffering and death avail for our deliverance as an equivalent substitute for penalty, and are therefore "for us," but not that these sufferings were legal penalty. They could not so be unless he were guilty, for penalty can be applied only to guilt.

And then to this it may again be objected, that the Scripture representation is, Christ does take our sins. "The Lord hath laid upon him the iniquities of us all." "He shall bear our iniquities."[2] "Who his own self bare our sins in his own body on the tree."[3] "He hath made him to be sin for us, who knew no sin."[4] To which again, here, it need only be replied, that Jesus took our sins in no such sense that he could suffer their legal penalty. This must involve penal demerit, and could not be transferred from us to him. Nor could this be putatively reckoned and voluntarily received, for no imputation of our sin could carry over their penal demerit. He was "made sin for us" in some other sense than made penally guilty for us. The reference in all these scriptures is to Jewish sin-offerings, and must be interpreted by them. The scape-goat bore away the sins of Israel in another acceptation than being made penally guilty, and legally suffering. If there be no alternative to the sinner than a standing on some foot of justice, there can be

[1] 1 Peter iii. 18.
[2] Isa. liii. 6 and 12.
[3] 1 Peter ii. 24.
[4] 2 Cor. v. 21.

no redemption for him; for neither God nor man can see any justice in suffering innocence.

2. In the Incarnation Penal Justice takes an Equivalent. — When man fell, penalty was due for sustaining the law in the honor of the lawgiver, and not because the penal infliction was what the lawgiver wanted. He wanted obedience; and that failing, no penal infliction could repair the loss. And when penalty is executed, it is not that the suffering of the punished may deter others from disobedience through fear, for such obedience could not please the lawgiver. The end of penalty, threatened or executed, is to disclose the full will and heart of the lawgiver, letting the subject know just how much he wishes his law to be fulfilled. There is no justice in a penal sanction which looks to any other end. The penalty, in this view, presses towards obedience, not through fear, but from reverent regard to the will of the lawgiver; and no obedience rendered from any other motive can consist with concordant communion between the subject and the heart-searching sovereign. When, then, precept is promulgated, and discloses what the lawgiver wishes, penal sanction must also be appended to disclose how much he wishes the precept to be obeyed. Precept without sanction is not law, but mere counsel; and the penalty which gives stringency to law is solely in the end of revealing the strength of the lawgiver's will, that obedience shall follow. The will of God thus disclosed is not, of

course, merely arbitrary, for it is the will of Absolute Reason; and when there is disobedience, this necessarily awakens in his heart disapprobation of the sin and compassion for the sinner. Absolute Reason cannot contemplate the subject as sinning without this double feeling of displeasure and compassion, for this only is reasonable. The strong term, wrath, given to divine disapprobation, is always tempered with pity; not the rage of the tiger, but "the wrath of the lamb." Penalty is ever threatened and executed by God with this spirit. Even judgment without mercy is by no means punishment without pity, but punishment in which compassion can put no reasonable mitigation. It becomes savage cruelty when the lawgiver has not reasonable sadness for sin.

On the ground of justice, then, when obedience is rendered, there is manifested God's approbation, but there is no opportunity given for manifested compassion; and when disobedience is rendered, there is manifested God's disapprobation in applied penalty, but there is no opening for manifesting the pity which God feels. Justice is adequate manifestation of displeasure, and that is in the penalty inflicted, and nothing else; and this must be, and in it pity may not make any change nor abatement. But in the incarnation and death of the Lord Jesus the ground of justice is totally given up, and wholly another mode of manifesting displeasure for sin is introduced. It is not Justice at all, but Grace, its directly opposite.

There is no room here for legal penalty to be exacted; that is excluded, and free favor is introduced.

But justice is not discarded and recklessly overridden; the whole provision has been made in such a way of wisdom that justice becomes fully satisfied in an equivalent substitute. God's wish for obedience, and displeasure for disobedience, are as strongly set forth as they could be by inflicted penalty. Jesus' interposition is not justice; it is a free gift, and yet as good for firm government as legal penalty. It is adequate to sustain law as well as justice, and it may be substituted for just penalty, and authority suffer no disrespect in the view of sovereign or subject. It is wholly another way of honoring law, but it puts as much honor on it as the punishment of the sin could. God sets this before the universe, and pardons the penitent sinner, and puts the honor and stability of his government upon it to stand the issue. When he lets a sinner go free for Christ's sake, he knows that neither man nor devil can disparage his government on that account, and stand justified in their own sight. That government is as venerable as if the full penalty had been exacted, and with this immense advantage to God and man, that it has given occasion for full scope to compassion. It is itself the offspring of God's compassion, and opens the way for his mercy to save every penitent and believing sinner.

3. The Word made Flesh has even magnified the Law. — In every view of governmental respect

and honor there comes out a glory in the incarnation, as reflecting upon the majesty of law, which is brighter in revealing how reverential its authority is, than any light which can be made to shine from penal justice. It was foretold that "the Lord was well pleased for his righteousness' sake; he will magnify the law, and make it honorable."[1] What has herein been done has made God's regard for his law more manifest, and added new honor to it. It appeals to the reason, and takes hold on conscience stronger than ever. The essence of what is given in the incarnation is self-sacrifice on the part of God himself. Nothing of this appears in giving law, nor in executing law. God's abhorrence of sin is marked in its punishment, but the suffering falls upon the guilty; while in "the Word made flesh," the sacrifice is on the part of God. Most affectingly it is here shown that God's pity for the lost has induced him to severe self-denial for man's sake. In the person of the Word, Deity has humbled himself to take on humanity, and in the body of Jesus to be born of woman. No so great self-sacrifice can in anything else be conceived. The glory of the Godhead is relinquished for ministering service in a body like the sinner's. And while the essence of divine condescension is in this taking on "the likeness of sinful flesh" in the sight of the universe, it is made to stand out in its most expressive forms. The assumed humanity begins life in a manger, opens into manhood in day-labor and poverty, and in public min-

[1] Isa. xlii. 21.

istration meets perpetual contradiction, reproach, and persecution, and terminates this suffering experience through the inflicted torture and death of the cross.

Animal sacrifice was instituted to foreshadow the sacrifice of the Lamb of God. But in the merely animal death, though strikingly significant, yet obviously how inadequate! If we might elevate the brute-sacrifice by putting into it human feeling and will, we should at once find greatly intensified expression. Take a lamb slain on a Jewish altar, and as the sacrificial knife enters and opens the vein, let there come the recognition that the soul of a dear human friend is incarnated in that animal body; suffering voluntarily all this cruel sacrifice for you; looking out, in love and forgiveness, for some remembered offence, from that meek, melting eye, as it is fading away from consciousness in the dying struggle, and telling to your spirit as plainly as the speaking voice could say to your ear, "This *I* do; this I willingly endure for *your* sake;" and in that human incarnation what new meaning immediately is seen in that flowing blood! Could you bend over such an applied sacrifice without emotion too deep for expression? But we go infinitely higher when we stand by the cross on Calvary. The true Deity is in that thirsty, pale, pierced, and bleeding man! He is there on your account! The Eternal Word made flesh is expressing the feeling of God's inmost heart in every groan and patient forgiving look of the Crucified, and telling how he pities your guilty state, while he dies to show how holy he deems that law to be which you have broken. He is suffering, "the just for the unjust, that he may bring you to God." "While we were enemies Christ died for us." What other possible scene can show so strongly how God wishes his law revered, and at the same time can say so well how much he wants the sinner saved?

Could all penal infliction enforce law so much as the death of the Son of God to redeem man from condemnation? To live in sin in the view of Calvary is more incorrigible in its rebellion than to sin on under the threatenings of the coming weeping and wailings of the lost. If the penalty of law be remitted to the guilty for the Saviour's sake, it has had its full equivalent in the Saviour's sufferings.

4. The Incarnation has its Equivalent for Piety as well as Penalty. — Penalty does not restore the end of the law when broken, as if disobedience and legal penalty were as satisfactory to the lawgiver as obedience and reward. Penalty is a mean, not an end; and its expediency is in upholding governmental honor and authority where the end of government has been subverted. The ultimate end of law is the loyalty of the subject, which in God's law is piety, as this is what God wishes; and there can be no reason in the case why there should be law, as expressive of God's will, but in order that his will may be done; and the doing of God's will from regard to his honor and authority is piety. When there is, then, disobe-

dience to law, which is impiety subverting the end of law, an equivalent for penalty cannot restore the end of law for that disobedience. Penalty itself cannot satisfy law; no more can an equivalent substitute for penalty satisfy law; for the sake of the substitute God may remit penalty, but this will not restore the lost end of law. There must be an equivalent for obedience to the precept, which God wanted and the sinning subject did not give; and this, when clearly apprehended, will be seen to be a righteousness which God may accept, in the place of the righteousness which the sinner should have rendered, and which, when applied, will satisfy the end of law.

This is the very point held in view by the apostle to the Romans:[1] "For they, being ignorant of God's righteousness, and going about to establish their own righteousness, have not submitted themselves to the righteousness of God. For Christ is the end of the law for righteousness to every one that believeth." The Jew's "own righteousness" was his attempted moral or ritual obedience; and "God's righteousness" was what he had established and substituted in the place of the righteousness the sinner should have rendered. God's righteousness is found in Christ, who has attained the end of the law for the sinner.

And specifically how Christ has done this, we have in the following scriptures. Prophetically David announced it when he presents the coming Messiah as

[1] Rom. x. 3, 4.

saying, "Burnt-offering and sin-offering hast thou not required. Then said I, Lo, I come; in the volume of the book it is written of me, I delight to do thy will, O my God; yea, thy law is within my heart."[1] This is more fully particularized by the apostle in saying of Christ, that "being found in fashion as a man, he humbled himself, and became obedient unto death, even the death of the cross."[2] And again, "Though he were a Son, yet learned he obedience by the things which he suffered, and being made perfect, he became the author of eternal salvation unto all them that obey him."[3]

Jesus' "perfection through suffering," includes the obedience in all things for the fulfilling of the mediatorial work, viz., his being made under law; his travail of soul in making an offering for sin; his finishing the work God gave to him to do. Not here looking to suffering as substitute for penalty, but to obedience in the face of such suffering as substitute for piety. There is here loyalty which does not shrink from taking a human body, and maintains steadfast obedience through life, under the temptations of the devil, the agony in the garden, and the torture on the cross. It is such unflinching loyalty as pleases God, and manifests how he loves obedience to his will, and which in no other manner could be so affectingly revealed. If all sinners had been perpetually devoted saints, and God had testified his love to it in legal reward, this could not have disclosed how much his

[1] Psalm xl. 6–8. [2] Phil. ii. 8. [3] Heb. v. 8, 9.

heart is set on having obedience to his will so strikingly as in this perfect suffering-obedience of the Son of God. It is God's expressed love to pious loyalty, and in this a righteousness that is the end of the law, and which no amount of human obedience can equal. There is here "wrought out and brought in everlasting righteousness," and which can satisfy the end of the precept as truly as Jesus' suffering can satisfy the end of penalty. But the satisfying obedience is not the legal righteousness, any more than the satisfying suffering is the legal penalty. The law demanded the subject's righteousness or the sinner's death, and here we have Jesus' righteousness and Jesus' death. What Jesus gave was not what was legally due, but it was more than an equivalent for legal piety and legal penalty. And so "what the law could not do, God's Son, in the likeness of sinful flesh, has done," that the righteousness of the law might be fulfilled in us, who walk not after the flesh, but after the spirit."[1]

5. Here is opened the new Principle of Obedience from grateful Love. — All rational creatures have occasion for gratitude. Their being is of God's favor, and his bounty supplies many things for their welfare which they could not claim. It is incumbent upon them that they be thankful. But they do not see in their favors any self-sacrifice on the part of God. All his bounty has flowed free to them at no expense to

[1] Rom. viii. 3, 4.

him. Life, and rational being, and righteous government, and providential bounty, are given as good beyond all desert; but God has not been impoverished, nor at all exhausted in their supplies. Their gratitude is due, but the full gratitude is an equitable return; and with this, justice between giver and receiver is equalled. There is no opening to a perpetually incumbent grateful love, which is beyond all paying.

But in the redemption provided in "the Word made flesh," there is a new claim opened, which the moral world could never before recognize. The Deity has voluntarily made himself empty of good for man's sake. He has purchased favor for his creatures at his own expense. He has laid by his glory, and humbled himself to servitude, that he might thereby minister to his creatures' welfare what could never reach them but through his self-denial. "Christ pleased not himself;" he subjected himself to reproach from those who had reproached the Father.[1] "Who, for the joy that was set before him, endured the cross, despising the shame."[2] A human susceptibility is here touched, which otherwise man could not have been made conscious was within him. Nowhere else does he see his Maker "put to grief" for him, and this while he is an enemy. The Deity has manifested self-sacrifice that the sinner may be benefited, and out of this the "new commandment," for a new form of love, has found its occasion to be promulgated.[3]

[1] Rom. xv. 3. [2] Heb. xii. 2. [3] 1 John ii. 8.

The requisition is a grateful love to God, and to all the children of God for Jesus' sake, because the Word made flesh has suffered for them.[1] The angels see God here in a new light, and must have by it new emotions; but the debt of grateful love is especially for human beings, for it was in human flesh, and especially in behalf of humanity, that the wondrous sacrifice was made. Hence the gospel is so full of the claim for love. It is the essential grace, and as in the gospel God has shown himself to be love, so none can be of the gospel and in the gospel kingdom who are not controlled by grateful love to God and benevolent love to man. By the one fact of the incarnation, there goes out the claim to a new duty upon the moral universe to love a self-denying God; and in the case of man, a debt beyond all power of cancelling is imposed, of gratitude to God and compassionate regard to all his race for Jesus' sake; and in the case of the saved sinner, a connecting bond is made to God, and a fountain of heavenly blessedness is opened in the immortal soul, which no merely just spirit can conceive, and in which his perfect righteousness does not qualify him to participate. The marriage supper of the Son of God has its wedding-garment, which no angel can put on. The Christian soul not only loves much, but he loves in a peculiar manner, because of the precious blood of Christ's redemption, whereby much has been forgiven him.

[1] John xv. 12-14.

6. REDEMPTION IS OPEN TO ALL, BUT THE RENEWED ONLY APPROPRIATE IT. — In itself, the Redemption wrought by Christ is no more for one than for all others, but essentially it is available for all. So much as Jesus has done would be necessary that one sinner should be saved, and no more than he has done would be necessary if all were saved. The full equivalent for both precept and penalty of law is found in the work of the Lord Jesus, and in nothing else, and no one of the saved can appropriate a part to himself, thereby leaving only so much less for others; but every saved sinner appropriates in his own case the full value of the entire redemption-purchase. The full manifestation of God in human flesh is necessary, in order that God may be just in justifying any believer; and when never so many have in this way been justified, the full manifestation of God in Christ's humility is equally available for more, and in itself is absolutely exhaustless. Hence everywhere the Scripture representation of the availability of Jesus' redemption for all sinners. He is "the Lamb of God, which taketh away the sins of the world."[1] And moreover, salvation is offered to all on his account, as in the representative of gospel salvation by the parable of a Marriage Feast, the messengers were required, "As many as ye shall find, bid to the marriage."[2]

[1] John i. 29, vi. 51; 2 Cor. v. 15–19; 1 Tim. iv. 10; Heb. ii. 9; 1 John ii. 2.

[2] Matt. xxii. 9; Mark xvi. 15, 16; John iii. 16, 17; Rev. xxii. 17.

Still, though thus available for and actually offered to all, its individual appropriation can be only on the return of the sinner to pious loyalty. The offer puts fully within reach of all that which only the renewed disposition will take or can make to be his own. The essence of gospel salvation is reconciliation with God; and with all that Jesus has done, peaceful communion between man and God can never come while the man hates and rebels. And also, on the other hand, what Jesus has done has honored the law; but the honor would become dishonor were the rebellious to be taken into communion. Redemption would be made self-contradictory; honoring God's government by Jesus' obedience to death on earth, and dishonoring it by fellowship with incorrigible rebels against it in heaven. The gospel message of free salvation to a lost world can apply its pardon and justification only to such as repent and believe.

And this makes it necessary that we look to the individual appropriation of redemption in these two aspects: —

1. *Of Pardon.* — Pardon is a remission of legal penalty. Gospel pardon is always represented as applied to the sinner solely on the ground of Christ's atonement. In his self-sacrifice the lawgiver finds an equivalent for the sinner's deserved punishment. The estimate is that of sacrificial value, and the view is that of an altar-scene with a pure victim and flowing blood. Christ's self-sacrifice is the expiation for sin.

But though this be adequate to sustain legal authority as well as executed penalty would, yet cannot this be while the sinner persists in rebellion. The atoning blood of Christ so appropriated would present the intolerable inconsistency of the sovereign upholding law with one hand and pulling it down with the other. The offender must confess and forsake his sin, and stand loyal to the government, or notwithstanding the adequacy of Jesus' sacrifice to sustain law, it may not, in the absence of godly sorrow for sin and return to loyalty, be put as substitute for his legal punishment. The heart of sincere loyalty must be the condition for appropriating the substitute, and the consistent index of such return to loyalty is the evidence of hearty repentance, which is the specific gracious exercise always put in the Scriptures as the requisite for obtaining pardon. "He that covereth his sins shall not prosper; but whoso confesseth and forsaketh them shall find mercy."[1] Repentance has in it an acknowledgment of guilty demerit, and also that remission of penalty is of favor, and alone for the sake of Jesus Christ.

2. *Of Justification.*—Justification is putting right towards law, which pardon as remission of deserved penalty cannot accomplish. In the sinner's justification there is more than an equivalent substitute for legal penalty, even an equivalent for the legal obedience the sinner should have, but has not, rendered. This is found only in Christ's obedience unto death, as he "is

[1] Prov. xxviii. 13. So also Isa. lv. 7; Luke xxiv. 47.

the end of the law for righteousness."[1] The estimate of this equivalent is in the satisfying the precept of the law, and not penalty as in pardon; and hence the view is wholly that of judicial inquisition in a legal trial, and not of expiation in an altar-scene.

Literally, justification is *a making just;* and personal sinless obedience to law is that which essentially makes the subject legally just. But when law has been violated, the sinning subject cannot make himself just with that violated precept; hence, if justified, there must be some substitute for that personal rectitude in which he has failed. This, as above shown, is Christ's obedience unto death, by which God's regard for righteousness is as fairly and fully manifested, and for which the sinner may be declared right towards law, as if he himself had obeyed the precept. In such case, it is the official declaration of the sovereign which makes just; and this justifying declaration justifies itself before the universe, and in God's own consciousness, on the ground of the unimpeachable equivalency of the substitute.

But God may not consistently so justify in a state of persistent disloyalty. Notwithstanding Christ's obedience and adequate righteousness, if the rebellious subject persist in rebellion and discard all interest in Christ's righteousness, God would be unjust to himself, to his subjects, and to Jesus in his suffering obedience, should he declare one to be right towards law who still hated the law himself and the equivalent

[1] Rom. x. 4.

substitution on which he must stand. The sinner must cordially trust the foundation he takes, or he cannot be permitted to stand upon it. Hence everywhere the Scriptures put faith as the indispensable condition of justification. "He is just in justifying him which believeth in Jesus."[1] And it is in "being justified by faith we have peace with God."[2] It is the faith which works by love, purifies the heart, and overcomes the world, that so unites to Christ as to be declared by God right in law on the substitution of Christ's righteousness. Neither is Christ's expiation legal penalty, nor Christ's righteousness that obedience which the sinner should have rendered, but on both sides they are equivalent substitutes appropriated on conditions of repentance and faith.

Justification is, therefore, of grace, for it is in Christ's name alone, and the faith which appropriates it is through the gracious influences of the Holy Spirit; still the law is left in full force and authority, since Christ has magnified and honored it. No sinner is justified *for* his works; and yet, as his works indicate the measure of his faith, he is justified *according* to his works.

[1] Rom. iii. 26. [2] Rom. v. 1.

CHAPTER IV.

THE HOLY GHOST SEALS REDEMPTION TO MAN.

THE same Third Person who wrought form and consistency in the physical universe, when the Second Person had created the material and ethereal atoms according to the eternal ideas in the First Person, must now be contemplated as consummating the plan of redemption which the Father has devised and the Son has actually exhibited. This Third Person is as essential for the consummation of redemption as for the completion of creation. The Second Person provides full redemption for all, but has not applied it to any; the Third Person takes the true meaning of this provision, and so works in the spirit of the lost sinner as to renew him in penitence and faith, whereby he is "sealed unto the day of redemption." The Son, having "obtained eternal redemption for us," "goes away," and then, "sent" of him and the Father, the Holy Ghost "comes," and consummates the work in the conviction, conversion, and sanctification of men, who may then be fully pardoned, and justified, and glorified.

Such is the depravity induced by the fall, that, notwithstanding all that Christ has done, no sinner will become reconciled to God, except by the special work of the Holy Spirit. The "going away" of the Son to the Father, and the "sending" of the Holy Ghost by the Son and the Father, inaugurate the new evangelical Dispensation of the Spirit, under which apostles and evangelists are fitted for their mission, and converted men are gathered into the church, and the church extended to the ends of the earth, until the "coming again" of the Messiah, who then accomplishes the last things in the mediatorial kingdom. This Dispensation of the Spirit is exclusive of his work in physical creation, and inclusive only of his spiritual operation in the redemption of humanity.

SECTION I.

THE MANNER OF THE SPIRIT'S COMING.

Antecedent to the incarnation, the Holy Spirit, as well as the Son, were each doing the work peculiar to his distinctive personality in the Godhead, in the moral as well as in the material world. In a similar way, and to the same end, the Spirit moved on human hearts in the Old Testament dispensation as in the New, and all the pious loyalty among men before the advent of Christ is to be ascribed to the Spirit's operation, as really as the piety in the race since Christ's death and resurrection. The Spirit's future coming and work were more difficult for human apprehension than even the coming and work of the promised Messiah; yet both were revealed in their respective offices for restoring lost men to Old Testament saints, and the more eminent and experienced among them recognized, in good measure, the reality and importance of the presence of the Holy Ghost. David earnestly prayed, "Take not thy Holy Spirit from me."[1] And Isaiah represents Moses and his people as remembered of God, saying, "Where is he that put his Holy Spirit within him?"[2]

1. The Mosaic Ritual prefigured the Spirit's Work. — The sacrificial blood was in expiation for sin, and prefigured the atoning blood of Christ; while the ceremonial application of water was for purifying from sin, and foretokened the cleansing efficacy of the Spirit's influence. And this use of water in the Hebrew ritual is usually connected with the sacrifices, and rendered almost as conspicuous as the blood.

Thus, when Aaron and his sons were consecrated to the priesthood, connected with the sacrifices and the sprinkling of blood, they were to be "washed with water;" and the sacrificial ram was to be cut in pieces, and "the inwards of him washed;" and a brazen laver between the tabernacle of the congregation and the altar was to be perpetually supplied with

[1] Psalm li. 11. [2] Isa. lxiii. 11.

water for the priests' purifying in their daily ministrations.[1] And in a similar manner all the Levites were to be cleansed by "sprinkling the water of purifying upon them."[2] And so with the sin-offering for defilement from varied sources; there were to be kept the burnt ashes of a red heifer that must be mingled in water, called "the water of separation," and which must be sprinkled upon the unclean for their purifying.[3] And the soldiers returning from war, and the spoils taken, were to have "the water of separation" applied, and what spoils would not stand purifying by fire were to pass through water.[4] And unclean vessels were to be "rinsed in water."[5]

These varied baptisms and purifications were extensively observed by the Jews at the coming of Christ.[6]

2. It was announced in Prophecy. — Ezekiel looked forward to the evangelization of Israel, and recognizes the Holy Spirit as the source of their cleansing, and author of a new heart and a new spirit within them: "Then will I sprinkle clean water upon you, and ye shall be clean;" "a new heart also will I give you;" "and I will put my Spirit within you, and cause you to walk in my statutes, and ye shall keep my judgments and do them."[7] And Jeremiah refers in prophecy to the same spiritual cleansing under the

[1] Ex. xxix. 4–17, xxx. 18–21, xl. 12.
[2] Num. viii. 7.
[3] Lev. xi. 32; Num. xix. 9, 18, 19.
[4] Num. xxxi. 23.
[5] Lev. vi. 28, xv. 12.
[6] Mark vii. 3, 4; John ii. 6.
[7] Ezek. xxxvi. 25–29.

representation of a new covenant: "For behold, the days come, saith the Lord, that I will make a new covenant with the house of Israel, and with the house of Judah;" "this shall be the covenant that I will make with the house of Israel in those days, saith the Lord: I will put my law in their inward parts, and write it on their hearts, and will be their God, and they shall be my people."[1] And especially Joel foretells the coming of the Spirit as securing inspiration and piety, and which was quoted by Peter as then fulfilled when the Holy Ghost came: "It shall come to pass afterward that I will pour out my Spirit upon all flesh;" "also upon the servants and handmaids in those days will I pour out my Spirit."[2]

3. The Holy Spirit was circumstantially Promised to his Disciples by Jesus Christ. — In that most tender scene on the night of the last passover with his disciples, when he let them know of his crucifixion just at hand, and his final departure from the world to the Father, among the most prominent and consolatory teachings was his promise of the coming Spirit, who should comfort, strengthen, and guide them to higher Christian experiences than they had yet attained. In various particulars, the results of this coming Spirit were presented for their consolation and encouragement. He would not depart from them. "I will pray the Father, and he shall give you another Comforter, that he may abide with you forever."[3] He

[1] Jer. xxxi. 31-34. [2] Joel ii. 28-32. [3] John xiv. 16.

should communicate new truth, and quicken their memory of past instructions. "The Comforter, which is the Holy Ghost, whom the Father will send in my name, he shall teach you all things, and bring all things to your remembrance, whatsoever I have said unto you."[1] His testimony will strengthen and confirm their witness of Christ's ministry from the first. This Comforter, "even the Spirit of truth, which proceedeth from the Father, he shall testify of me: and ye shall bear witness, because ye have been with me from the beginning."[2]

It was better for them and for the world that Jesus should depart, for the Spirit, who would not otherwise come, would work graciously and extensively in the world, and in making Christ himself more clearly known by his people. He would make the sin of all unbelief in Christ conspicuous, and give assurance that Christ's work on earth was an acceptable ground of justification with God, and that Christ had utterly vanquished the devil; and also besides new revelations of truth, he would add new glory to Jesus by making brighter exhibitions of him; all which is taught in his saying, "When he is come, he will reprove the world of sin, and of righteousness, and of judgment; of sin, because they believe not on me; of righteousness, because I go to the Father, and ye see me no more; of judgment, because the Prince of this world is judged." "He shall glorify me, for he shall receive of mine, and shall show it unto you."[3]

[1] John xiv. 26. [2] John xv. 26, 27. [3] John xvi. 7-15.

And at a former time Christ had foretold their coming persecutions, and that they need have no anxiety about answers to charges in their arraignments before courts and councils, for the Spirit would inspire them. "When they bring you unto the synagogues, and unto magistrates and powers, take ye no thought how or what thing ye shall answer; for the Holy Ghost shall teach you in the same hour what ye ought to say."[1] And after Christ's resurrection and his commission to the apostles, just at the hour of his ascension, he refers to this promise of the Spirit in saying, "Behold, I send the promise of my Father upon you; but tarry ye in the city of Jerusalem until ye be endued with power from on high."[2] And then Luke enlarges upon this charge in another writing, that, Christ and the disciples being assembled together, "he commanded them that they should not depart from Jerusalem, but wait for the promise of the Father, which, saith he, ye have heard of me. For John truly baptized with water, but ye shall be baptized with the Holy Ghost not many days hence." "Ye shall receive power after that the Holy Ghost is come upon you, and ye shall be witnesses unto me."[3]

According to this charge there given, the disciples went back from the Mount of Olives, after Christ's ascension, and took an upper room in Jerusalem, and abode in that city, having constant communion and prayer "with the women, and Mary, the mother of Jesus, and with his brethren."[4] Here also at the

[1] Luke xii. 11, 12.
[2] Luke xxiv. 49.
[3] Acts i. 3, 5, and 8.
[4] Acts i. 13, 14.

counsel of Peter, they cast lots, and appointed Matthias to the place in the apostleship "from which Judas by transgression fell."[1] All were thus in expectancy, waiting the coming of the Holy Ghost.

4. The Actual Descent of the Holy Ghost. — The Passover prefigured redemption by Christ, and thus, as it was, the crucifixion appropriately occurred at the hour for killing the paschal lamb. Fifty days after the institution of the first Passover and Israel's departure from Egypt was the giving of the law from Sinai, and the annual feast of first fruits was instituted afterwards to occur at the same period. The sacrifices of burnt-offerings, peace-offerings, and the sin-offering were made at the time of this "feast of weeks," so called because the fifty days made an intervening week of weeks, and which Pentecost feast was in perpetual remembrance of deliverance from Egyptian bondage,[2] and of which the Spirit's freeing the soul from the bondage of sin was the antitype, and so appropriately the descending power of the Holy Ghost was on the day of Pentecost. The full account is given in the second chapter of Acts.

The hundred and twenty disciples of Christ, then made, were by agreement together in one place, and a sound like the roar of a strong wind filled the room where they were, and flickering flames appeared on the heads of the disciples, and the power of inspiration, and miracles, and speaking with tongues, was at

[1] Acts i. 15-26. [2] Lev. xxiii. 15-21; Deut. xvi. 9-12.

once communicated to them. The wondrous event drew the multitudes from all lands at the feast to this meeting of Christ's disciples, and each nation, in its own tongue, heard from these Galileans the Christian truths to which "the Spirit gave them utterance." Some mockers said it was drunkenness from new wine, but to most the phenomenon was inexplicable. Peter stood up, and so expounded and applied the occurrence, and the truths involved, that three thousand believed in Christ, were baptized, and added to the one hundred and twenty as a Gospel Church the same day. The Holy Ghost thus signalized his first special descent, and from that time forward the church has depended on the presence of the Holy Spirit to guide her ministry and membership, and make their evangelical work and example effectual in converting the world to Christianity. Jesus Christ appeared to Saul supernaturally after this, and thus qualified him as an apostle, to be a witness to Christ's resurrection; but with this exception, the divine authority and power of the Christian church have been under the immediate dispensation of the Spirit. In the apostolic age miraculous gifts, prophecy, and speaking with tongues, were communicated by the Spirit for eminently accrediting some disciples, but the mass of Christians and Christian ministers then and since have relied on his indwelling in the heart.

SECTION II.

THE MANNER OF THE SPIRIT'S AGENCY.

THE Spirit came like the Saviour's representation of it to Nicodemus; a "wind," that one might "hear the sound thereof, but could not tell whence it came nor whither it went."[1] No sense perceives the Holy Ghost, nor is there any consciousness of his presence, and we can know directly nothing of him except as reason sees him in his moral effects, just as reason sees the Creator in his works, or except as revelation may describe him. All communion of disembodied spirits is beyond our sense-consciousness, and especially must the communications of the Absolute Spirit be a secret to human experience, as to the mode of giving over what is his to be an impartation to us. And yet the facts given in experience and divine revelation do permit the insight of reason to determine many things with strong positiveness about the manner of the Holy Spirit's operation upon the human soul. Our creed here need not, and should not, be mere credulity.

1. IT IS AS MORAL POWER DISTINCT FROM PHYSICAL FORCE. — Like the life-energy, the Spirit uses and

[1] John iii. 8.

controls force, without itself being force; and as a user of forces, his agency is properly power. But as his power is not a control of forces in building up organisms, as the plant-instinct, nor a mover to locomotion, as in sense-appetites, which, though spontaneous, are still in nature, and as it is wholly in the end of fulfilling reasonable behests, so is it wholly moral and not mechanical power. The Spirit is free personality in conscious will, and he works in mind as will, and not at all as instinct, or appetite. He controls the man only through imperatives and affections, and it is exclusively in this moral field that we are now to contemplate the manner of the Spirit's agency. We put aside all mechanical force, and blind instinct, and sense-craving, and all analogies with such moving energies, — for they are all bound in the necessities of nature, and have no alternatives in their sequences, — and contemplate the Holy Spirit as supernatural, working on that which also in man is supernatural, and with activity in himself, and securing activity in man, which is solely reasonable and responsible.

"That which is born of the flesh is flesh, and that which is born of the Spirit is spirit;" and these two are no more to be confounded in their modes of working than in their manner of being. The Spirit is reason working on reason, and controls the sense only through reason. The Holy Ghost can find nothing in man's animal nature with which he can deal in directly gaining his spiritual ends, but subjects what is animal in man to God's commandments through conscientious convictions of what ought to be, and loving constraint in the choices of what is right to be. He works not as on sense to crave, and in executing the craving to gratify; but he works on reason "to will," and in executing the will "to do," that which reason approved.

2. The Spirit's Action is direct upon the Human Mind. — God's Spirit and man's spirit come directly and immediately in communion. All media of sense-apprehension are overpassed, and the Spirit finds man's immortal spirit itself, and deals face to face with that. We have already seen that pure spiritual communion is not within human consciousness. We cannot get beyond the exercises of our own spirits, and while, by careful introspection, we may discriminate these exercises, yet we never get the light of consciousness down under them, and descry the spirit itself putting forth these exercises, and of course we shall never get God's immediate communings with our spirits into consciousness. But, from the very fact that this is below all conscious exercising, and not through any media of phenomenal activities, it must be that the Holy Ghost and the human soul are together in these transactions, with nothing between them. And such is clearly Scripture statement, that the Holy Ghost works here exclusively from all intervening instrumentalities. "Which were born, not of blood, nor of the will of the flesh, nor of the will of man,

but of God."[1] The apostle says, "I have planted and Apollos watered, but God gave the increase; so then neither is he that planteth anything, neither he that watereth, but God that giveth the increase."[2] It is also an agency distinct from the action of truth; though both may concur, yet is not the Spirit's action the truth's action, for God's choosing to salvation is "through sanctification of the spirit and belief of the truth."[3]

3. IT PRECEDES AND TENDS TO THE RIGHT WILLING OF THE MAN. — The power of the Holy Ghost meets the mind of the sinner with his spirit disposed already on sense and self-gratification, and not on the ends of reason and self-approbation. There may be alarming apprehensions and stinging remorse, but no disposition that is a return to God and righteousness. The fear and conviction of guilt may be the first intimations that the Spirit has already met the careless soul. The end of the Spirit is in the sinner's disposing his voluntariness aright, and which will be the beginning of piety in the sinner, and the increase of piety in the saint; to the former the Spirit's work is precedent to any holiness, and to the latter it is precedent to the increased degree intended, and in both the end is to this disposing the soul loyally. Not at all as if the soul had begun and was doing the work, and the Spirit of God co-operated in helping, but in all cases it precedes the voluntary disposing, whether anew in piety, or to a

[1] John i. 13. [2] 1 Cor. iii. 6, 7. [3] 2 Thess. ii. 13.

new degree of steadfastness. But for the Spirit's power, the disposing in holiness, either in the renewing or in the growing sanctification, would never occur. God works on the mind "to will" and "to do," and thus before the willing and doing.

4. The Power of the Holy Spirit may be resisted by the Sinner. — All moral power on mind leaves still to that mind the alternatives of compliance or resistance open. It never overbears the liberty and responsibility of the mind. A careful analysis reveals clearly that so it must be in the application of any moral power to the human spirit. When the truth in reference to any natural sensibility reaches the mind, that truth itself works an effect in the mind spontaneously, without the mind's willing anything about it. A man hears of the misfortune or death of a friend, and the sad message does its work in the mind irrespective of the man's agency. And so, when any divine truth, as an enunciation of God's will, is clearly apprehended, it makes its spontaneous impression, and quickens intellect and sensibility, ere yet the will has been reached. The conscience starts into conviction of obligation, and of guilt at not having fulfilled a long incumbent duty, and in this conviction the will has had nothing to do. The rebellious and the loyal wills are alike in this respect; that applied truth works its own convictions in the soul, independently of the soul's willing whether it shall so be, or not. And this is the meaning of Christ's declaration, "The

words that I speak unto you, they are spirit, and they are life."[1] There is a living efficiency in truth to quicken and kindle mental susceptibility, without the mind's willing it should do so.

And now, as a moral power, the action of the Holy Ghost on mind is strictly analogous. That spiritual power has its own efficiency in modifying the mind on which it works, aside from the mind's will helping or hindering. The truth and the Spirit may affect the mind together, and each in its own way distinct one from the other, and that mind not have willed at all in the matter. So far forth, either with the Spirit or the truth, there has been no occasion for resistance. But this quickened susceptibility by the truth and by the Spirit prompts to its execution, and urges the fulfilment of the obligation; and just here comes the occasion for responsible action. The human spirit must now yield to or resist the striving. The will must now come into exercise, and the human spirit dispose itself with or against the Holy Spirit and the truth. The alternatives are both open to it, and it must take one or the other; and as its disposing is, that is its will, and this disposing for or against is of the human spirit's own origination. This disposing is not the truth's, nor the Holy Ghost's disposing, but solely the man's spirit disposing, and wholly at his responsibility. His spirit is not like his sense-appetite, which, as of nature, must go towards highest gratification, and has no alternatives but degrees of happiness,

[1] John vi. 63.

of which the higher must prevail against the lower; but his spirit is above nature, competent to control natural appetite and all its gratifications, and to sacrifice and reject any degree of happiness for self-approbation in righteousness. And to this the Spirit strives, and the truth prompts, and neither can go any further, for the pious yielding or the impious resisting must be of the human spirit's originating. Hence the earnest caution against "resisting the Spirit," "quenching the Spirit," and the manifest accounting the sinner himself guilty in doing it.[1]

5. The Effectual Calling of the Spirit induces a complying Will. — The human preacher calls and warns, invites and persuades, but he necessarily stands outside of the minds he addresses; and can only do his work through the truth he uses. He can only use means, and be himself but an instrument in saving sinners. The Holy Ghost most gloriously reverses this order of working on human hearts. He comes directly to the human spirit, and beyond all means works on it, and quickens every faculty and susceptibility of the man. He rouses conscience that it cannot sleep, and quickens convictions of guilt the man cannot repress, and stirs sympathies that soften and melt the soul's obduracy, so that he cannot but sigh and weep over his sins. In this effectual working, though the spirit is competent to struggle on and cleave to its sensual bondage, it takes a new disposing,

[1] Acts vii. 51; 1 Thess. v. 19; Eph. iv. 30.

and renounces flesh and sense, and wakes and acts in the recovered freedom of its own sovereignty. It now rules, and does not serve, the lusts of the flesh; and the will is in it, and the choice upon it. With all the power of the Holy Ghost effectually working, the human spirit also has as freely worked in the change as in any act in his life when no special power of the Holy Spirit was present. What the Spirit has done has secured what the sinner has done, but the Spirit's doing has been his own, and the sinner's doing has been his, and without the former the change would not have been, and without the latter the change could not have been, for the change is just this new disposing.

6. The Assenting Will must be to the Truth.—The power of the spirit is not on nor through truth, but directly on mind; yet the truth must be also on the mind in order that the assenting will may be. No intelligent willing can be in darkness, and this assenting spiritual disposing is in the end of known truth and conscious obligation. The operation of the Holy Ghost is other than the action of truth; and if it were conceived to be when truth was not, and sufficient for securing the change when the new disposing shall come, yet could not that new disposing occur but in the presence of truth. The willing must have its end as truly as the knowing and feeling, and the very end of the pious willing is the truth itself. Hence conversion of spirit, and growing sanctification of spirit,

must be by the Holy Ghost, as effectually working in mind, and must also be through the truth as that to which the mind turns and embraces; and hence, too, the propriety and consistency of the prayer of the Saviour, "Sanctify them through thy truth; thy word is truth."[1] God sanctifies as God renews — by the power of the Holy Spirit; but neither is done except in the presence and to the end of truth, which is the word of God.

SECTION III.

THE WORK WHICH THE HOLY SPIRIT ACCOMPLISHES.

In creation, no substantial forces are made by the Son which are not systematically arranged in connection by the Spirit; and so in redemption, no work wrought by the Son is overlooked by the Spirit, but in his own time and manner he puts it in available communication with the human mind for executing the eternal plan of the Father. It was foretold that he should "not speak of himself," but should "take of the things of Christ and show them unto us." What power Jesus Christ has put in the world of humanity by his incarnation, life, and death, the Spirit applies by his power in obtaining the designed result in

[1] John xvii. 17.

human salvation. In the sphere of redemption the whole work of the Holy Spirit is upon mind, and in full consistency with human freedom and responsibility; but without his working the work of the Son would be unavailable. His agency is as necessary, and as lovinglygracious in the interest of human salvation, as that of the suffering Saviour.

1. The Work of the Holy Spirit in Inspiration. — The Incarnation, and thereby the open manifestation of God in humanity, was in one age and among the people of one country, and yet this was destined to become known and felt in every age and among all people. In order to reach coming ages and distant lands, it was necessary to so embody and retain the living truth in its power that it might be perpetuated and transmitted to all future generations. The wisest way conceivable for this was purposed by inspiring some selected minds with the divine communication, and prompting them to record, as was needed, the heavenly messages, and duly authenticate their record, that it should be received and work its power out upon the world wherever it should be sent. The essential thing is the truth of the record, and that it is *the* truth which God designed to communicate to men; hence the prime importance of the attestation of this divine inspiring in the men who received and recorded the messages. The writers claim for themselves inspiration on the face of the record itself, and they have given valid proof for it; but with this proof

we are not now concerned, and only with the consideration of inspiration itself as a work of the Holy Spirit. It is the work of Absolute Reason within the individuality of finite reason, and so a work of the divine Spirit in the human spirit, and which cannot be phenomenally perceived, but must be spiritually discerned.

We may be much assisted in rendering this spiritual work intelligible by following out its fair analogy in the field of rational art, inasmuch as the work of reason in and through sense in any one case is very far explanatory of all other cases. The artist must first be fully possessed with the idea he is about to embody. He will never get out in expression more than is contained in his archetype. The pattern-thought may be an origination of his own genius, or an adopted and perhaps modified form from some other, but the idea must stand clear in his own mind as the necessary pre-requisite of his communicating anything to others. And when such bright ideal is in possession, it ever proves an inner stimulus, strenuously prompting in some way to its outer manifestation. It makes a mental unrest that cannot be quieted except as there is given to it some fitting state of fixed expression. And in doing this the artist's hand is guided by the inner eye of reason intent on this created or adopted ideal.

Even so with the inspired Messenger from heaven. He must have the divine idea in clear contemplation, and as it must be no original of his own, but wholly that which Jesus has embodied already for him in some experience of his life, these facts of Christ's originating must be exactly imparted to him. The event must have been once witnessed and then accurately recalled, and the meaning intended unmistakenly disclosed, and for this "the inspiration of the Spirit must give him understanding," and set in clear insight the mind and will of the Lord Jesus. With such clear impartation of the quick and stirring vision, there rises the irrepressible impulse to communicate it. It is as "a burning fire shut up in his bones," and the uneasiness of forbearing wearies so greatly that he cannot stay the expressing.[1] And in this communicating he must be guided as unerringly as in apprehending, so that the very received Idea shall be lodged in the literal record. As in the case of Moses with the Tabernacle and its sacred furniture it must be made "after the pattern which was shown thee in the mount."

For all this the Holy Spirit works in the mind, effectually securing that mind freely to accomplish just what in the inspiration is intended — clear possession of the truth and correct expression of it. The power of Jesus Christ still inheres in his living experience, as divinely communicated to the mind of the Evangelist, both of deed and word, and their "spirit and life" rouses him to his work of recording, and then goes into his record to quicken future readers; but while thus recording, he needs the constant

[1] Jer. xx. 9.

present Spirit directly working on his mind, to quicken every faculty, that it may take truth accurately; to stimulate to intense urgency, that it may write promptly; and then to keep the intensified vision on the imparted pattern, that it may copy exactly the heavenly meaning. In this way the inspired man works in entire freedom, while the Spirit gets the work done, as he intends, without error.

Truth so expressed is no merely honest human record of what is sensibly or studiedly apprehended, just as all carefully written profane history is; a sacred power is here superintending the whole transaction for its own purpose, and making the record, though freely written, yet so written as the superintending Spirit designed it should be. One in his free characteristic mode of expression gives his peculiarly marked revelation; another gives his spontaneous record of what has been vivid in his mind; but the Holy Spirit has so wrought on each as to get from all just the sacred Book he purposed.

Any mind in any age may be influenced by theHoly Spirit to sharper insight and intenser zeal in expressing, and more clear and effective communication of his message, and for this the good man, and especially the gospel minister, may earnestly and believingly pray; but such assisted message cannot claim the authority of plenary inspiration without the attesting supernatural signs which must convince others that God has sent him. No one may arrogate for himself, nor may others claim for him, the prerogative of infallibility without the seal of supernatural powers.

2. THE WORK OF THE HOLY SPIRIT IN MIRACLES. — If philosophy can only logically judge from experience, any valid conclusion of miraculous occurrences is impossible. No experience can then reach beyond nature, and nothing can be known out of nature that can interfere with nature; and any strange occurrences which may come into experience must be just as much of nature as the ordinary onflow of successive events. Indeed, from mere experience can be deduced no laws of nature to be miraculously subverted; all phenomenal changes are mere facts perceived, and the order of occurrence as marked a fact as the phenomena themselves and their changes, and no experienced invariable order can be logically raised above fact, and made to be law; and all assumptions of necessary connections in experience, because nature itself has necessary connections, rest solely on the habit which events have taken on, and which they may at any time break up. It is only when we recognize an Absolute Reason, regulating experience through a regulated series of events, that we come to any valid knowledge of fixed connections in nature from the control of reason put into nature, and thus making nature the subject of law, and a legitimate field for philosophy. As the creature of reason, and subject to reason, nature may have outside interferences, and newly introduced events into its old order whenever

reason itself may demand it. And such is the meaning of a miracle, viz., an interference in nature by the Author of nature, when he has reason for it.

And now, the whole redemptive work for humanity is supernatural; as much above nature, and from a source out of nature, as was the origination of nature itself; and the carrying on of such a work in nature must, in varied ways, reasonably interfere with and designedly make changes in the orderly connections of nature. When such an interference as only the Author of nature can effect is wrought in nature, to give his own sanction to a message or messenger assuming to come from him, then is the occasion reasonable, and the accredited authority valid. But the condition of the interposition of divine power is essential to such validity. An animal interferes in one part with nature when he overcomes gravity, and makes a weight move up hill; but animal sensibility is nature, and the motive to move the weight has been some appeal to sentient nature, and thus as much one part of nature interfering with another part, as when the force of falling water or condensed steam moves machinery. There is here no introduction of power from beyond nature. Still further, a man, as rational, may overrule sense, and act from reason in taste, philosophy, morals, or religion, and so work on nature, and make changes in nature that originate in a source wholly beyond nature; and thus human interferences in nature are oftentimes completely supernatural; but such human changes can give no valid accrediting to any assumed authority from heaven, and so these man-made changes are properly no miracles. Even magical enchantments, and satanic "lying wonders," are no attesting miracles; but to give valid warrant, the attestation must be superhuman, supersatanic, even divine; just as Moses' rod devoured the serpents which Egyptian magicians exhibited, and Paul dispossessed the pythoness of her "spirit of divination." When that which only God can do is truly done in nature, to give his own authority to his own commissioned ministers, then is the occasion reasonable for the miraculous interposition, and the clear interposition valid for the claims of a divine commission. So true prophecy is a miracle of foreknowledge; and reading the heart, a miracle of "discerning spirits;" and dividing the sea, or raising the dead, a miracle of omnipotence; but the reasonable occasions can seldom only occur, for the frequent repetition of divine interferences miraculously must soon subvert the very end designed; but on reasonable occasions, human agents may do truly divine deeds.

But conditional that man should be a miracle-worker, is special faith in the impartation to him of a divine power. No man could do the mighty work unless he had the peculiar faith; and the genuine faith, though small in degree, secures the possession of the power. "If ye had faith as a grain of mustard-seed, ye might say unto this sycamine-tree, Be thou plucked up by the roots, and be thou planted in the sea; and it should obey you."[1] And the exercise of this faith was secured by the inworking of the Holy Spirit upon the human mind. Many cases of Old Testament miracles had occurred, and the apostles in Christ's day wrought miracles, and all from an inworking principle of faith which the Holy Spirit had quickened in them; but the abundant and effective attestation of divine authority for human ambassadors from God was after the ascension of the Saviour and the descent of the Spirit at Pentecost. This was one part of the power the disciples waited at Jerusalem for.[2] The inward trust prompted the expecting of the energizing, and the divine efficiency accompanied the human act, and the miraculous result followed. This faith could not be, except as grounded in a divine promise, and influenced by a divine presence; and hence the human working of miracles can be only in an age and place divinely appointed and rationally approved, and not at the caprice of human curiosity or selfish interest. At times the faith requisite for the exigency came only by special "prayer and fasting,"[3] and sometimes also the persons to be miraculously helped must have the peculiar faith;[4] but always the presence of the faith availed to secure the miraculous interposition. And as yet further to be noted, the faith available for working the miracle was not that requisite for saving the soul, since even men of carnal dispositions and disobedient lives have worked

[1] Luke xvii. 6; Matt. xxi. 21, 22.
[2] Luke xxiv. 49; Acts i. 8.
[3] Matt. xvii. 20, 21.
[4] Matt. xiii. 58; Acts xiv. 9.

miracles. Balaam prophesied,[1] and the sons of the Pharisees cast out devils,[2] and a faith that may remove mountains can be without Christian charity;[3] but no worker of miracles in Christ's name, though not following him, could lightly speak evil of him, and was thus to be allowed in prosecuting his miraculous working as, so far at least, in Christ's interest.[4]

So the canonical Scriptures stand, attested by miracles from the Holy Spirit for their inspiration and authority, as the only rule infallible for faith and practice; and when any new claims of infallibility are made, the miraculous seal from the Holy Ghost can alone fix their validity. Such accrediting the church and world have needed, and have had; but the need for such may probably never again occur.

3. THE NECESSITY FOR, AND THE WORK OF, THE HOLY SPIRIT IN REGENERATION. — When our first parents fell, they took on a disposition to the ends of sense which was a radical perversion and depraving of moral character, and sure permanently to be perpetuated by them if left to their own course; and still further, their fall so vitiated their sentient nature as to secure its universal propagation in the race, and this sentient corruption was sure to induce the free moral disposing of all their descendants, upon sense-gratification as end of life, if no gracious remedy were provided. Natural vitiation would carry with it uni-

[1] Num. xxiv. 15–19.
[2] Matt. xii. 27.
[3] 1 Cor. xiii. 2.
[4] Mark ix. 38, 39.

versal free moral depravity, if God himself did not help. The help needed, and the only help available, was the introducing of a moral power, which should secure the disposing of the spirit away from self-gratification as end of life to self-approbation, and therein attain a moral character which God could approve, and through Christ's mediation could meet with his favor. This change of the character which was certain to follow from natural birth, when secured by God's interposition, was known as the "new birth," and involved within it the conditions of repentance for pardon, and of faith for justification. Under whatever influence secured, the disposing of the spirit is the person's own agency, either sensually or spiritually, and solely on his responsibility; but having bowed in bondage to sense, and become "carnally-minded," the human spirit will persist in his carnal disposing, and live on sensually and sinfully. "The carnal mind is enmity against God," and in its persistent carnality "cannot be subject to the law of God;" and the disposition depraved, the entire life is perverse.

And now, after the redemption-work of Christ, laying the ground for pardon and justification, the grand condition for its appropriation to any is this new spiritual birth; and the obstinate guilty resistance of the old carnal disposition to it, and the yielding in no case to any other influence than the direct agency of the Holy Spirit upon the carnal mind, make the work of the Holy Spirit a necessity, if any one is to be "born again." The strength of the depraved disposition is manifest in many ways. Legal authority may press guilt and awaken remorse and fear in the perverse spirit, and threaten speedy application of deserved penalty; yet this is made by the sinner rather to intensify his hatred to law for its stern restraint, and the aggravation of its carnal lusting by the rebellious heart, and the pressure of law exasperates rather than subdues the mind to God. This conviction of obligation and guilt must be awakened by the application of law, but if the authority of law only be applied in any way, the disposition of the rebel will not become loyal by it.

Then appropriately comes the application of the power of the cross. Here is a ground of pardon from penal infliction, and a righteousness which may stand in stead of the obedience the sinner should have rendered, and the stern authority of law may still stand without the sinner's punishment, and in the loss of his personal righteousness; and so even under the pressure of law, the sinner occupies a place where peace and reconciliation lie open. Yea, still much deeper strikes this power of Jesus' redemption. It is the fruit of tenderest pity for you, and kindest compassion; it has been attained through deepest self-humiliation and painful self-denial for you. The laying by of heavenly glory and taking your humanity, and suffering the shame and death of the cross, have all been his for your sake; and this "speaking blood" of Calvary pleads with tenderer efficacy for submission and reconciliation than the stern voice of command and threatening. And yet this pleading pity and patient suffering must still teach as deep abhorrence for sin, and as strenuous claim for a disposition set on righteousness, as does the authority of law. The man must come back with a new disposition in spiritual integrity; and when it is openly seen that sense-gratification as end of life must be wholly renounced, and self-serving give place to full-hearted devotion for God, this deeply convicted and affected soul can, and will, put away all soft impressions, and cut short all sympathy in the Saviour's suffering, and forget his compassion, and despise his love, and as determinately as before push his own way on in carnal gratification. He will not only hate the law, but will resist the power of Christ crucified, and smother convictions of sin and all sympathetic relentings in returning sensual indulgences. Praying saints and pleading friends may all add their affectionate and anxious solicitations, and before the strength of this carnal disposition, all will fail.

The power of the Holy Ghost, on such as he sees reason effectually to operate, here comes in, in concurrence with all else which without him is ineffectual. Face to face with the human spirit, he works directly on mind in his own distinct and peculiar way, which, so far as our insight into all revealing can go, we have before described, and wakes the life and intensifies the energy of every faculty. Memory is quickened to call up anew past sins, and mercies, and persistent neglect, and ingratitude, and the soul cannot shut down its convictions of guilt and desert. Self-reproach, and conscious claim, and short opportunity lay their burdens upon the spirit, which the soul can neither put down nor carry along. Old sense-indulgences cease to please, and from no quarter comes any peace to the troubled heart. In this arrest and suspension of all joy, the Holy Spirit further "takes the things of Christ and shows them" to the soul whose mental eye is now opened to see the suffering, and mercy, and waiting wish to receive, and longing interest to save; and to this power of the cross he additionally works with his own direct power, which knows the chords to touch, and how intensely to make them vibrate; and so, in this "day of his power," that mind becomes "willing," and the human spirit now as freely disposes itself towards God as it before did towards self-gratification. Old idols are discarded; a new master is taken; "the old man is put off," and "the new man is put on," which after God is created in righteousness and true holiness.[1] In this new disposing is the new life, and at once flow out new affections and new volitions. "Old things are passed away; behold, all things are become new; and all things are of God, who hath reconciled us to himself by Jesus Christ."[2]

When we speak of this change as from the sinner's agency, we employ terms expressive of his activity; when in view of the divine agency, we speak of the

[1] Eph. iv. 22-24. [2] 2 Cor. v. 17, 18.

sinner as acted on; but the complete change effected includes both; and the active "conversion" is also the being "born again," and the regeneration is in no way completed but in the new disposing of the man's spirit under the working of the Holy Spirit. Henceforth, the ongoing is in a new direction, and the life has a new experience. The consciousness when the change occurred may be less or more retained, but the consciousness that the change has occurred is daily to grow clearer. "One thing I know, that whereas I was blind, now I see."[1]

4. THE WORK OF THE HOLY SPIRIT IN SANCTIFICATION. — Christian life begins in regeneration, and subsequently matures through the natural life. The new-born soul must not merely persist in holy living, but must grow in holiness; gaining intenser devotion and loyalty to God by the discipline of daily experience and the prayerful cultivation of all Christian graces. The physical faculties of body and soul may augment by age and experience in good and bad men, and doubtless there is intellectual and emotional growth of faculty in an angel; it is not, however, this growth in the being itself of the agent that we here regard, but the growing strength in the spirit and disposition, and increasing energy of purpose and fervent zeal in all good, which is now contemplated as involved in Christian living. The beginning activity of the new-born soul is never in full maturity. The new

[1] John ix. 25.

disposition is never as full and fixed on God and truth as it should be, or as in future experience it must be. Intruding appetites call out desultory volitions for sense-gratification, and difficulties and dangers oftener daunt and discourage than they ought, and temptations and crosses are borne less patiently and steadily than is right. The spiritual control must grow firmer, and colliding sense-inclinations must be held in more complete subjugation to the will of God than the first Christian experience ever exhibits. This growing energy and stability of the new disposition in regeneration, and which gives augmenting integrity of Christian character, is what we here mean by sanctification. It distinguishes itself from other Christian states by just this fact of growth. Regeneration begins Christian life; sanctification is Christian life growing. Pardon is official remission of legal penalty, justification is official declaration of the satisfying of legal precept, and adoption is official admission to God's family; but sanctification, in reference to each of these respectively, is less and less desert of penalty, more and more conformity to precept, and increasing filial affection and obedience. The others are complete at once and at the start; sanctification ripens on till the presentation "without spot to God." Aside from growth, sanctification has other peculiarities to be noted.

The work is within the human spirit. — External conformity of life is not it, but comes from it, and the former may be without the latter. So pharisaical self-righteousness may constrain the outer life to great exactness in religious rites and ceremonies, but merely cleanses and whitens the outside, leaving the inner defilement unmitigated. Ritualism may punctually observe every imposed rite, and school itself in bodily exercises "profiting nothing," but "he is not a Jew who is one outwardly, and circumcision is of the heart."[1] The burden of the prayer which is to shape the Christian life in growing sanctification must cry with the Psalmist, "Search me, O God, and know my heart; try me and know my thoughts, and see if there be any wicked way in me, and lead me in the way everlasting."[2]

It is persevering. — From the reason in the case, the man alone considered, perseverance in holiness could not beforehand be affirmed. Adam fell; some angels fell; the restored sinner is freely holy, and the alternative of falling away is fully open. But the reason of the case is far otherwise when the honor and power of God are considered. The new life is from God, and shall he begin and not be able to finish? Shall Satan pluck his redeemed children from his hand? And yet strongly as reason may affirm that God's begun work must be carried on to its consummation, the importance of the doctrine has secured for it God's direct declaration in addition to speculative reason. Under inspiration Paul thus reasons: "For if when we were enemies we were reconciled to God by the death of his Son, much more being reconciled we shall be saved by his life."[3] And again, "Being confident of this

[1] Rom. ii. 28, 29. [2] Ps. cxxxix. 23, 24. [3] Rom. v. 10.

very thing, that he which hath begun a good work within you will perform it unto the day of Jesus Christ."[1] And so reason all the inhabitants of heaven, who "rejoice more over one sinner that repenteth than over ninety and nine just persons which need no repentance."[2] They take the assurance that true repentance is persevering, and they rejoice unquestioningly so soon as it begins. Direct declarations are exceedingly numerous in the Bible, and probably no doctrine is more repeatedly asserted than that of persevering sanctification. "Whoso liveth and believeth in me shall never die."[3] "Whosoever drinketh of the water that I shall give him shall never thirst; but the water that I shall give him shall be in him a well of water springing up into everlasting life."[4] "After that ye believed, ye were sealed with that Holy Spirit of promise which is the earnest of your inheritance."[5]

Those texts asserting perdition if one falls away are the stronger modes of asserting that the saint will not fall, since so improbable a consequence cannot have its occasion. Just as in Paul's hypothetical declaration, "Though we or an angel from heaven preach any other gospel, let him be accursed,"[6] was no admission that apostles and angels would preach another gospel, but rather the curse if they should, was its greatest improbability; and so with this other

[1] Phil. i. 6. [2] Luke xv. 7. [3] John xi. 26.
[4] John iv. 14. [5] Eph. i. 13, 14. [6] Gal. i. 8.

declaration, "For it is impossible for those who were once enlightened, and have tasted of the heavenly gift, &c., if they shall fall away, to renew them again to repentance."[1] It means not that such experienced saints shall fall, but rather that the impracticability of renewing them again, if they did, was the strongest expression of its improbability. None who finally perish were ever saints, for of the best of such Christ says he "never knew them."[2] And John says, "They went out from us, but they were not of us."[3]

Sanctification will be perfected at death. — Different notions of perfection have occasioned different opinions of complete sanctification in this life. One may deem his own state perfect, which another sees to be very imperfect. The new disposition may be sincere in end and aim, and truly towards God and righteousness, but the sincere change is not, as such, evidence that the disposing is "with all the heart, mind, and strength." That strength of disposition which has kept sense in good subjection for a time, so that the man may not have been conscious of sin, may still be very imperfect and fall into grievous sins in other trials at other times. Perfection in faith and love, so as properly to be complete sanctification, must be so whole-souled that no trial shall overcome, and no temptation lead astray. This ought so to be in all cases, at all times, and a failure to stand so firmly at all times is at the responsibility of the sinner. So firm every Christian should be, and hence it is possible for

[1] Heb. vi. 4-6. [2] Matt. vii. 23. [3] 1 John ii. 19.

him to be; but possibility and duty are not evidences that the fact yet is. The inquiry is, will such perfection be till after death?

No present consciousness of overcoming strength can be consciousness of strength which shall always overcome. No possible present experience can be the ground on which to determine all future experience, even in cases of entire liberty and responsibility. It will not, thus, be right for any one to assume that he now has such perfect sanctification. All probability is against him, and the decision of revelation is squarely on the other side. Sinless perfection has been in no human experience but in the man Christ Jesus. The Lord's Prayer is meant for all living, and it makes confession of sin. Paul proves, from the Old Testament Scriptures, "that all, Jews and Gentiles, are under sin."[1] And John affirms that "if we say we have no sin, we deceive ourselves, and the truth is not in us."[2] And Solomon of old affirmed, "There is not a just man on earth that doeth good and sinneth not."[3]

But at death, we are informed, all sin passes away, and complete sanctification reigns. Not because a completely sanctified man could not longer live, do we put perfection to be at death; nor is it because death has itself a sanctifying efficacy; but, dropping the body of sense and retaining only the spiritual body, and coming into direct communion with the Holy Spirit, the whole soul comes into complete and

[1] Rom. iii. 9. [2] 1 John i. 8. [3] Eccl. vii. 20.

ecstatic consecration and beatitude. Nothing within hinders, and nothing without defiles, and even the coming resurrection body is wholly incorruptible.[1]

5. ALL THE WORK OF THE HOLY GHOST IS IN FULL SOVEREIGNTY. — The Holy Ghost has been sent of the Father and of the Son, and executes his commission as third person in his own conscious voluntariness; and thus the regeneration and sanctification of sinners have, in their procuring, the agencies of all the personalities in the Godhead concurrently operating, and the whole work is in the absolute sovereignty of the Deity. Sovereignty is not arbitrary purpose without reason, but purpose wholly in the end of reason. What the Holy Spirit does is determined in its absolute reasonableness. It accords with his reason; it satisfies his reason; it is absolved from all other interests than reason; and this makes the action to be in pure sovereignty. He chooses among sinners with the end of reason in view, and so his election is in sovereignty, and all is the same as to say that the ultimate is his own excellency or glory. The operation of the Spirit in saving men comes in under these following conditions: The whole race were in a hopeless state. Jesus' incarnation and death opened redemption for all. God would have all freely accept this salvation. Man's perverse disposition universally rejects the offered salvation. Some effectual agency must just here come in, or the redemptive sacrifice

[1] 1 Cor. xv. 42-44; Rev. xxi. 27.

utterly fails. And as, when God would not have Jewish offerings, the Saviour said, "Lo, I come to do thy will, O my God," so when all human souls reject, the Spirit is sent "to convince of sin, of righteousness, and of judgment." He convicts, converts, and sanctifies men according to the divine will. He does just what in the whole case is reasonable should be done. As already seen, his work on the mind is a moral power, and not mechanical force; and he executes his own purpose through the freedom of the human spirit.

How, then, it may be asked, does he secure the salvation of any? The answer is, that his work on mind, in quickening and rousing every faculty, secures the sinful spirit's working in the change from sense-disposing to spiritual-disposing. The old disposition on sensual gratification becomes the new disposition on spiritual approbation. If he so turn some freely, it may be further asked, Why not turn more? Why not save all? The answer comes from the very being of the Absolute Reason in his sovereignty, that something higher must be regarded than human salvation. That must be secured, if at all, in a way that shall consist altogether with right and reason, and to save other, or more, will require action which somewhere must violate reasonable claims, and be doing wrong. If sinners, more or all, will themselves come, they may and welcome. But if they will not, and the Spirit must work on them for their disposing, then must he guide his work by perpetual regard to its universal reasonableness, rightness, respect for his own excellency's sake. He so does this, that in keeping to what is "good in his sight," he forever shuts off all just complaint, and secures coming universal assent to his integrity.[1] What is done by the Spirit in electing in time had the same reason for the purpose in eternity.[2] So with election to eternal life; it is direct, and in the sovereignty of Absolute Reason, to the end that the elected be secured in holiness. But, on the other hand, election to eternal death, which is the doctrine of reprobation, must not be viewed in the same way as a direct and eternally designed work of the Holy Spirit. There is no direct, designed influence of the Holy Spirit to secure and perpetuate a depraved disposition. The Holy Spirit must needs work upon depraved hearts if they are to be renewed, and he does this to the end and in the way of its eternal reasonableness; and so doing, he finds such as it would be unreasonable he ever should have chosen, and who must be left in their own determined disloyalty, and their final rejection is of their own procuring. To each of such determined rejecters of Jesus and his offers must come the time when longer waiting shall be unreasonable, dishonorable to God, and inviting to universal disrespect of the Spirit's authority; and at such time all further gracious striving must cease. With some, this may be before life closes, and as incorrigibly "joined to their idols," they are "let alone." And in all other cases,

[1] Isa. v. 4; Matt. xi. 26; Rom. iii. 19.
[2] Eph. i. 4; 2 Thess. ii. 13.

the divine striving must terminate with the natural life. The end of the Spirit's work is a new spiritual disposition controlling all carnal inclination, and which must be in the day of fleshly probation. When the sinner is cut down by death, it must be as with the fruitless tree, pruned a while, but when proved hopelessly barren, it is cut down, to lie as it falls. No culture succeeds with the sinner in the absence of divine influence, and with it some only become new-born, while others reject and resist all that it is right the Spirit should do for them, and they are necessarily lost as their own destroyers.

So the dispensation of the Holy Spirit will last, and his work extend over the ages, till all which may be done by him for human salvation will have been exhausted. The gospel will be preached, and the missionary sent, to all nations, and converts be made in all lands, and the word of life and the church and its ordinances be given to all people. Ancient prophecy, and revealed promise and purpose of God, shall have their complete fulfilment, when also the Spirit's work shall be finished, and all that God's plan of redemption can effect for human conversion and recovery to spiritual life, under the righteously applied power of the Holy Ghost, will have been secured; and then the last things must occur in the closing of human history. We do not need to trace the course of Christian ecclesiastical history in detail up to the present time, nor attempt to settle where in the process of prophetic fulfilment our age stands. We only need to know the

Holy Ghost will preside over and guide the church, and show the things of Christ to her members, and convince the world of Christ's true Messiahship "to the glory of the Father," till his second coming.

We may well believe, from the increased missionary zeal and prayer of the church, and the Christian enterprise of the age, and the faith and expectation of Christians, that we are near to auspicious events, and extensive changes for good to mankind. One wide-spread iniquity after another is attacked and abolished, and the hope and courage of good men, notwithstanding prevalent infidelity and abounding iniquity, were never so high and strong as now. The nations of the world are to become the one kingdom of the Redeemer, and in his own time he shall come and stretch his sceptre over them.

CHAPTER V.

THE LAST THINGS IN THE REDEMPTION OF HUMANITY.

IN the interest of the Absolute Reason himself it behooved him to people this earth with human beings, constituted in the union of sense and spirit; and so constituted, the fair trial for the control of the spirit over sense became also a claim of reason. This trial, we have found, eventuated in the progenitors of the race voluntarily subjecting the spirit to the bondage of sense, and which so vitiated the sentient nature as to insure the disposing of the spirit to the ends of sense in all their posterity. A gracious plan of Redemption then opened a second probation for man, in full satisfaction with every claim of reason and under stronger influences for spiritual integrity than in the first probation; and with an assurance that the Redeemer should have a seed whose service should satisfy him for all his sacrifice. We have followed the history of humanity through this gracious probation, "founded on better promises," under the dispensations of the Son, and then of the Holy Spirit; and now, as the mediatorial work is to close, the issues must be as accordant with reason as the whole process has been. The Universe must know that all has been rightly ordered.

From the reason in the case itself, the whole probation of man must pass while the spirit is in union with the flesh, since the end of the probation is to bring the body in subjection to the spirit; but a state of retribution necessarily involves a change in the mode of being. "Flesh and blood cannot inherit the kingdom of God, neither doth corruption inherit incorruption," and yet the change in the mode of existence must admit of full conscious identity and personal individuality in this passing from trial to final award. What our speculation has already attained will enable us intelligently to follow the conscious experience of humanity over from a gracious probation to a final retribution, and to clearly note the Last Things in the closing mediation which opens into direct face-to-face beholding. As in the history thus far we have kept our insight constantly to the facts of nature and revelation, so in what is to come we must carefully note the few but emphatic annunciations of the word of God, as the grand source of light and authority in searching for and establishing the truth and doctrine of a carefully considered Eschatology. Reason can read the facts which are to close time and open eternity only in God's revelation: but such revelation is a sealed book to sense, and has no meaning but for a spiritual discernment.

SECTION I.

SPECULATIVE VIEW OF HUMAN DEATH.

HUMAN probation terminates in death. The first trial and fall would have eventuated in eternal death, as originally threatened, but for the merciful interposition of a redemptive plan, and on the ground of which a second state of probation was secured. It behooved God to indicate his displeasure for the first sin in lasting consequences through the ages, and in the delay of the original penalty, among other items of the divine disapprobation was the curse of temporal death. "Dust thou art, and unto dust shalt thou return." In some sense the animal dies as truly as man, and yet in the animal kingdom death has reigned perpetually from before the creation and fall of man, and was thus neither a result of man's sin, nor a curse following any moral probation. Death to the brute is something quite other than death to man. The brute was designed to be mortal, but man's original immortality was both indicated and secured by his free access to "the tree of life," while on his fall the indication and certainty of coming death to him was in the barring up the way to the tree of immortality. It was a curse to him consequent upon his sin, and when it occurs it terminates for him his new state of probation. The opportunity of subduing appetite to the governing spiritual disposition passes, and the way opens for final retribution in a new state of being appropriate for it. In some respects man's death and dissolution is like that of animals, but in reality it essentially differs from all other forms of dying.

1. All Death differs from Natural Decomposition. — In nature there is perpetual alteration as substitution of one thing in the place of another, and also continual change as modification going on in the same thing. The fluid stream congeals to a solid, or passes utterly away in evaporation, but in such change there is no death. The mechanical forces in nature are ever combining and dissolving, but nature's forces are in constant conservation, and from nature nothing dies out. Death in any form is more than chemical decomposition, for in no chemical or crystallizing combinations has there been life.

2. In the Vegetable Kingdom is the Lowest Life, and hence the Simplest Form of Death. — The plant has been built up by the life-instinct, and organized according to the specific type in the ends to which the original want refers; and through all the vegetable kingdom the life-power which builds and inhabits and uses the organism is instinctive only, going out to its end, with never a return upon its agency in self-recognition. It has no capabilities for concentrat-

ing its activity in any point, where the activities might meet in self-feeling. Superinduced upon ethereal force, as is the life-want, for the end of assimilation and combining of material forces into its own corporeity, it uses the ethereal force for that end alone, and never organizes its combinations in any capacity for conscious activity. In its original want, it has no such typical end as attaining sentiency, or conscious agency. Hence, when it has exhausted itself in assimilations and reproductions, its organism dissolves, and the life-want departs from it. The continued organism was the individual plant, or tree, during its continuance; and when the organism is gone, the individual is lost forever. The plant so lives, and in dissolving dies; and that plant has no reviving. The life-want, separate from the old organism in the propagation of a new plant by sex-generation, goes on in its new organism as a new individual; but when the organism itself dissolves, the life-want has no individual manifestation. Its history ceases with the organism it constructs; and such history is only for another, for it never finds nor leaves any conscious experience. We can say nothing of the life-want, independently of its working in the end of an individual body, and thus plant-death is individual plant-dissolution.

3. In the Animal Kingdom there is Sentient Consciousness, and thus a Death of Sensation. — The assimilating agency, building and perpetuating the

animal organism, is as purely instinctive as that which builds up the plant; the conscious sensation comes after the organizing instinct has done its work. But that instinct has originally an end in its construction, beyond that which builds the plant. It works for an organism, in which it may come to itself in conscious recognition. It adds to its organization a fixed centralization, and thus makes occasion for complete circulation about and through the fixed points where its agency may come in upon itself. Its peculiarity is an organism of nervous irritability, with its ganglionic centres, and outlying afferent and efferent filamentary communications. The incoming report from the exterior to the ganglion gives opportunity for reaction in sensation, and this again is occasion for an answer to the same in some conscious form of execution. The central ganglion has a point of reciprocity, where action to and action from may have mutual meeting, and come into communion, and so be felt by the one irritable life-organ. And when this nervous organism is complicated with many ganglia, and all these nerve-centres have their co-ordinating sensorium, and in this a prime ganglion of all ganglia, we have animal life, competent to feel its own agency, and direct that agency again from its own feeling.

But this nerve organism is the necessary condition for sentient activity. Only through it is there a conscious appetite, and a conscious executive in its gratification; and when the nervous organism dissolves, and ganglionic centres and co-ordinating sensorium all fall in pieces, the sentient life dies in the same stroke which dashes down the system with its ministering members. The living instinct not only ceases working in assimilating and incorporating, as in the death of a plant, but much more; the whole work of recognized self-feeling, and active self-gratifying, dies in the same organic dissolution. Just as in the plant the individual is lost in death, so here, both instinctive life and sentient consciousness together go out, and the conscious sentient individual is no more.

4. HUMAN DEATH LEAVES THE SPIRIT STILL IMMORTAL. — Man does not live, nor can man die, as does the brute. To him the identity and individuality are retained in and through death. He has an outer body of flesh, like the animal, in which sense and sex distinctions and natural affections have their source; and this may be dissolved and pass away like the brute body, when it has subserved its designed end. But this body of "the earth, earthy (*choikos*),"[1] has its substantial base of material forces, which the claims of the spiritual in man will not permit shall at any time be dissolved. The ethereal life-instinct has assimilated matter to itself by infusing its own vital energies, and made the matter to be living and sentient nature, just as the animal body; but this ethereal-instinct and sentient-consciousness has the still higher endowment of rationality in man, making

[1] 1 Cor. xv. 47.

him to be free personality, and responsible for the character of the disposition he forms; and this will not allow the substantial basis of his sentient nature to pass away. The interest of the spirit must hold the sentient soul in immortality, and that must hold a material body together for itself in perpetual unity. And this has been abundantly confirmed in the revelation God has given, and the meaning which the reason reads in the written word.

The divine inspiration sending life into the nostrils of the first man sent, moreover, a rational spirit in the Maker's image along with it. The living soul which man thus became was other than the sentient nature of the brute. The sense became imbued with spirit, and while the spirit's own abode was in its retained ethereal forces, it also infused its agency through the animal sense, making this to be persistent human soul, the tabernacle for which was the substantial material forces that was the basis of the animal body. There is thus the occasion for comprehending the Scripture analysis of man's whole being. The ethereal forces held as the pure temple of the spirit, constitute Paul's *pneumatikon*, translated "spiritual body;"[1] and the working of the spirit through the sentient soul, and holding permanently about the soul the material basis of the animal structure, constitutes Paul's *psuchikon*, translated less discriminatingly, in the same text, "natural body." The first is the body of the *pneuma;* the second is the body of the *psuche;*

[1] 1 Cor. xv. 44.

and then over and beside this is the *choikos*, as the "earthy,"[1] and which is the mere animal nature that perishes. The *pneumatikon* is the inner penetralium of ethereal forces which the spirit directly controls and uses; the *psuchikon* is the permanently held material forces which the sentient soul occupies, and on which the changing elements of the bodily members gather and dissolve, and so linked by the spirit, the soul and soul-body are made co-existent and immortal with the spirit and the spirit-body.

But this soul and spirit, *psuche* and *pneuma*, each of which the man has, but neither of which the brute has, and which during probation have been in living connection, are now in the closing of probation to be sundered; and in this separation of soul and spirit beyond the dissolving of the animal body, is the peculiarity of human death. "The word of God," through the probationary period, has been "as a sharp two-edged sword" in its living truth, discriminating accurately between appetites and obligations, utilities and duties, gratifications of sense and approbations of conscience, and has thus intellectually "divided asunder the soul and spirit;"[2] but now, that which has been intelligibly so clearly distinguished is to become an actual dissevering, and by the stroke of death, soul and spirit are literally to be divided, and their long intimate union violently parted. There is to be all the going out of life from the animal body, and the dissolution of its elements, as with the perish-

[1] 1 Cor. xv. 47.

[2] Heb. iv. 12.

ing beast; and so the *choikos*, as earthy body of flesh, and blood, and bones, will decompose, and such sense-want and animal appetite as have been subservient to nourishment, and organic growth, and reproduction, and sympathizing interaction, pass away in the elementary disintegration; but the soul and soul-body as the basis on which the mere sentient animality has temporarily rested will survive, and not the dissolutions of the animal, but the sunderings of the psychical and the spiritual will be that which gives to human death its pang, and both to soul and spirit their dread and dismay in the terrible execution of the primeval curse for sensual depravity. The soul and the soul-body go their way together, and the spirit and the spiritual body go their way to God who gave the spirit to the ethereal living forces. The real death for man is in the parting of soul and spirit, while both are separately perpetuated.

SECTION II.

THE INTERMEDIATE STATE.

The individuality of existence in both the vegetable and animal kingdoms is in the persistence of the life instinct in holding the organism in combination. The dissolution of the organism is the final loss of the individual. The individuality of man is in the perpetuity of the rational spirit to hold the ethereal living forces together as its spiritual body, and at the same time to hold the sentient life perpetual in the assimilated material forces as the psychical body. So long and so far as the spiritual and psychical bodies stand in union, there is complete individuality; but at death this union is interrupted, and in so far there is an interference with the human individuality. Inasmuch as the separation at death is repugnant to both soul and spirit, and reluctantly endured, it awakens the rational anticipation that the separation is not final and forever. The reason of the case opens a view in which is the requisition for a reunion that shall be permanent. The speculative inquiry, then, at once arises respecting the condition of man after death, and preceding this future reunion of soul and spirit. Here is an intermediate state for man: what is that state? and the experience of the man in it?

Revelation gives short but expressive hints in reference to such experience, while it is full and explicit that man is to pass such an intermediate state of existence. These revealed facts must guide the speculation, but they determine directly nothing of locality, and little of personal agency and experience; and yet, what is said involves much that a careful insight may clearly gain relatively to individual communion with God and other spirits, and in the future of inner personal consciousness. The Scripture notices not merely consist with, but quite fully confirm, the speculative attainments hitherto made, since these declarations cannot apply but to such peculiar modes of being.

1. The Conscious Individuality after Death.—The animal body of flesh and blood dissolves at death, and were there nothing in man but his sentient consciousness, his individuality would be as the brute which perisheth. But the hold of the spiritual upon the sensual has immortalized it, and the substantial forces in which it abides. There is no longer occasion for mastication and digestion, heart pulsation and circulation, respiration, reproduction, and recuperation of wasted forces; all organs designed for such functions in the probationary state dissolve, and their material forces are no longer retained in the individuality. But the basis of all sentient life and consciousness in the substantial material forces on which the fleshly organism has rested, still remains undecomposed and perfect. In these essential forces of the material body abide the undying life and sentiency of the individual, and all the record of his previous sense-history and experience is left indelible within and upon them. The spirit has so imbued the sense with rationality and responsibility, that it cannot be allowed to fade away, nor its essential material organism to fall in pieces. So much of the spirit inheres in the sentient soul and the psychical body, that it individualizes and immortalizes them, and they cannot dissolve as the flesh falls back to dust. There is a

spiritual interest in them, and a future demand for them, which must keep them entire in their identity. And yet in their separation from the spiritual, they are not so held in it as to partake of its personality. The sentient soul in its indissoluble body is separated from the personal reason in its spiritual body, and were it active in a conscious experience, it could be only for sense-gratifications, and using its material body so far as it might for sentient happiness. Such activity would have no rational importance, and its life may be left where revelation leaves it, safely abiding the coming morn when reason shall call loudly for it. Subject as it is to all the mundane forces, they cannot hurt, but only keep it in the world where it had acted till the spirit departed from it.

But the spirit, separate in death from the soul and its psychical body, has its body of living light, and in it is a free citizen of the ethereal universe. It is purely personal, and its own disposing, accordingly as formed in probation, governs the spiritual body in which separately it now abides. It uses the living light of its own body in working on and through the light about it at its pleasure. It changes the equilibrations of diremption in its own forces to any measures of excess on any side, and so has locomotion in the ethereal universe at will, in any direction, and with any measure of velocity. The inner reason is identical in the same forces, and so individualizes them in perpetually holding them in one; and such spiritual individual is the identical personality, once linked to and working in and through its own soul-body in its state of probation, but which at death it left behind in the terrestrial sphere where the trial together had been made, now traversing the universe through any field of light it pleases. Its personal individuality is in and with the spiritual body, but it has its rational interest in and claims upon the sentient soul in the soul-body, and recognizes that this soul is, and is alone, for it, and not another.

2. THE SPIRIT-WORLD. — The material worlds move in their places in their respective systems, and each must have for its own inhabitants the periods of time measured from its own revolutions; but the spiritual body is held by no single world, and is not to be conceived as limited within any definite locality. To it there are no material nor spacial restrictions. The universal ethereal sphere is open to the spirit in its spiritual body. The light is everywhere diffused, and wherever a spirit in its ethereal body may be, the universe is in panorama about him. The ages from all particular worlds, as standing in their particular histories, may be estimated by him, and disregarding all special times of particular worlds, the absolute universal time, as determined by the moving of all systems about the universal centre, is the ultimate measure to which he must subject all partial particular periods. Every spirit, good and bad, is let out in full freedom into the common ethereal universe. The

material worlds are held in their places in the peripheral portion of the universal sphere, while the interior region is pure ether surrounding the central creating and managing source of all. The spiritual body is susceptible to all ethereal action, and its communications for conscious recognition are from all quarters and through all light-vibrations. What we have learned of the universe, from the work of Creator and Creation, opens at once to our comprehension the outer freedom and expanse of spiritual existences.

3. All Restriction is from Personal Disposition. — Spiritual life is essentially free life. The universe is open to it. But each man has his controlling disposition, fixed in the period of his probation, and his very freedom determines his communions and exclusions. There are no outer bars, and only inner likes and dislikes. If reason's end has been taken as the guide of all action, then nothing hinders in all that reason approves. If self-indulgence has been taken as end of life, then has the spirit lost its rationality and become unreason, and shut itself off from all rational interests. The person knows his own disposing, and the spiritual body is no disguise to another's discerning, and thus every man's disposition limits for him his moving and his resting. Reason's rule is reason's right, and the righteous will be where the approbation of conscience determines. Self-gratification rejects all right, and thus subjects its own spirit to perpetual disapprobation. This fixes

the separating gulf between the good and bad, and shuts off all annoyances from the one side and all alleviations from the other. The righteous can make no ministrations to the wicked, and the wicked can give no disturbances to the righteous. They have all passed into the one invisible state, from mortals, known as Hades; yet such invisible world to mortals has no local restrictions, but the more effectual moral separations.

4. There is no Opportunity for Purgatorial Experiences. — So far as all moral change in purification of spirit from selfish purposes is concerned, the one influence of Christ's redemption by the Spirit's application gives all that can be effectual, and that belonged to the probationary state which has now gone by. And so far as withdrawing from the influences of carnal appetites is concerned, the dissolution by death has made a complete purgation, and the earthy body of flesh and bone has been wholly left behind. The disposition acquired and retained fixes the character, and no experiences in the intermediate state change that, nor can any discipline there cleanse the spirit from its impurities. "He who is holy will be holy still, and he who is filthy will be filthy still." Nothing can here be done to the spirit or the spiritual body to cleanse from any pollution; the moral stains are all from the spirit's own agency, and the fountain of its activity in the permanent disposition remains after death entirely the same.

5. The Spirit at Death goes to its Final Home.—The intermediate state changes for a permanent state only in the mode of existence by the reunion with the soul, but the home is unchanged. The dying thief went at once to "paradise," and paradise is the "third heaven."[1] Stephen expected to go, at death, to heaven as he saw it open.[2] Jesus Christ is in heaven, but saints at death go where Christ is.[3] And saints come with Christ at the judgment.[4] And so also in John's prophetic vision.[5] And if thus the saints at death go at once to heaven, the wicked also, like Judas, go to their "own place." It is not a sound conclusion, that somewhere there is a place of two apartments for the dead, which will be emptied at the resurrection; but the open universe receives all spiritual bodies, and then takes back again the same when the sentient soul is reunited to its own personality.

[1] Luke xxiii. 43. Confer 2 Cor. xii. 2–4.
[2] Acts vii. 55–59.
[3] 2 Cor. v. 8; Phil. i. 23.
[4] 1 Thess. iv. 14.
[5] Rev. vii. 13–17.

SECTION III.

THE RESURRECTION.

THE New Testament Scriptures have two words expressive of the resurrection; one *an arousing*, as if from sleep, and the other *a standing up again*, as if from a reclining posture; the latter being the more frequent. The doctrine means more than restored consciousness to the soul, and implies the return of the spirit to the body. The full import of the Christian doctrine of the resurrection is, *a raising of the bodies of the dead, and a reunion of each with its own spirit.*

1. THIS IS INDICATED IN THE ANALOGIES OF NATURE. — In the vegetable kingdom, the vital energy has its first exhibition in the seed, but it attains its full maturity only through dissolution. "The blade, then the ear, afterwards the full corn in the ear," all come after the old seed has passed away in its corruption. This analogy to human change from the mortal to the immortal was early observed. In reference to his own death Jesus Christ said, "Except a corn of wheat fall into the ground and die, it abideth alone; but if

it die, it bringeth forth much fruit."[1] And so the apostle Paul: "That which thou sowest is not quickened except it die."[2] There is ever the passing through this form of death by the seed, in its development to the new and complete plant; and the analogy not merely illustrates, but fairly indicates, the resurrection of the human body, which "is sown in corruption, and raised in incorruption." Human death is not annihilation; something of the old passes over from the former state, and stands out again in a new and more perfect state of maturity, and the two are identified in one individuality. If revelation had not used the analogy, there would have been the indication of man's resurrection in the germinating plant from the dying seed; and this Scripture use was because the index was already there.

And so, in some forms of animal transformation to a state of fuller development, we have equally striking indications of man's change in his coming resurrection. The worm passes into its chrysalis form, and lies in torpor, out of which it emerges and lives again in vastly augmented beauty, and with capacities for a new experience, into which it could not before enter. Aside from revelation, the thinking mind from such suggestions could scarcely help rising to a belief in his own resurrection to a wider sphere of life and activity.

[1] John xii. 24. [2] 1 Cor. xv. 36.

2. Man's Instinctive Anticipations give Premonition of his Resurrection. — The human spirit not merely forecasts its own immortality, but it instinctively assumes that the body it inhabits will again be its abode. No man can well put off the conviction that his body is more to him than common dust, and that his interest in it must be perpetual and enduring. Hence the respect in all ages for funereal rites, and reverential regard for places of human sepulture. Even savage tribes carefully bury their dead, adorning the body, and accompanying it with what may minister to its uses in its future blessed abode. Ancient people costly embalmed the dead body, to preserve its form, and others purified it by fire, and carefully collected in precious urns the indestructible ashes. Such instinctive prompting foretokens the coming event; and the prophecy uttered in nature carries in it the assurance of future fulfilment. *Vitulus percutit fronte inermis* — and the butting calf is sure to have the future horns. Divine precepts regulate the human premonitions, but they neither repress the instinct nor forbid its working. God manifestly meant that man should regard these inward teachings.

3. Reason establishes a Claim to the Reunion of Body and Spirit. — Essentially, humanity is sense and spirit. In this complexity it has been tried and fallen; and as sense and spirit, the human has had redemption, and been put upon its second probation. Under the gospel, a spiritual disposition has been

made, and the character formed, either in the subjection of sense or the enslaving of spirit. In no other manner than by the conflict of the spirit with the flesh, could confirmed virtue and permanent integrity of personal character be attained; and the issue in such trial must be fairly joined, and the result must be freely settled by the self-originated act of the individual. When the first pair fell, they thereby settled what would come for the race. And when a gracious redemption opened a new probation, the issue must again be individually joined and freely settled by a renewed disposition to subject the sense under the influence of the Holy Ghost, or by a persistence in carnal servitude in spite of the strivings of the Holy Ghost; and which way soever the trial has eventuated, the sentient body and the spiritual personality have been both involved, and as participating in the probation, they should also participate in the retribution. The appropriate awards cannot be made, but as the complex humanity still exists in readiness to take the gracious blessing or the deserved punishment. The same body must be present with the spirit it once held, or that which in reason ought to be, in executed fact still cannot be. No possible alternative can thus rationally be interposed to the fulfilment of the coming universal summons, "Arise, ye dead, and come to judgment."

4. The Authority of Revelation is here ultimately conclusive. — The Old Testament is less ex-

plicit than the New in its declarations of a resurrection; yet may the teachings of it be satisfactorily found from several passages. God seems to have revealed it in similar language to both Moses and Samuel: "I kill and I make alive."[1] "The Lord killeth and maketh alive; he bringeth down to the grave, and raiseth up."[2] Job speaks doubtingly, yet a prevailing faith in his coming resurrection is manifest. "Man dieth and wasteth away; yea, man giveth up the ghost, and where is he? Man lieth down, and riseth not; till the heavens be no more, they shall not awake, nor be raised out of their sleep." Yet in the end he expects his awaking. "Thou shalt call, and I will answer thee; thou wilt have a desire to the work of thine hands."[3] David also was assured of his own resurrection in the foreseen resurrection of the crucified Messiah. "My flesh shall rest in hope. For thou wilt not leave my soul in hell; neither wilt thou suffer thine Holy One to see corruption."[4] Daniel foretells that "many of them that sleep in the dust of the earth shall awake, some to everlasting life, and some to shame and everlasting contempt."[5] And Hosea represents the Lord God as saying, "I will ransom them from the power of the grave; I will redeem them from death; O death, I will be thy plagues; O grave, I will be thy destruction."[6] But all this is made more clear by what the New Testament affirms Old Testament people believed. "They desired a

[1] Deut. xxxii. 39. [2] 1 Sam. ii. 6. [3] Job xiv. 10, 12, 15.
[4] Ps. xvi. 9, 10. [5] Dan. xii. 2. [6] Hosea xiii. 14.

better country, that is, a heavenly;" and "Abraham believed that God was able to raise up, even from the dead."[1] And Paul says of his persecuting Jewish brethren, "that they themselves also allow that there shall be a resurrection of the dead, both of the just and unjust."[2] And Martha knew her brother Lazarus "shall rise again in the resurrection at the last day."[3]

The New Testament abounds in direct declarations of the resurrection of the body, and in full measure "brings life and immortality clearly to light:" a few only of the many are here cited. Jesus Christ affirms of both good and evil, "The hour is coming in which all that are in their graves shall hear his voice, and shall come forth; they that have done good unto the resurrection of life, and they that have done evil unto the resurrection of damnation."[4] Of Christians Paul says, "If the spirit of him that raised up Jesus from the dead dwell in you, he that raised up Christ from the dead shall also quicken your mortal bodies by his spirit that dwelleth in you."[5] John, in the Revelation, "saw the dead, small and great, stand before God. And the sea gave up the dead which were in it, and death and hell delivered up the dead which were in them."[6]

As Jesus Christ is mediatorial king, so, as is fit, he is the direct agent in calling all the dead from their sleep. "I am the resurrection and the life; he that believeth in me, though he were dead, yet shall he

[1] Heb. xi. 16-19. [2] Acts xxiv. 15. [3] John xi. 24.
[4] John v. 28, 29. [5] Rom. viii. 11. [6] Rev. xx. 12, 13.

live."[1] "I am he that liveth, and was dead; and behold, I am alive for evermore, amen; and have the keys of hell and of death."[2] It is not to be correctly understood that the resurrections of the righteous and of the wicked are at separate periods. John saw "the souls" of the martyrs "beheaded for the witness of Jesus," who "lived and reigned with Christ a thousand years," and which was called "the first resurrection;"[3] but this means that the spirit of the martyrs lives in the millennium, as Elijah's spirit and power lived in John Baptist, and not that their bodies had been seen to be made alive. The universal representation of the resurrection otherwise is, that it is one and the same event for the world of all the dead.

5. There will be a Special Change in the Resurrection Body. — The living at the time of the resurrection are not to "prevent," i. e., go to Christ before, "them which are asleep." "For the Lord himself shall descend from heaven with a shout, with the voice of the archangel, and with the trump of God; and the dead in Christ shall rise first. Then we which are alive and remain shall be caught up together with them in the clouds, to meet the Lord in the air; and so shall we be ever with the Lord."[4] And to the same purport is the apostle's explanation of the "mystery," that "we shall not all sleep, but we shall all be changed. In a moment, in the twinkling

[1] John xi. 25. [2] Rev. i. 18. [3] Rev. xx. 5.
[4] 1 Thess. iv. 15-17.

of an eye, at the last trump, the dead shall be raised incorruptible, and we shall be changed. For this corruption must put on incorruption, and this mortal must put on immortality."[1] The manifest order of events, in the one transaction of transferring the dead and living to their spiritual state, is, the descent of Christ, the sound of the trump, the awaking of the dead, the instant change of the living to be like that of the raised dead; and so, in arrangement and result, the whole human family are made ready for the judgment.

In what this change consists, the Scripture recognizes in distinct summary declarations. The dissoluble elements which are combined in the flesh and frame of the body fall away at the resurrection, since "flesh and blood cannot inherit the kingdom of God,"[2] nor has a spirit "flesh and bones."[3] So the organic arrangements for digestion and assimilation are left behind; for while "belly and meats" are for each other here, both are then to be "destroyed."[4] Sex-distinctions and relations then pass away, "for when they shall rise from the dead, they neither marry nor are given in marriage, but are as the angels which are in heaven."[5] "The corruptible puts on incorruption," and the natural body sown is raised a spiritual body,[6] and yet the spiritual body retains still its hold on the sentient soul, and as that was at death, so its moral state continues after the resurrection, since,

[1] 1 Cor. xv. 51-53. [2] 1 Cor. xv. 50. [3] Luke xxiv. 39.
[4] 1 Cor. vi. 13. [5] Mark xii. 25. [6] 1 Cor. xv. 42-44.

when that time is at hand, "He that is unjust is still unjust, he that is filthy is still filthy, as truly as he that is righteous still remains righteous."[1] And so the man has either the "fleshly mind" or the "spiritual mind" controlling all his eternal experience.

The reason of the case also determines that organic functions, now needed and there needless, will be accordingly dispensed with. On earth, the growth and restoration of the body require many extensive material arrangements. A great proportion of the body consists of that which ministers to the nourishing and perpetuating the body. The entire physiology of mastication, digestion, respiration, circulation, secretion, assimilation, and excretion, relates to the supply of new, and the elimination of used-up material. All the members for locomotion, manual ministration, and organs of sense-perception, are adaptations to an earthly state of being, and can have no relevancy to the abode of the resurrection-body. All media of sex-generation, and reproduction, and alimentary sustentation for infantile life, belong to the world of human probation, and have ceased forever this side of the world for human retribution. All these are the corruptible "flesh and blood," which will have been dissolved and put off when we come to "put on incorruption." They are organic combinations of assimilated elements, which have rested on the essential sub-forces of the body in this mortal state; but they utterly fall away when "this mortal puts on immortality." These sub-forces of the body have in them

[1] Rev. xxii. 11.

the essential sentiency which came out in the organic nerve-irritability, but in the spirit-world are open to impressions from only spiritual adaptations.

The first great change is in the material body, from what, as given by the apostle Paul, is "the earthy" to the purely psychical body. The *psuchikon* puts off all earthy organic elements, which had been superimposed upon it for the ends of its temporal state, and retains only the essential material forces, which have been the permanently balanced basis of the entire bodily organism. The pure psychical body is the sentient soul's tabernacle, when all the ministering members meant only for this life have been dissolved and passed away, leaving these fundamentally combined forces indissoluble and indestructible, with all the soul's sentient capacity abiding in the fixed body. And this change is thoroughly completed in the reunion with it of the *pneumatikon*, or spiritual body, which had departed from it. The rational spiritual energy goes through and combines both the material and ethereal, making the whole resurrection-body to be one, and henceforth under the control of the one spirit, according to its determined disposition. Here is, thus, the same sentient soul, the same rational spirit, and the perduring substance of the same living material and ethereal body; making the identical and individual personality which dwelt on earth, and formed his disposition in time, now fitted to take the retributions of eternity. The past is in memory, the present disposition is in full consciousness, and the accountable being now stands awaiting the coming issues of the Final Judgment.

6. THE RESURRECTION AS PRESENTED BY THE APOSTLE PAUL. — Prophets, apostles, evangelists, and the Lord Jesus speak of the resurrection of the body as a certainty, but with little particularity in detail, while the circumstances of Paul's ministry lead him to be earnest and minutely exact in enforcing and teaching the doctrine quite beyond any other inspired writer. The incarnation of the Lord and the resurrection of the dead body were specially obnoxious to such philosophers as restricted all knowledge within experience. The whole *cultus* and control of life was by two eminent Grecian sects of philosophers of that day derived wholly from nature; either, on one side, seeking all practicable pleasure, or, on the other side, indifferent to either pleasure or pain, since nature would surely send both; and Paul's missionary life and experience in Grecian cities necessarily brought him often in conflict with these objectors to such spiritual truths. When he went to Athens and preached in the market, these new doctrines at once provoked opposition. "Certain philosophers of the Epicureans and Stoics encountered him. And some said, What will this babbler say? and others, He seemeth to be a setter forth of strange gods, because he preached unto them Jesus and the Resurrection;" and they took him to the Areopagus for further discussion.[1]

[1] Acts xvii. 18, 19.

Timothy was sent by the apostle to labor, and set in order churches, among the same class of cavillers and disputers; and in the last part of his First Epistle to Timothy, Paul very strenuously charges him, "O Timothy, keep that which is committed to thy trust, avoiding profane and vain babblings, and oppositions of science falsely so called, which some professing have erred concerning the faith."[1] And the repetition of the charge in the Second Epistle, with similar but more pointed and explicit terms, explains fully that this urgency to maintain his commission means, that he strenuously uphold the Christian doctrine of the resurrection. "Shun profane and vain babblings, for they will increase to more ungodliness. And their word will eat as doth a canker; of whom is Hymeneus and Philetus, who concerning the truth have erred, saying the resurrection is past already, and overthrow the faith of some."[2] The "oppositions," or intrinsic contradictions, which such sciolists might readily urge, as making the raising of the same body an absurdity from its perpetual changes, wide dispersion of particles, and perhaps participation in the construction of other bodies, would naturally lead to the profane and vain babblings, which were to be avoided; but the true and important doctrine must be held as standing on "the sure foundation of God"

This disputation, among false scientists, and scepticism even among professed disciples, induced Paul not

[1] 1 Tim. vi. 20, 21. [2] 2 Tim. ii. 16–18.

only to enforce the doctrine by apostolic authority, but more largely and philosophically to expound its meaning and consistency to the intelligent apprehension of his converts. The church of Corinth was in the midst of these pretentious, empirical logicians, and one long chapter of the First Epistle to this church[1] is wholly devoted to the defence and exposition of this doctrine of the resurrection, basing it upon the truth of Christ's resurrection, and then meeting empirical objections by higher spiritual instruction. When they incredulously and contemptuously inquire, "How are the dead raised up? and with what body do they come?" Paul in effect answers, "Get a little wiser, and your logic will be clearer." Even the wheat-seed dies and comes up again in a new body of its own; and every seed has its own body, which it renews by dying. God gives different terrestrial and celestial bodies to be of different grades of glory as it has pleased him, and to man he has given a natural body and a spiritual body; the natural body is sown in death, and comes up a spiritual body in the resurrection. "So when this corruptible shall have put on incorruption, and this mortal shall have put on immortality," the doctrine will have its highest vindication, for "then shall death be swallowed up in victory."

And another most difficult portion of Scripture,[2] finds in its application to this Pauline view of the saints' resurrection its only clear exposition. We give our commentary in a very general paraphrase.

[1] 1 Cor. xv. [2] Rom. viii. 18-23.

— The sentient part of humanity is for the present continually suffering, but it is truly of no account when compared with the coming glory. For this "creature," as sentient soul, waits in expectation "for the manifestation of the sons of God." For the sentient soul was made subject to "vanity," or emptiness, poverty, misery, not of choice, but of God's appointment for discipline and trial, by which the "hope" opens for deliverance from this "bondage of corruption" to "the glorious liberty" of Christian sonship. For we know that the animal creation, and as subject to the primeval curse "the whole creation," groans and travails in pain up to this time. Yea, even we children of God, who have tasted "the first fruits of the Spirit," even we groan inwardly, waiting our inheritance in the final resurrection and "redemption of our body." — This is Paul's estimate of this great doctrine. All suffering and subservient nature is waiting with earnest longings for it, and all redeemed saints are in hasting "expectation" of it. To them creation shall no longer be a mere sense-show, but known and used in its essential reality; all sense-infirmity, weariness, sickness and pain, will have forever passed away, and both sentient soul and material body become spiritualized in a blessed immortality.

7. Revealed Resurrections and Translations. — The Scriptures notice a number of cases of persons raised from the dead, and also of some translated to the world of spirits without dying, and it is desirable

to note what bearing these instances may have upon the doctrine of the general resurrection.

The prominent cases of raising from the dead are Elijah recalling the spirit in the case of the widow of Sarepta's son;[1] Elisha restoring to life the Shunamite's son;[2] Jesus raising the widow's son,[3] the nobleman's son,[4] the synagogue ruler's daughter,[5] Lazarus;[6] and Peter's raising Dorcas.[7] These cases were strong manifestations of God's power and benevolence, and bore testimony to the divine mission and authority of those who wrought the miracles, as in other cases of supernatural signs and wonders; but they have no special import in confirmation directly, nor as affording any illustration of the Resurrection at the last day. The old bodies of flesh and blood were reanimated, and the persons restored to natural life, and were again to pass through death, as before.

Then we have the translation of Enoch,[8] and of Elijah;[9] and because Moses died alone with God on Nebo,[10] and appeared in glory with Elias on the mount of transfiguration,[11] it has sometimes been taken that he was removed to heaven, though the record is, that the Lord "buried him," but no one knoweth of his sepulchre. Such cases of translation without dying have this bearing upon the doctrine of the bodily resurrection, that their bodies were transferred to the eternal state, as those of the raised dead at the

[1] 1 Kings xvii. 21, 22. [2] 2 Kings iv. 34, 35. [3] Luke vii. 11-15.
[4] John iv. 46-53. [5] Luke viii. 49-56. [6] John xi. 43, 44.
[7] Acts ix. 40. [8] Gen. v. 24; Heb. xi. 5.
[9] 2 Kings ii. 11. [10] Deut. xxxiv. 5, 6. [11] Matt. xvii. 3.

last day will be; though the comparison must rather be with the quick and great change the living will undergo when the universal dead are raised. Corruptible flesh and blood fall away, and only the substantial forces of the material body rise with the spirit in permanent union.

The earthquake, at Jesus' dying hour on the cross, broke open the sepulchres of some of the recent dead in the neighborhood, and at Jesus' resurrection "many bodies of the saints which slept arose, and came out of their graves, and went into the holy city, and appeared unto many."[1] Here seems a full presage of the general resurrection, and as it were the first fruits of Christ's awaking from the dead. They went into Jerusalem and were known to their old acquaintances; but no more is said of them. The probability is, they ascended to glory, as the raised saints will at the final resurrection. The indication is quite strong that a raised body for the state of glory, with its corruptible portion removed, will still possess permanent material forces that will present the old bodily likeness, though entirely at the unresisting control of the indwelling spirit; and the same may also be gathered from the glorified forms on the mount of transfiguration.[2]

Jesus' resurrection would seem to have partaken of both a reanimation of flesh and blood, and a permanent reunion of soul and spirit. His resurrection was to be established before the living, and must not

[1] Matt. xxvii. 50–53. [2] Luke ix. 28–36.

only be visible, but tangible and audibly communicative. "His flesh saw not corruption," and the entire body lived again, and was touched and handled; it spoke, walked, and ate; and as he said, "A spirit hath not flesh and bones, as ye see me have." His body, like Lazarus' body, could be fully identified by the living, and for the forty days after his resurrection he would seem to have been as fully in the flesh as before his crucifixion. But that body was not to die again. The human spirit was reunited, no more to be dissolved; and when the ascension hour arrived, and the body went up from the mount at Bethany, it was changed in the cloud that received him from the corruptible .and mortal to the incorruptible and immortal, and which is to have a second coming in like manner as this first ascending. His human body went to the right hand of power, a truly spiritual body as the glorified saints shall be.

SECTION IV.

THE FINAL JUDGMENT.

REDEEMED Humanity, as now viewed, has finished its second probation in mortal flesh, and raised to an immortal reunion of soul and spirit in a spiritual body, awaits the final Judgment. The fall of man was connected with the sin of angels, and all moral beings have an interest in the divine manifestations made in the work of redemption; the intelligent universe must be intensely attentive to the disclosures and issues of the last mediatorial official function.

1. The Design of the Final Judgment. — The intermediate state has occasioned experiences which have given full disclosures of character and condition; and all the living, in their entire change to the spiritual body, have come into full consciousness of the disposition they have settled each for himself; the last judgment is not, therefore, needed nor designed for making any new discriminations of state and affection of heart towards truth and God. But in the wide administration of the divine government, many inscrutable measures have been taken for fulfilling eternal purposes, and measures of justice and judgment, patience and favor, have been so often mysteriously mingled, that it has been impossible for finite spirits to comprehend the equity of many transactions; and the great interposition of God in human flesh, making redemption for a lost race, and requiring many sovereign interpositions of providence and interferences of divine influence, which the consummation of God's design can alone clear up; all must now be reconciled with reason, and stand out clear in conformity with righteousness and truth. Both for the sovereign's and subject's sake, such final and universal vindication of sovereign authority in its dispensation of judgment and grace is important.

The new basis laid for human probation, the entire system of doctrine and evangelical ordinances, and all the mediatorial administration, must be made convincingly correct and just to every conscience. God will be justified when he speaks, and clear when he judges; every mouth stopped, and all cavilling dissent shown to be guilty before God.

2. The Evidences of the Final Judgment. — The aspirations of quickened and ardent piety "look forward and hasten to the coming of the day of God;"[1] and burdened with indwelling and surrounding sin, exposed to detraction and persecution, the longing soul cries, "Even so come, Lord Jesus," quickly.[2] On the other hand, the guilty have dread forebodings of its coming. Felix trembled at Paul's preaching of the judgment to come,[3] and the devils anticipate their time of torment.[4] These inward premonitions are sure foretokens that the day is coming. The reason of the case calls for such vindication and deliverance of the good, and such destructive rejection of the bad; but beyond all, the direct revelation of God has kept the fact perpetually before the world. David says, "The Lord shall judge the people;" and prays, "O, let the wickedness of the wicked come to an end; but establish the just; for the righteous God trieth the heart and the reins."[5] Solomon warns the thoughtless youth of the judgment,[6]

[1] 2 Peter iii. 12. [2] Rev. xxii. 20. [3] Acts xxiv. 25.
[4] Matt. viii. 29. [5] Ps. vii. 8, 9. [6] Eccl. xi. 9.

and urges on all to keep God's commandments: "For God shall bring every work into judgment, with every secret thing, whether it be good, or whether it be evil."[1] And Daniel had it fully announced that all things should be fairly redressed in the end.[2]

The New Testament is much more particular. "When the Son of Man shall come in his glory, and all the holy angels with him, then shall he sit upon the throne of his glory. And before him shall be gathered all nations; and he shall separate them one from the other, as a shepherd divideth his sheep from the goats; and he shall set the sheep on his right hand, but the goats on the left."[3] "For we must all appear before the judgment seat of Christ, that every one may receive the things done in his body, whether it be good or bad."[4]

3. THE DAY WILL COME SUDDENLY AND UNEXPECTEDLY. —There are considerations by which we know the world is not yet ready for the judgment. The gospel is to be "first preached to all the world,"[5] and the man of sin is to be fully exposed, before the judgment.[6] But if not now ready, when these events shall have passed, it will still be left uncertain when the Judge shall come. Before the destruction of Jerusalem, it was foretold that portentous precursors should be given; and the manifestly double representation

[1] Eccl. xii. 14. [2] Dan. xii. 2-13. [3] Matt. xxv. 31-46.
[4] 2 Cor. v. 10; see also Acts xvii. 31; Rom. xiv. 10.
[5] Matt. xxiv. 14. [6] 2 Thess. ii. 3.

of the destruction of the temple and the end of the world in the prophecy Matt. xxiv. 15 to 33 has induced the opinion that forewarnings of the judgment will also be given. But that generation was not to pass before the signs should be fulfilled.[1] History declares these signs appeared before Jerusalem was destroyed, but the sign preceding the judgment is the appearing of the "Son of Man in heaven," and the sounding trumpet, and the sending the angels to gather the dead together,[2] which only immediately precede the judgment scene. All representations referring to the mode of Christ's second coming make it to be a surprise, from its being unheralded by any indications. "Watch, therefore, for ye know neither the day nor the hour wherein the Son of Man cometh."[3] "But the day of the Lord will come as a thief in the night, in the which the heavens shall pass away with a great noise."[4]

4. THE JUDGE WILL APPEAR IN GREAT MAJESTY.— In this respect the second coming of Christ strongly contrasts with the manner of his first appearance. All manifestations of weakness, poverty, suffering, and degradation have forever passed away, and the exhibitions of great splendor, terrible majesty, and glorious authority are made. All judgment is committed to the Son;[5] and he is "ordained of God to be the judge of quick and dead;"[6] and he comes in fitting honor

[1] Matt. xxiv. 34. [2] Matt. xxiv. 30. [3] Matt. xxv. 13.
[4] 2 Pet. iii. 10; see also 1 Thess. v. 2, 3.
[5] John v. 22 and 27. [6] Acts x. 42.

for such an office. It is in "the glory of his Father with the holy angels;"[1] "in flaming fire, taking vengeance on them that know not God."[2] "Every eye shall see him, and they also which pierced him;"[3] "thousand thousands ministered unto him, and ten thousand times ten thousand stood before him; the judgment was set, and the books were opened."[4]

5. THOSE WHO ARE TO BE JUDGED. — The work of redemption has had special reference to men, and their probation has been justified through the Redeemer's mediation; the judgment day must on this account specially concern humanity. But all intelligences have been spectators of the redeeming work, and are participants, in some form, in its influence; and hence the disclosures made and the convictions secured are to reach all moral beings. "Every knee shall bow, and every tongue confess that Jesus Christ is Lord, to the glory of God the Father." And this not only of "all in heaven and on earth," but "all under the earth;" universally, all intelligences shall, by the judgment disclosures, be made to approve of Christ's work as honorable to God.[5] Holy angels have from the beginning been ministering spirits to men, and to Christ in the days of his flesh; nor could the judgment of men be complete without including that of angels, both elect and fallen. All orders of moral beings — angels, devils, and men — are to be present and

[1] Matt. xvi. 27. [2] 2 Thess. i. 8. [3] Rev. i. 7.
[4] Dan. vii. 9, 10. [5] Phil. ii. 10, 11.

interested participants in the transactions. Good angels come with Christ;[1] fallen angels have been reserved compulsorily for this day;[2] and all the human race are there.[3] The grand end is, a complete and universal vindication of God towards all, and in the presence of all; forever settling the integrity of the government of God as extending over all worlds.

6. ALL SECRETS THEN LAID OPEN. — Isaiah represents God as saying to his people, "I, even I, am he that blotteth out thy transgressions for mine own sake, and will not remember thy sins."[4] On this account, and as if to save from degradation to themselves and dishonor to Christ, it has been surmised that saints shall not have their secret sins disclosed. But the meaning of the text is exhausted, in that God will not remember his people's sins so as to punish; and the grace of Christ to his children cannot appear but in the amount of sins forgiven. The full declaration is, "God shall bring every work into judgment, with every secret thing, whether it be good or whether it be evil."[5] And not only the conduct of the subjects shall be brought to light, but the dealings of God the Sovereign shall have their explanation. The many unaccountable and mysterious providences, wherein God hid his counsels, shall so be fully unfolded that all shall acquiesce and praise. God has

[1] Luke ix. 26. [2] 2 Pet. 2, 4; Jude 6. [3] Rev. xx. 12.
[4] Isa. xliii. 25. [5] Eccl. xii. 14.

beforehand said, "What I do thou knowest not now, but thou shalt know hereafter."[1]

7. FORM AND PROCESS OF THE JUDGMENT. — From the several representations of the judgment we may obtain the following particulars in form and process, after the manner of human judicial proceedings: There will be the throne, or judgment seat, and this occupied by the Lord Jesus Christ as Judge.[2] There will be evidence received, as if from accredited affidavits and recorded depositions in "books," indicating the disclosures of omniscience.[3] "And the dead were judged out of those things which were written in the books according to their works." Judicial decisions and official sentences will be given;[4] and besides the books of testimony, the Judge has kept his record of all the names he justifies in his own "book of life."[5] It was an ancient practice, after trial, to arrange the acquitted and the condemned in opposite ranks, and so at the judgment it is "as a shepherd divideth sheep from goats;"[6] and the respective allotments follow.[7]

These representations, instead of being taken as literal transactions, are rather a mode of expressing full, impartial trial, and righteous decision and execution. All iniquity is uncovered, and every person's

[1] John xiii. 7. [2] Matt. xxv. 31; Rev. xx. 11.
[3] Dan. vii. 10; 1 Cor. iv. 5; Rev. xx. 12.
[4] Matt. xxv. 31 and 41.
[5] Mal. iii. 16; Rev. xx. 12 and 16; Rev. xxi. 27.
[6] Matt. xxv. 32. [7] Matt. xxv. 46.

disposition and character revealed, and all divine dealings with both righteous and wicked through the universe are put full in the light. The disclosure will carry conviction of God's rectitude to every conscience.

8. THE GENERAL CONFLAGRATION OF THE WORLD. — Job speaks of a time when "the heavens shall be no more;"[1] and the Psalmist affirms of the earth and heavens that "they shall perish;"[2] and Isaiah declares "the heavens shall be rolled together as a scroll;"[3] thus indicating that of old it was believed the present order and movement of nature would at one time be subverted; but of the fact and manner the revelations of the New Testament are particularly clear and exact. Christ says, "Heaven and earth shall pass away."[4] And Peter foretells that the heavens shall pass away with a great noise, and the elements shall melt with fervent heat, and the earth and the works that are therein shall be burned up."[5] And John, in the Revelation, saw the judgment throne and him that sat upon it, "from whose face the earth and heavens fled away, and there was found no place for them."[6] This does not mean annihilation, but a making over in a new heavens and a new earth; and as once the world was destroyed by a flood, so at last it is to be renovated by flame. And this appropriately concludes the judgment, which forever disposes of

[1] Job xiv. 12. [2] Ps. cii. 26. [3] Isa. xxxiv. 4.
[4] Luke xxi. 33. [5] 2 Pet. iii. 10. [6] Rev. xx. 11.

sin, and then cleanses by fire the guilty world in which so much sin has been. The groaning creation finds deliverance in "the glorious liberty of the children of God."[1]

SECTION V.

THE ISSUES OF THE JUDGMENT FOR BOTH THE RIGHTEOUS AND THE WICKED.

FROM history and prophecy we have been able to trace the leading interpositions of God in human experience from the creation to the final judgment, and find in the consummation that what the reason of the case required should be, that in God's acts ever has been. Bible eschatology and speculative reason are one and the same, in completely vindicating the equity and integrity of the divine government through the whole process of human probation. But here probationary history ceases, and speculation goes over into the world of retribution; and in this complete overturn from the sensual to the spiritual, it is to be expected that there must be greater obscurity in tracing particular consequential results, in divine interferences with the experience of humanity. The same

[1] Rom. viii. 21, 22.

stream still flows on, but it here passes through such a chasm, and is to emerge from the gulf into so altered a region, that we more hesitatingly say what the future channel from the past current determinately must be. And yet, since in the resurrection humanity is still soul and spirit reunited, and coming retribution is for the disposition and character formed in past probation, reason may see in general what the issues of the judgment should be in the retributive experiences of both the good and the bad. Revelation also sends gleams of light beyond the judgment, and discloses something of the coming occurrences between God and man in this spirit-world.

It may both clear the insight of reason, and strengthen our faith in revelation, if we get in a position to take in both together, and see how completely, in the world of retribution, the revealed dealings of God tally with the determinations of reason. Standing, then, at the closing of the judgment scene, and from an insight of the past attaining a clear contemplation in reason of what humanity then is, we can speculatively there see what the future of humanity must be; and can there, also, read the record of divine revelation, declaring what the future of humanity shall be; and very certainly we shall not find any contradiction between them.

1. All the Dealings of God with Man, preceding the Judgment, have been Reasonable. — Both an æsthetic and an ethic interest prompted to an

outer manifestation of the inward ideal of the universe, and thus the overt creation of the worlds was in the end of Absolute Reason alone; nor could the creation of intelligences be arrested by anything short of the full expression of the complete Idea. However variously other intelligent beings may be constituted, it was reasonable that in some world soul and spirit in union should exist, and give occasion for sense-gratification to be brought under the rule of spirit; and thus it was worthy of God to constitute humanity with the open way to a spiritual disposing in righteousness, and that he should be put upon our earth and have dominion over it. He must be tried in order to be virtuous in a confirmed character, and it was reasonable that man's trial should be made an occasion for the adequate trial also of other intelligent beings; and such mode of trial was all reasonably arranged. The best possible test for man, and in him the best trial for other intelligent spirits, was given, in which the devil sinned, and induced man's fall; and God's disapprobation and pity followed just as in reason it should; and such rational abhorrence of sin, and pity for the tempted sinner, rationally provided the way of Gospel Redemption.

Under the conditions of a promised Deliverer, involving his incarnation and crucifixion and the Spirit's mission, it was reasonable that a new probation should begin, and tnat the human race should multiply and be disciplined for an eternal state; and in this new probation for humanity, God has done at his own self-sacrifice all that reason prompts and permits for restoring the lost and confirming the faithful in loyal allegiance. In all ages some have been reclaimed, and some would not be inclined to reformation; and the judgment day, as we have now contemplated it, comes and brings out to universal conviction God's honor, truth, and righteousness in all that he has done, and all that he has forborne to do. And now, all means of grace, hitherto reasonably applied, are here reasonably arrested. Patience, and inviting, and soliciting, must now stop or be unreasonable. As a righteous moral Ruler, God can allow pity no further scope; for compassion must be reasonable, and it has reached its limit. All could have returned, but many would not; all now can come back of their own accord, but none that have not returned now will; and in this the issue settles itself, just as the free disposing of the human spirit fixes it; and the compassion which bled and died on the cross can do no more, without bringing conscious reproach to God himself. The universe has seen the cup of divine self-sacrifice drained for sinners, till reason is constrained to cry out, "It is finished."

The reclaimed are by the judgment acquitted and saved; but it is of grace in Christ Jesus that they have come back, and been pardoned and justified. The incorrigible are condemned and cast out; but it is for the stubborn hate that did, and does, reject all the blood-bought overtures of reconciliation. Divine pity for the condemned is as deep as ever, but it would be unreasonable that God should act from pity any further, and he satisfies reason in henceforth manifesting exactly rational displeasure towards them. All sinners now stand precisely in the point of just desert before God, and the universe, and in their own consciences; and the Judge is clear in his judging, and just in his condemning. He did reasonably and rightly in creating, trying, redeeming, and again proving mankind; he had that "joy set before him" when "he endured the cross and despised its shame," which he now has in possession when he welcomes "the seed" he saves to his kingdom, and he is "satisfied." He pities now, as he has ever done, the stubbornly self-ruined; but he holds his pity subordinate to his integrity, and in this also he is satisfied. The number of the irrecoverably lost among men and devils may be small, compared with the unsinning in all worlds, and the recovered in this world; and the confirmation of the holy in allegiance may result, from what of God they have seen in his redeeming or punishing such as despised his redemption; and so in his own reasonably doing and using what his creatures have freely but unreasonably done, he stands whole in his honor and glory before the universe, and thoroughly self-consistent and complacent in his own consciousness. He has secured as many converts as in reason he could, and he has done as much and waited as long for the wicked as in reason he might, and he knows that every saved and lost spirit has the full light of his eternal integrity.

2. THE FUTURE WILL EVER PRESENT GOD AS REASONABLE. — The sense-world and the spirit-world widely differ, but in both the same Absolute Reason holds sway; and in this respect God's government in retribution is but a perpetuation of his government with probationers. The "new heavens" and the "new earth" are a renovation from the old, — not that the old have been annihilated. The material and ethereal forces are all conserved, and the recombinations are only for a more complete application of reward and penalty to spiritual being.

The righteous have their resurrection-body in complete subserviency to the spirit, and it moves and rests as the spirit determines. The material and ethereal forces are the identical substances which stood as the basis of the earthy body, and the one spiritual life now goes into the sentient soul and resurrection-body, individualizing it as "spiritual body," and yet the same body that was on earth; and the blended material and ethereal forces move unhindered at the spirit's will, free and rapid as the light in its own vibrations. The universe is open, and they traverse or contemplate its worlds and their interspaces at pleasure. They also recognize the accordant sympathies and dispositions of the heavenly society as clearly as the beauty and harmony of the material systems; and there is perpetual fellowship and also immediate communion with the good, and in full assurance that there can be no social disruptions, for all are in conscious agreement with the Absolute Spirit. While the outlying material worlds move, in their respective systems, in the peripheral spaces of the universe, and the pure ethereal sphere holds them out in balanced security, the great central source of this creating power and guiding wisdom is the true Shechina, or brightest manifestation of the Triune Jehovah; and yet with no excess of light, for the purified vision of the blessed is made adequate to stand face to face before it. Since Christ has made them right towards God, God has only serene loveliness towards them.

But to the incorrigibly wicked the same Absolute Reason, in which the redeemed have become one, makes the Divine Presence a most terrible adversary. Their resurrection-bodies are also indissoluble, and spiritually subservient, like the righteous; but the radically different disposition changes the whole experience. This has been in bondage to the sense, and the end of the soul is still made to be sentient and selfish gratification. Though the carnal instruments are dissolved, and all fleshly members are left behind, the sentient inclinations are still retained, and the stubborn spirit keeps its perverse disposing in their interest with even intenser obstinacy than in the flesh. Their determinately perverted reason has become incorrigibly confirmed unreason, and this madness of the spirit now works itself out in the baser folly and wilder frenzy of the sentient soul. That sets itself towards gratifications it cannot get, and aims at ends it cannot attain, and the captive spirit puts its own immortal energies into these tantalizing enterprises, the continual issue of which is disappointment and shame. Nothing is so repugnant to such unreason as the witness of the Absolute Reason, and they will turn away, both in hate and fear, from all that manifests his wisdom and holiness. They flee from the bright central light and glory of that presence, to them so dreadful, and hide as they may within the shadows of the material worlds, to their sentient seeking the more grateful. And even material nature in its truth and beauty is made hateful to the wicked; for it cannot gratify lost carnal senses, and it does reproach and offend the spirit now turned to folly.

And still more than with the beauty and truth in universal nature are the wicked displeased with the reasonably-disposed life and society of the righteous. There is no communion with the blessed, and they must associate with the guilty; and even here, as in everything else, their own perverseness makes their wretchedness. No one can trust or love his fellow, for they well know each other's selfishness. In their determined wilful unreasonableness, it is reasonable that they distrust and disturb one another. There must be a retributive method in their very madness. It is not the part of Absolute Reason to attempt correcting incorrigible unreason, but rather to display the terrible irony which sets unreason reasonably to punish itself. It is even so that God "laughs at the calamity of the ungodly, and mocks when their fear cometh." He pities, but it is not the place for pity to help them; he may not even annihilate them, for what they have already been and done cannot be annihilated. They must, in their own retribution, perpetuate the only counteraction to their guilty folly. They might at any moment repent, confess, and come into reasonable allegiance, and receive all reasonable alleviation; but since they will not, compassion may not help them; it would only make the divine pity itself unreasonable.

3. Revelation also makes the Future determined by the Character. — To live for the end of reason is to be righteous and godly; to live for sentient gratification is to be wicked and selfish; and these two ends of living characterize humanity in its two grand distinctions, besides which there can be no third class. And the Bible accords with rational speculation in making the future experience to be determined by the character found at the judgment. The separation is according to these distinctions.

Of those "that feared the Lord" it is recorded, "they shall be mine, saith the Lord of Hosts, in that day when I make up my jewels; and I will spare them as a man spareth his own son that serveth him. Then shall ye return and discern between the righteous and the wicked, between him that serveth God and him that serveth him not."[1] Jesus Christ declares, "The Son of Man shall send forth his angels, and they shall gather out of his kingdom all things that offend, and them which do iniquity. And they shall cast them into a furnace of fire; there shall be wailing and gnashing of teeth. Then shall the righteous shine forth as the sun in the kingdom of the Father."[2] And again, Christ says the dead "shall come forth, they that have done good unto the resurrection of life, and they that have done evil unto the resurrection of damnation."[3] "Behold, I come quickly; and my reward is with me, to give to every man according as his work shall be."[4]

4. The Purport of the Bible is, Probation in Life, and endless Retribution after the Judgment. — This is true both of the righteous and the wicked; but since there is neither the wish nor the attempt to question this in reference to the righteous, we need only give attention to the general representations of Scripture regarding the probation and retribution of the wicked, and this as to general drift without adducing particular texts.

Life is everywhere presented as the period of trial; a prison of hope; a day of grace; an accepted time; and thus urgently to be improved as the only opportunity for reformation and reconciliation with God. After death and the judgment, the representations as

[1] Mal. iii. 17, 18.
[2] Matt. xiii. 41, 42.
[3] John v. 29.
[4] Rev. xxii. 12.

invariably are penal endurance; prison of darkness and despair; judgment without mercy. Chastisement, disciplinary correction, is for the probationary state; but after the judgment comes penalty, vindication of authority, as if there were no expectation further of return to loyalty, or fitness in using means for recovery. It is as if patience were exhausted, and pity in vain, and forbearance had found its limit; for the wicked are so irrecoverably lost as to refuse all correction, and can be dealt with further only in perpetual retribution. Reason can to them have further application only in holding them in the attitude of penal warning, and vindictive admonition of the sanctity of law and the heinous guilt of standing out stubbornly against both mercy and authority. All this is just in accordance with the reason of the case, and the full scope of revelation cannot fairly be interpreted by any other meaning. This is proved:—

i. *By the Scripture record of Providential Judgments.*—With all the examples of patient expostulation and paternal discipline and correction, there are manifest cases in the Bible of providential punishment exclusive of all design for chastisement. The stroke was purely in judgment, irrespective of all regard to the good of the suffering sinner. The wicked have been smitten down in their sins with no end in reclaiming them, but with the clear intent of vindicating the majesty of despised authority. They are examples like those of the Flood; the destruction of Sodom; of Pharaoh; of Jerusalem after Christ's crucifixion, when the Christians followed their Master's direction,[1] and fled to the mountains of Pella and were saved. In all the above cases some were saved, and suffered only in chastisement; the wicked retributively perished. So we must interpret such cases, and understand that punishment still followed on after the temporal judgment, else were the real severity on the good who were spared, and the greatest kindness towards the evil who went at once into eternal favor. So of Judas, and Ananias and Sapphira in their lying unto God; if their death were only chastisement, and not judgment, the dealings of God were better towards the dying bad than towards the living good.

ii. *The Feeling manifested by the Inspired Teachers.* — The inspired prophets, apostles, and evangelists knew what the truth was in reference to probationary continuance and retributive commencement, and their earnestness in their work discloses what they knew. They were sincere men, and their zeal bespoke their true feeling, and their feeling told their honest conviction. Their pressing invitations, and sharp admonitions, and personal sacrifices tell how strongly they felt the urgency of the sinner's case, that he be immediately reconciled to God, and the terrible risk in all procrastination of repentance and of faith in the Lord Jesus Christ. Such zeal and sacrifice could not con-

[1] Matt. xxiv. 16.

sist with any other conviction than that life was the short probation, and that the life to come was settled by it.

iii. *So also by the Conduct of their Hearers.*—The effect produced is abundantly evidential of the doctrine declared. There can be no more mistake in determining the tenor of the apostles' preaching from its results than in the case of any modern ministry. Plain, simple, direct, earnest, clearly apprehended, their hearers took the intended truth of the message, and the result in their life and practice tells us what its meaning was. Some were converted to an entirely new life, after the deepest sense of sin and guilt, and inward struggle to renounce all selfishness, and return to truth and righteousness. When the sinner did not yield and renounce his sin, he showed the pressure he had felt on his conscience by the intense hatred and hostility to the obligation. Pressing upon men the obligations of immediate repentance and holiness, and offering a free salvation through Jesus' grace alone, will induce such conduct on both sides now; and never in any age, nor in any way of preaching universal salvation, will such effects follow. Whether he obeyed or rejected, the primitive hearer of Christ's gospel knew it offered salvation now, and endless retribution if he rejected it.

iv. *The plainest direct Scripture declarations affirm the Retributions after the Judgment to be end-*

less. — Of many alike explicit and emphatic, it is sufficient to cite the following: "Some shall awake to everlasting life, and some to shame and everlasting contempt."[1] "These shall go away into everlasting punishment, but the righteous into life eternal."[2] "Who shall be punished with everlasting destruction from the presence of the Lord, and from the glory of his power."[3] "He that believeth not the Son shall not see life, but the wrath of God abideth on him."[4] And as the Holy Ghost has the last dispensation in human probation, and so all preceding sin and rejection may, under this last dispensation, be remitted, yet, if the Holy Ghost be sinned against, and its influence stubbornly and finally resisted, the last overture is herein rejected, and there can be no deliverance. "Whosoever speaketh a word against the Son of Man, it shall be forgiven him; but whosoever speaketh against the Holy Ghost, it shall not be forgiven him, neither in this world, neither in the world to come."[5]

[1] Dan. xii. 2. [2] Matt. xxv. 46. [3] 2 Thess. i. 9.
[4] John iii. 36. [5] Matt. xii. 32.

SECTION VI.

END OF THE MEDIATORIAL REIGN.

Redemption, planned in eternity, promised at the fall, and opened in Christ's incarnation, was consummated, as now considered, at the final judgment. The wonder of wonders in the whole universe, "the mystery of godliness, God manifest in the flesh," has now its complete development and perfect explanation in its own fulfilment. The mediatorial work in the offices of prophet, priest, and king has here been finished. But scarcely is this divine scheme in its devising and unfolding a deeper mystery for finite reason, than the disposal of it must be when its end is accomplished. In what shall the Messiah's reign terminate? Immanuel, God in humanity, has perfectly executed and thoroughly completed all that was in the original Idea; he has saved a multitude no man can number, satisfied his own soul for all his atoning travail, and justified the way of God before the universe; and after this, what next?

This mediatorial reign has been means, not end; and finite reason may see in it that which forbids its perpetuity, while no human reason may be able to say what shall be done *with* it, when God's purpose has been entirely done *by* it. Mediatorial sovereignty is delegated authority. "Head over all things," as Jesus at the right hand of the Father is, and glorious as this royal majesty is made to be, yet is the sovereignty in its glory and majesty still a part of Christ's humiliation, and it should be sustained only for the attainment of the Father's design. It takes the Redeemer out of the poverty of his earthly life, and above the reproach of his crucifixion; yet is it given to him as the reward of his obedience unto death, and is but the splendid badge that in doing service for another and a higher, he is thereby pleasing the other. Can, then, Deity everlastingly abide in humanity, and reign only in vice-regency? If the normal co-equality of persons in the Godhead may, for a reasonable end, take positions of voluntary subordination, yet even finite reason can firmly say, the subordinate must again rise to its normal dignity so soon as that reasonable end has been gained. And yet inherently there are deep difficulties and dark mysteries. How abolish the mediatorial administration, and keep the distinctive church? How the song of the blood-bought be eternal, when he who washed them in his blood is no longer in humanity? Reason sees a change must be, but finite reason will never devise what the change is, and how it must be effected.

One human mind, and but one, has been so opened and elevated by the Spirit of omniscience as to see through this mystery, and state the way of its clear-ing-up for other careful readers of his revelation. The manner of moving back from the wondrous episode of human redemption to the eternal order of God's normal administration, is given in one short and clear statement; besides which, nothing of inspiration relieves the necessary perplexity in our ascertaining how this gracious digression can wisely be brought in again to the one Absolute Dominion. In his prophetic exposition of the doctrine of the coming resurrection, the apostle Paul opens one clear flash of light upon the darkness beyond the revealings of the day of judgment, and in this alone, of all inspired seers, Paul shows us how the needed subserviences and delegated authorities in mediation lapse again in the Absolute Sovereignty of the Godhead. But while Paul only tells how the mediatorial reign passes into the one Absolute Kingdom, the beloved disciple, John, has the crowning prophetic prerogative of expanding human vision within the opening brightness and blessedness of this one eternal Realm for all heavenly immortals. It will most help our comprehension of the whole revelation to see how the success of the mediatorial reign, according to Paul's fuller vision here, culminates in Triune Absoluteness; and then, to contemplate this eternal heavenly Reign, as John was given to behold it.

1. The Mediatorial Kingdom fully committed to Christ. — In the second psalm, David introduces the Lord as speaking of his Anointed, saying, "I have

set my King upon my holy hill of Zion. Ask of me, and I shall give thee the heathen for thy inheritance, and the uttermost parts of the earth for thy possession." And in the eighth psalm he speaks of Christ's dominion in a way applicable to the dominion given to humanity over other creatures, saying, "What is man, that thou art mindful of him, and the son of man, that thou visitest him? For thou hast made him a little lower than the angels, and hast crowned him with glory and honor. Thou madest him to have dominion over the works of thine hands; thou hast put all things under his feet." And when Christ ascended, after his resurrection, he said to his disciples, "All power is given unto me in heaven and in earth."[1] But the apostle Paul makes all this more clear and full. If we take him to have been the author of the Epistle to the Hebrews, — and that he was, this exclusive Pauline manner of setting forth the mediatorial authority is strong proof, — we have him largely expounding the above words of the eighth psalm as God's delegation of kingly authority to the Divine Mediator in his humanity. And his comment on the passage is, "For in that he put all in subjection under him, he left nothing that is not put under him. But now we see not yet all things put under him. But we see Jesus, who was made a little lower than the angels for the suffering of death, crowned with glory and honor, that he by the grace of God should taste death for every man;"[2] and his experience in

[1] Matt. xxviii. 18.

[2] Heb. ii. 8, 9.

human nature and life fitted him to be King, as well as "merciful High Priest," for every purpose in the work of human redemption. And then, again, in the first chapter of Ephesians, we have Paul saying of "the God of our Lord Jesus Christ, the Father of glory," that he hath "set him at his own right hand in the heavenly places, far above all principality, and power, and might, and dominion, and every name that is named, not only in this world, but also in that which is to come; and hath put all things under his feet, and gave him to be the head over all things to the church, which is his body, the fulness of him that filleth all in all." Such, then, from the Father, is the Mediator's full investiture of authority over the entire Universe.

2. The End fulfilled in Christ's actually subduing all Things. — In the last of the psalms ascribed to David we have the full execution of this universal subjecting of all earthly sway to Christ, under the representation of a prayer for Solomon, but which is comprehensive of David's greater Son and King. "All kings shall fall down before him; all nations shall serve him." "His name shall endure forever; his name shall be continued as long as the sun, and men shall be blessed in him; all nations shall call him blessed."[1] And so all through the eighty-ninth psalm, but especially in saying, "I will make him, my first born, higher than the kings of the earth. My mercy

[1] Psalm lxxii.

will I keep for him forevermore, and my covenant shall stand fast with him. His seed also will I make to endure forever, and his throne as the days of heaven." And also in the one hundred and tenth psalm, "The Lord said unto my Lord, Sit thou at my right hand, until I make thine enemies thy footstool." John, in the Revelation, sees prophetically this progressive, and in the end complete subjugation. The Lamb leads the church and defends the chosen, and subdues the nations, and crushes all enemies from age to age, till finally, at the judgment, "death and hell were cast into the lake of fire," as the destruction of all opposition.

But in Paul's representations we have wider views of mediatorial accomplishment, including not mankind and this world only, but also angels and universal being. In taking human nature, Christ not only redeemed man, but subdued the devil and destroyed his work, and subjected all the enmity that sin anywhere induces. "Forasmuch as the children are partakers of flesh and blood, he also himself took part of the same, that through death he might destroy him that had the power of death, that is, the devil, and deliver them who through fear of death were all their lifetime subject to bondage."[1] In his kingly authority he redresses all wrong, subdues every hostile power, and forces all opposition to bow beneath him in all worlds. "Wherefore God hath highly exalted him, and given him a name which is above

[1] Heb. ii. 14, 15.

every name; that at the name of Jesus every knee should bow, of things in heaven, and things in earth, and things under the earth, and that every tongue should confess that Jesus Christ is Lord, to the glory of God the Father."[1] Here is the conclusive proof, than which nothing can be stronger, that all sin in the universe has its connection with the sin which ruined humanity. Man's Redeemer, in doing his mediatorial work as between God and man, subdues the devil, destroys death, and brings every sinner in the universe at his feet. Righteous angels and renewed men willingly bow, and fallen angels and lost men are crushed in penal retribution beneath him, and every enemy in God's dominion is subdued to our Mediator, because he humbled himself in our nature; and on his one judgment-seat, he redresses universal wrong in the same right as that with which he squares man's account with God. And then, in another announcement, Paul affirms the necessity for this delegated mediatorial authority to last till all hostility is subjected; and the very last of all that offends God's majesty, in all worlds, is the death inflicted on humanity for Satan's temptation and man's sin in this world. "For he must reign till he hath put all enemies under his feet. The last enemy that shall be destroyed is death."[2] All sin had such connection with and participation in man's sin for which man was cursed with death, that in the Redeemer's abolishing death at the resurrection and final judgment, the last

[1] Phil. ii. 9-11.

[2] 1 Cor. xv. 25, 26.

enemy's head was bruised; and this fatal blow on the devil was not direct from the absolute Godhead, but from the avenging hand of the Mediator, within whose reach God the Father had put the devil. And so Paul further says, "When all things are put under him, it is manifest that he is excepted which did put all things under him."[1] As Mediatorial King, the Lord Jesus Christ, in human personality, literally subjects all but the God who gave him authority, willingly or compulsorily, to his sway, in whatever world it may be. All that dishonors God anywhere, when taken in hand by Jesus and put in the light, which his mediation empowers him to do, is made to minister to "the glory of God the Father." So much is all sin allied with human sin, that one mediation between God and man can reach over and take care of all sinners, in such a manner as to eternally and universally vindicate God in his disposal of them.

3. When finished, Paul reveals the giving up of the Mediatorial Kingdom. — Among the later prophecies of Christ's advent was the following: "Yet once, it is a little while, and I will shake the heavens, and the earth, and the sea, and the dry land; and I will shake all nations, and the Desire of all nations shall come, and I will fill this house with my glory, saith the Lord of hosts."[2] Commenting on this prophecy, and its reference to the previous shaking of Mount Sinai at the giving of the law, the

[1] 1 Cor. xv. 27. [2] Hag. ii. 6, 7.

writer to the Hebrews says, "Whose voice then shook the earth; but now hath he promised, saying, Yet once more I shake not the earth only, but also heaven. And this word, yet once more, signifieth the removing of those things that are shaken, as of things that are made, that the things which cannot be shaken may remain."[1] And this inspired interpretation of the prophet Haggai is thoroughly Pauline, when we understand its meaning to reach beyond all the changes which Christ's coming made on earth, to the removing of what could not permanently remain in his kingdom of heaven. The shaking earth signified that the law had in it a ceremonial portion which could not be lasting, but must pass away on earth at Christ's advent; and so the shaking heaven signified that the redeemed kingdom had also in it a mediatorial part temporarily constituted, and which at last must pass away, while the things which cannot be shaken shall remain. With such interpretation, how supremely striking the appeal following! "Wherefore let us have grace, whereby we may serve God acceptably, with reverence and godly fear; for our God is a consuming fire."[2]

And now, this momentous fact, of the literal removing from the everlasting kingdom what is not stable within it, is recorded by the prophetic pen of the apostle Paul, and by no other inspired penman. Most concisely, and yet most clearly, is this astonishing transaction given in the following record: "Then

[1] Heb. xii. 26, 27. [2] Heb. xii. 28, 29.

cometh the end, when he shall have delivered up the kingdom to God, even the Father." "And when all things shall be subdued unto him, then shall the Son also himself be subject unto him that put all things under him, that God may be all in all."[1]

In this plain declaration much is directly expressed, and much also is with certainty implied. Here is the official surrendry of the endless kingdom to God, the Father, so that as a redeemed church it still remains, but as the direct possession of the first person in the Godhead. With this presentation of the church to the Father, there is also the resignation of mediatorial authority, by which the God-man Redeemer has ruled over it and over all things, under God, for the sake of it. Moreover, it is the direct assertion that Christ, having all things subdued unto him, becomes, as Son, himself subject to the Father in a new sense from the old mediatorial subordination. And then finally, as direct assertion, this subjection of the Son to the Father secures a new peculiar sense in which God is all in all. The above directly asserted facts make necessary the following facts by implication. The latter are woven in with the web of the former. The union of Deity and humanity in the person of Jesus Christ becomes dissolved, and the human alone, as the Son, miraculously created by God in the womb of the virgin, hence onward with no divinity, is, like all created human personalities, subject to God. It is

[1] 1 Cor. xv. 24 and 28.

also implied, that the Word made flesh, but now disunited with humanity, takes the glory that he "had with the Father before the world was," and the Godhead has tripersonality in intrinsic unity as before the incarnation. And finally, the necessary implication is, that the Son in pure humanity has no delegated authority, and neither capacity for nor investiture with the offices of God's anointed Prophet, Priest, and King; and so the glorified church, presented to the Father, stands now face to face with the Triune God, needing and having no official Mediator; and thus to it, and to all the holy, God is all in all. The perpetuity of Jesus' high priest's office, as given in the Hebrews, "forever after the order of Melchisedec," is fully satisfied by the consideration that it endures so long as intercession and sacrificial mediation are needed; for this High Priest, "after he had offered one sacrifice for sins forever, sat down on the right hand of God; from henceforth expecting" all enemies to be subdued, and the sanctified to be perfected.[1] The prophetic and priestly offices both fall off in the surrendering of the kingly office; but they all last till mediatorial teaching, and expiation, and ruling have done their work, and the redeemed church has been presented spotless and complete before God; henceforth to "see him as he is," and "know as they are known."

It is also a fair implication for the speculative reason to read in this record, that after the abdica-

[1] Heb. x. 12, 13.

tion of the mediatorial throne, and the assumption by the Word of the glory he had with the Father before the world was, the purely human Son of God must still sustain peculiar relations to the glorified church and the universal spirit-world. No other being can be altogether like him. He has been directly God-created, as were angels and Adam; yet was he created man, and not angel, and created in the womb of the virgin, and not by inspired dust from the earth, as was Adam, nor in ordinary generation, as are all other human beings. In all these respects he stands alone; and yet more peculiarly unique than in anything else, that he has the conscious reminiscence of human experiences which have been modified by their union with the divine. He is still the very human person through whom temptation, and suffering, and dying came to the divine, and in whose human consciousness the divine energy came back in vigor and virtue, which kept his heart from sinking, and his will from sinning. The impressions thus given can never fade from his own recognition, nor be lost to the contemplation of other intelligences. The human saved and the human lost must stand to him, and he to them, as no other beings reciprocally can; and ministering angel and tempting devil must have an attitude towards him which puts each to each in aspects exclusively peculiar. With no authoritative representation either way from God to man, or from man to God, his very mode of being and past experience make him a sacramental sign to good and bad, in which is a savor, not as once of divine efficacy, but yet of high memorial intensity, and which forever must so be, a savor of life unto life to the holy, and a savor of death unto death to the unholy. His peculiarity makes him universally conspicuous, and every eye that turns towards him looks on the pierced one, and in him eternally is Calvary presented in sacramental symbol, and every spirit, from the reason of the case, and in his own conscious disposition, is obliged, with no power of avoidance, perpetually to "eat and drink," either his own "damnation," or his gracious justification.

4. JOHN SAW THE ABSOLUTE KINGDOM BEYOND THE MEDIATORIAL. — Paul only has prophetically seen and stated the mediatorial resignation; yet it is fully manifest the beloved disciple, John, also looked quite up to this closing scene of temporary mediation, and if he did not behold the actual surrendry of the mediatorial sceptre, — as certainly he has nowhere affirmed that he did, — he was even more eminently favored in prophetic exaltation to look beyond this marvellous consummation of redemptive expediency, and have the broader vision of eternal life, where all see the Absolute ELOHIM as he is. But while his view is more extensive, probably from the very necessity of the case, he describes what he saw much less definitely. The sphere is so far removed from, and so much unlike to, the scenes of earth, that all attempts at de-

scription for us must needs be vague, and only through the use of symbols.

In the successive visions given in the Revelation of John the Divine, we have, near the commencement, presented to us "a Book sealed with seven seals" in the right hand of Him who sat upon the throne. "And in the midst of the throne, and of the four beasts, and in the midst of the elders, stood a Lamb as it had been slain; and he came and took the Book out of the right hand of Him that sat upon the throne," and the heavenly choir "sing the new song, saying, Thou art worthy to take the Book, and to open the seals thereof."[1] This sealed book holds the future, and the slain Lamb opens the seals and makes the revelations, which John records. All along the prophetic announcements, it is this Lamb, who has been slain and is alive, that leads and defends the saints, and arranges the events, and controls all the agencies involved, as the successive seals in human history open. Among the closing judgments belonging to the providences in human probation is the destruction of mystical Babylon, and the introduction of millennial peace and purity, represented as the coming of "the marriage of the Lamb, and that his wife had made herself ready."[2] After this millennial period of triumph and joy, "the loosing of Satan," and his "deceiving the nations," and the gathering of "Gog and Magog" to the last battle, there is the final destruction of God's and man's enemy by the

[1] Rev. v. [2] Rev. xix., xx.

"casting of the devil into the lake of fire, to be tormented forever, with the beast and the false prophet." Then follow the scenes of the general resurrection, the final judgment, and the retributions of "the second death" upon "whomsoever was not found written in the Book of life."[1]

And now, just here, whether John's vision caught or not the event he does not describe, must have occurred the relinquishment of the mediatorial administration, which we have above considered as so clearly but concisely given by the apostle Paul. The redeemed church was here, by the Redeemer, given over to the Father; the divine and human in the Messiah were disunited, and the Word, which had been incarnated in humanity, returned to his former glory. After the fulfilment of those wonders, whether within John's prophetic ken or otherwise, we have his further revelation of transmediatorial glories, but in highly figurative representation and in the use of mystical symbols, and yet admiringly grand and pure. "I saw a new heaven and a new earth, for the first heaven and the first earth were passed away, and there was no more sea." Created nature, as appearing in sense, has all gone out, and the merely phenomenal qualities have passed away, since the sense-organism has been put off for the resurrection "spiritual body."

The bride, the Lamb's wife, appears as a glorious city; the new Jerusalem, coming down from God

[1] Rev. xxi.

out of heaven, and within which the espoused saints abide. "They shall be his people, and God himself shall be with them, and be their God."[1] And here we have the enigmatic but brilliant picture of the saints' eternal home — to the imagination a scene of blessedness inexpressible, and only to be known in its reality when we shall be changed into the same image from glory to glory. There is no need of any sense-media, as of the sun or the moon to give light; yea, there is no divine Mediator, for God *and* the Lamb, as now both one, immediately give light in their one glory. "A pure river of life; a tree of life, with its monthly fruit and healing leaves; no curse, and no night; the Lord's face open to them, and his name in their foreheads, and they reign forever and ever."[2] All this is in full accord with Paul's account of mediatorial resignation, for all is post-mediatorial, and one God is all in all. The river of life comes out of *one* throne, and this throne has *one* sovereign; for God and the Lamb are now but one Being, and "*his* servants shall serve *him*." Reason in speculation and reason in revelation come, ultimately, each to each, in full conformity; the one saying that we need, and the other that we have, immediate communion with God in Eternal Glory

[1] Rev. xxi. [2] Rev. xxii.

CPSIA information can be obtained
at www.ICGtesting.com
Printed in the USA
LVHW041226160323
741693LV00036B/1650

9 783382 130008